"You're still looking for someone to protect you."

Hadn't he been listening to her? "I can protect myself. I've learned that much."

He made a disbelieving noise. "Listen, sweetheart, don't mistake a bit of spunk for the ability to keep yourself safe."

Anger roiled inside of her. Helen stalked across the few feet that separated them and grabbed his arm.

"I'm not mistaken about anything. Besides, Nick Thorndike, you can't protect me, because you're too busy pushing away those who give a damn, just so they won't hurt you. You're too busy being an island and not getting involved with anyone."

"Too late for that," he muttered. "I'm already involved."

Dear Reader,

Welcome to another fabulous month of the most exciting romance reading around. And what better way to begin than with a new TALL, DARK & DANGEROUS novel from *New York Times* bestselling author Suzanne Brockmann? *Night Watch* has it all: an irresistible U.S. Navy SEAL hero, intrigue and danger, and—of course—passionate romance. Grab this one fast, because it's going to fly off the shelves.

Don't stop at just one, however. Not when you've got choices like *Fathers and Other Strangers,* reader favorite Karen Templeton's newest of THE MEN OF MAYES COUNTY. Or how about *Dead Calm,* the long-awaited new novel from multiple-award-winner Lindsay Longford? Not enough good news for you? Then check out new star Brenda Harlen's *Some Kind of Hero,* or *Night Talk,* from the always-popular Rebecca Daniels. Finally, try *Trust No One,* the debut novel from our newest find, Barbara Phinney.

And, of course, we'll be back next month with more pulse-pounding romances, so be sure to join us then. Meanwhile…enjoy!

Leslie J. Wainger
Executive Editor

Trust No One

BARBARA PHINNEY

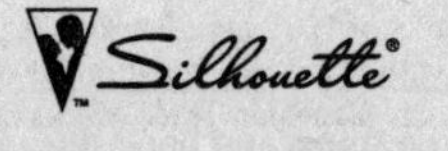

INTIMATE MOMENTS™

Published by Silhouette Books

America's Publisher of Contemporary Romance

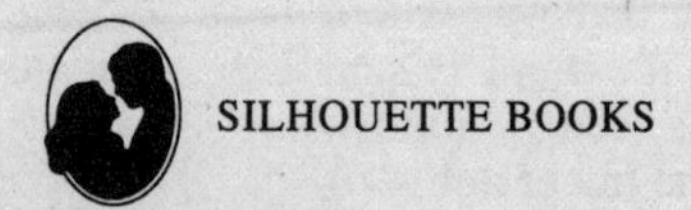

ISBN 0-373-27318-5

TRUST NO ONE

This edition published by arrangement with Harlequin Books S.A.

Visit Silhouette at www.eHarlequin.com

Printed in U.S.A.

BARBARA PHINNEY

was born in England and raised in Canada. She has traveled throughout her life, exploring the various countries and cultures of the world. After she retired from the Canadian Armed Forces, where she had been a mechanic for seventeen years, Barbara wanted to do something different and decided to try her hand at romance writing. During a camping trip to New River Beach in New Brunswick, she fell in love with life on the beautiful Bay of Fundy, and she knew that was where *Trust No One* had to be set. She found it extremely satisfying to create a small town, down to its scenery and friendly local culture—and it scratched the travel itch.

Barbara spends her weekdays writing, gardening and building her dream home with her husband. The rest of the time is spent with their fast-growing children, numerous relatives and a dozen silly but lovable chickens.

To my family, and to Lucie, a friend now gone.

Special thanks to Carol, Dorothy, Joy,
Kate, Lina and Norah for all their help
and encouragement. You gals are the best.

Prologue

The attraction struck Helen Eastman square in the chest with such force that she nearly reached out to grip Jamie for support.

She caught herself in time. Heaven only knew how he would interpret such an action. Instead, she chose to smooth down the soft material of her evening dress, hoping the furtive touch would allay the impact of…

…of her single glimpse of *that man.*

Smoke blurred the crowded cigar bar a few feet ahead, its blue haze intensified by several well-dressed men enjoying long, ugly stogies. Abruptly, they closed ranks, obliterating her view of the man, and for once she was grateful that Jamie had so many acquaintances.

''This way.'' Jamie took her arm. Their relationship wasn't serious, but he'd adopted the irritating habit of squeezing her elbow. She gritted her teeth and suppressed a shudder. She should say something, but now, heading into the party that was so important to him, wasn't the time to dislodge her arm and demand he not touch her.

Helen flicked back her long hair and allowed Jamie to guide her over the threshold into the private salon of his most exclusive restaurant. He paused to speak with another couple lingering nearby.

Her gaze drifted and she caught a glimpse of the man again. He stood across the room, not even looking her way, for Heaven's sake.

And yet…

Oh, mercy. The attraction walloped her again and she froze, uncertain of whether she should laugh or cry or give into the insane desire coursing through her.

No. No way. She swallowed, unable to thrust off the sudden, ridiculous image of the man pressing his long frame down on her, all too easily coaxing out a heady response….

With a hard clamp of her jaw, she forced herself to look at the couple facing her, a tight smile superglued to her face.

Jamie still gripped her elbow, his fingers digging into the bone. Oh, how she'd love to tell him to let go. But the request would imply he'd made a mistake and from the few times they'd dated, she knew he didn't like mistakes.

Blinking away the acrid smoke, she scanned the room. She'd seen some of Jamie's guests before, here or there, but not the man who'd sent her senses reeling out of control, while still several yards away.

She tried to clear her throat, but the effort was futile with it so tight and dry. When the small clique of cigar-puffing men broke toward the bar for refills of their whiskeys, she stole another glance across the room. At the man who still nursed a bottle of imported beer. Jamie's favorite kind, she noticed. The one with the green label.

He began to turn toward her and she snapped her attention back to Jamie so quickly that her long hair swung out and slapped her face.

She hadn't given a total stranger a second look in a long time. Unlike the other women here, she wagered. Indeed, the cigar-smoking woman in front of her had stolen her own share of lustful looks at the man.

With his image seared into Helen's mind, she replayed it again. Taller and more muscular than Jamie, he possessed an edge of danger that made Jamie's own dark looks seem insipid.

Good heavens, this attraction was insane. And risky, to say the least. If Jamie found out, he'd…

What would he do? Even as she asked herself the question, something inside warned her not to test that water. Jamie had begun to show his jealous streak. Another reason to end whatever they had.

Just as well. She didn't have relationships. She…she couldn't.

And she didn't want one with Jamie, either. They didn't seem to have much in common, but the girls at work had encouraged her.

Anyway, time to end it. She'd begun to see behind the charming mask to his unpleasant and controlling personality.

How good it would feel to walk out on him tonight, but it wouldn't suit Jamie, she realized with a wash of apprehension.

This time she managed to clear the smoke from her dry throat.

"What's wrong?" Jamie asked.

"Nothing." She lifted her eyebrows to convey some sense of nonchalance. "It's smoky in here."

Jamie scanned the crowd, raising his hand once to wave hello to someone in the far left corner. Then his gaze settled on the man she couldn't look at anymore and a smile spread across his plain features. "Come, Helen, I want you to meet someone."

Panic flared in her chest. "W-who?"

"Nick Thorndike." Jamie's smile turned sly. Over the course of the past few dates, she'd noticed the look several times and disliked it. But tonight it offered comfort compared to the thought of extending her hand to that dark-haired devil across the room. If a mere look at him could plunge her into uncharacteristic longing, how would she handle his handshake? Would the heat of her attraction spill into his open palm?

Would he see the desire in her eyes?

"Nick's a cop." Jamie's thick growl scraped into her ear and she fought the urge to lean away. "But he got tired of drawing mediocre pay. Look at him, sweetheart. A real-life bad-boy cop searching for a piece of the action." He chuckled and Helen caught a disagreeable whiff of the single malt whiskey he'd just finished. "And you want to know something? He's not the only one."

The air grew thick and choking. She wanted to gasp out loud for a decent, clean breath. Instead, she ground the slim point of her sandal heel into the burgundy carpet and faced Jamie. "I'm sorry, but this smoke is murder. I've had a headache all day. Would you mind taking me home?"

Jamie's brows knitted together for a moment and a cold panic crested inside of her. He'd just as likely refuse her, as he would relent.

She held her breath. Then he smiled that condescending

smile of his. The one that grated on her nerves. For a brief second, she weighed the risks of telling him she no longer wanted to date him. But again, this wasn't the place.

Finally, he shrugged. "All right. I'll introduce you to him another time."

She practically fled through the door to the main salon of the restaurant, ignoring the curious stares of the other guests. In that relieved minute, she didn't care what Jamie Cooms or anyone else thought of her.

Outside, fog from the harbor slid in, chilling her enough for her to draw up the wrap that matched her only long gown. After Jamie unlocked his car, she sank into the seat, lowered her eyelids and drew in a deep, pacifying breath of damp air to compose herself.

So that was Nick, the bad-boy cop. For weeks, Jamie had hinted about his newest pal, disclosing only the man's first name.

Until tonight.

When she'd taken one look at him and nearly melted.

Oh, yes, she'd been wise to leave. She didn't need to meet Nick Thorndike, the handsome, dangerous police officer who wanted "a piece of the action."

It was almost as if Jamie was into something shady, the way he talked about Nick Thorndike.

Why hadn't she realized this before?

Because Jamie rarely took her to meet his friends, that's why. And since she hadn't considered their relationship serious, she hadn't bothered to look for anything beyond the norm. Anything shady.

She watched Jamie settle behind the steering wheel, wondering again why he had asked her out in the first place. Had he been using her for something other than a casual escort? If so, what could it be?

She shivered, her suspicions settling over her like a wet,

woolen coat. Was Jamie Cooms not doing things by the book? And what kind of action would a dirty cop want a piece of? She didn't really know Jamie, or any of his many businesses, be they warehouses or restaurants, though the girls at work had said such details weren't important.

Evenings with Jamie were just dates. And hadn't her past gut instincts about men been wrong?

The ache in her head intensified, and she blinked watery eyes to dispel *that* former humiliation.

The wipers slashed across the windshield, removing the night's mist. *Forget him.* And forget this whole evening. His activities were no concern of hers, and she'd soon be clear of him.

Without a backward glance to the restaurant, she buckled the seat belt inside Jamie's expensive import. All things considered, she should forget Jamie and his suspicious activities.

And stay away from Nick Thorndike.

Far, far away.

Chapter 1

Suspended.

The word had threatened to surface between him and his chief throughout Nick's not-quite-regulation role in the undercover investigation, but now that Chief Dennis Hunt had said it—and enforced it—the word damn well hurt.

Suspended. Nick slapped the steering wheel of his sport utility vehicle and gunned it out of the police parking lot. Within minutes, he was halfway home.

Everything in Lower Cove, New Brunswick, was only minutes away, including the city of Saint John, where he'd been part of a drug investigation. The investigation had been running as expected until a body washed onto the shore of the Bay of Fundy, just inside Lower Cove's jurisdiction.

Bile collected in his stomach. He hit the power window button to let the cool, autumn air fill his lungs, hoping to prevent the memory of the unzipped body bag from resurfacing.

It didn't work.

The deceased had been identified as Tony DiPetri. His murder had all the earmarks of Nick's chief suspect, Jamie Cooms. The victim had also been Cooms's best friend for years, or so the fool must have believed.

DiPetri had been last seen alive in Cooms's office, with Nick standing next to the unlucky man less than an hour before his death. Just him, the victim and Cooms.

Nick automatically flexed his fingers, trying to work a cramp out of the swollen knuckles. He'd done more than just stand beside the man.

Now he waited for the autopsy report to exonerate him....

No. He wouldn't worry about clearing his name, not when Tony DiPetri's murderer roamed free.

When the chief had called him in for an update, he'd had to explain all the nauseating, illegal crap he'd done. Lower Cove's police policy dictated that if a member was participating in a Joint Task Force with another police department, the member must obtain express permission from his police chief before jeopardizing any civilian's life.

He sighed. All right, he'd roughed up DiPetri only an hour before the murder, simply to show Cooms how tough he could be. After all, his cover was that of a disillusioned police officer looking to pad his pension. As far as Cooms was concerned, he'd do anything for money, even "straighten out" a guy who suddenly had cold feet.

He muttered another curse. He'd assaulted a civilian, a guy who might have been ready to spill his guts to the police.

Hell, he couldn't water down his explanation to a simple assault. It was aggravated assault, plain and simple.

As a result, the chief had no choice but to suspend him.

Nick had argued back, anyway. ''Come on, Chief. I hardly had time to call for permission.''

The chief shook his head. ''You know the rules. And you can't keep breaking them.''

''But I'm close. Cooms is responsible. Not just for DiPetri's death, but for every gram of narcotics in Saint John.''

He wanted to add a word about the corruption he suspected, but Chief Hunt curled his lip. ''Yeah, well, I'm responsible for this police force, Thorndike. I don't want to even think what the mayor would say if he found out I'd covered your ass when you broke one of his pet regulations. Hand 'em over.'' He'd held out his hand.

Stone-faced, Nick had relinquished his weapon and badge. Then, without a backward glance, he'd stormed out of the office.

Now, fifteen minutes later, Nick turned down a secondary highway, a chip-sealed road worn down to the gravel in spots. What was he supposed to do while the rest of Lower Cove's police officers investigated him? They were already short-handed and hardly inclined to investigate one of their own.

Besides, the Saint John Police Department had accepted the risks involved with the undercover operation. Why couldn't this police force? Every law enforcement agency in New Brunswick wanted suspected drug dealer and money launderer Jamie Cooms behind bars. They knew the price that had to be paid.

He rotated his tight shoulders. And how were Lower Cove's finest going to investigate him, anyway? Ask Cooms what happened?

He should be on duty, working the investigation, not twiddling his thumbs at home. He'd been close to securing the overwhelming evidence against Cooms, despite the misgivings of his chief and some of the officers with the Major Crimes Unit of the Saint John Police Department. Not just for the illegal drug trade, but for corruption somewhere high in the ranks of the city's officials—maybe even a cop or two. Nick had insinuated himself in close to Cooms. He knew the mealy-mouthed bastard better than anyone in either police department. And he could have had the guy for DiPetri's murder and for trafficking. For everything. It would have been a piece of cake.

Until his suspension, that is.

He turned his SUV at the next right. The black spruce trees, stunted by poor soil and a constant Bay of Fundy wind, clung to the rocky ground, obscuring his narrow driveway. He bumped over the potholes left by the spring rains. Finally, home.

A simple two-story log house, built years ago by his uncle and willed to him by his childless, widowed aunt, his home stood stark and cold along the tiny cove. A short stretch of sand smoothed the landscape between two high, wooded cliffs, but there wasn't enough beach to lure other potential homeowners, a fact for which he was grateful.

For a moment, he remained in his vehicle and watched the nearly full tide batter the cove. A nasty fall storm loomed to the west, something left over from the last hurricane that had skirted the eastern seaboard of the United States. Until now, he'd been too busy pandering to Jamie Cooms to catch the latest news and weather reports.

After the storm, he'd have to fix those rickety stairs leading down to the beach. Being suspended, he now had the time.

Yep, nothing to do really meant nothing to do in Lower Cove. But the town was good to live in, even boasting its own police force when other towns around the province had bowed to fiscal pressure and hired the Royal Canadian Mounted Police. Lower Cove had its own six officers.

Make that five.

He climbed out of his SUV, wondering with a bone-weary sigh if his partner, Mark Rowlands, would be willing and able to salvage Nick's part in the investigation. Mark hadn't met Cooms, though some of the undercover officers had. How would they explain his sudden disappearance?

Should have thought about that before. Nick hadn't kept Mark up to date. If his partner was smart, he'd let Saint John handle the investigation and slip back into an easy routine of cruising the quiet streets of Lower Cove.

A gull screamed overhead and with his vehicle door still open, he glanced up. Thick, burgeoning clouds whipped past, low and dark and cold. A fat raindrop hit his cheek. He slammed the door and stalked toward his house.

A movement of light against the dark sky caught his attention. Squinting into the moist wind, he peered over at the east cliff directly ahead, but saw nothing more than churning white-capped waves hurling themselves at the rocks. With nothing to do, he walked to the corner of his house and stared up at the cliff.

It was probably a hungry gull, diving down for a morsel of food. He watched for the bird to be driven skyward by the updrafts slamming against the cliff.

Instead, a figure appeared at the top, briefly, before stooping down again.

Nick slammed himself against the logs of his house, instinct surging inside of him. One of the reasons scum like Cooms made New Brunswick their home was because of coves like his. Too dangerous for pleasure craft, these secluded coves were perfect for smuggling in drugs.

And perfect for eliminating the kind of evidence that could speak out in court against them. Like witnesses.

The heavens opened, pelting him with cold rain. He stared through the sheets of water, not wanting to lose sight of the figure trespassing on his land.

There! A small, slight woman, busying herself with something at her feet.

What the hell was she doing? His suspicious mind automatically focused on the worst. Was she getting rid of evidence? Or flagging in a boat?

Wild speculation, brought on by his suspension, he told himself. But hell, the hairs on his arms tingled, a sure sign his instinct had just kicked into overdrive.

Keeping low, he made a dash for the largest outcropping of rock beside his house, the one that hid his SUV from view and grew into the east cliff. He knew every pebble in the cove and he easily judged the distance to the figure. Three hundred feet, no more.

The figure seemed to wipe her eyes against the wind and rain. He hugged the treeline, thankful his dark jacket matched his surroundings. Then he ducked into the woods, following the narrow path that climbed to where the woman stood. Hidden by the trees and muffled by the wind, he knew he'd reach her in a matter of seconds and she would never know he was there.

Tiny hairs tingled at the back of his neck, chilling him more than the rain. He was in full-blown goose bumps by the time he reached the end of the path.

Something was out of whack. His instinct had never failed. Until now, it had kept him alive and he anticipated no change. He stepped carefully onto the small precipice.

There she was. He froze, not wanting her to catch his movement in her peripheral vision.

Slowly, shakily, she peeled off her jacket and dropped

it onto the sneakers she'd removed. He caught her drenched profile. A smooth face, pert ski-jump nose and pouty lips parted to show straight, white teeth.

Lips, lush, delivering a moist heat to his bare skin.

Desire pumped through him, hard and fast enough to cause him to jolt back against a dead tree in astonishment.

Damn, he had to get himself laid if the sight of a bedraggled bit of a woman turned his crank so quickly.

He squared his shoulders. Pretty face or not, she was up to no good.

When she turned to confront the onslaught of howling wind and storm, he stepped past the edge of the trees. She still couldn't hear him over the gale, despite being only a few feet away from him.

Her hair had been brutally hacked off and Nick felt a surge of indignation. Who had cut off such a thick, dark mass that even now defied the downpour with lush curls?

Shivering, the woman tugged up her knit sweater. His heart spasmed. What the hell? Autumn was hardly the time for public nudity.

She slipped the soaking sweater free of her slender body.

Each hair on his arms danced as he watched with fascination. Would she reach around and peel away her bra as well?

She didn't. Instead, she dug her ringless fingers into the soft sweater and with unexpected violence, rent it in two. Then stooping, she dragged the pale pink knitted material over the point of the sharp outcropping.

Wearing only a sheer bra and hip-hugging jeans, she flung the sweater over the cliff. Heavy with rain, it sailed outward for a mere second before dropping from his view.

Was this woman insane?

Her shoulders stiff, the woman stepped closer to the

edge. She leaned over, her frame weaving slightly in the strong wind.

"Stop!" Nick didn't believe he'd shouted the word until she whirled around to face him. He stepped farther from the shelter of the trees and reached for her.

The woman focused on his face, paling to the color of ashes.

Her mouth formed a soft plea of something he didn't quite catch.

Then she fainted.

As soon as she reached the cliff, Helen removed her shoes. Too bad she had to leave them here. They were comfortable and had cost her almost a month's worth of groceries.

Not that she'd needed too many groceries, lately. All too often, Jamie appeared at her apartment door with Chinese takeout, or orders to put on a classy dress because they were going uptown to one of the many restaurants he owned.

Remembering her socks, she tugged at them, turning them inside out. Some days, it seemed like Jamie owned half the city of Saint John. And a few of its politicians, too. He'd told her so himself one night after a few too many drinks. Another night, at one of his fancy parties, he'd even hinted he owned a few cops.

It had made no difference to her, she'd kept telling herself. He was merely a casual boyfriend, not a long-term lover. She couldn't have anything long-term. No way, not after the mistakes she'd made a few years ago.

All she'd wanted was someone to be close to. She thought she'd had it with Scott Jackson. But he'd taken her fragile state and swept it away like the tide below would do to her clothes.

She shut her eyes and the pouring rain sluiced away the tears that had squeezed free.

Things were different now. Bad. Worse than bad, as the horror of last week churned inside of her.

She'd decided to break it off with Jamie and had walked into his office the very second he put a gun to the back of his friend's punched-in head.

And pulled the trigger.

She'd turned and fled, like the devil himself was at her heels.

Indeed he was. She fought the memory of Jamie screaming at her, warning her she couldn't run. Warning her he'd find her. Catch her. Kill her.

He hadn't so far. She'd worn the sneakers she'd just removed, while Jamie had struggled to keep up in his usual Armani suit and slippery Italian loafers.

She didn't go home. Nor did she go to the police. Not after Jamie's veiled confession that he was paying off a few of Saint John's finest.

Including Nick Thorndike—the tall, muscular man with a charming, rough-edged appeal to his dark features, who she'd first seen at Jamie's gala affair. She recalled the terrifying, hot slam of attraction that had both intrigued and appalled her. What insanity to be attracted to one of Jamie's crooked cops. If Jamie had found out…

She'd pleaded a headache and escaped for home before Jamie could introduce her to Nick.

The second time she'd seen him had been even more terrifying. Last week, as she'd stepped off the elevator, she'd spied him shutting Jamie's office door, with *blood-stained hands.* Not wanting to be seen, she'd ducked into the stairwell.

Her fingers flew to her mouth to check a gasp. Why were his knuckles bloodied? What had he done?

And yet again the crazy fascination resurfaced. Minutes after that, she'd learned how he'd bloodied his knuckles. Horrible.

Now, a week later, shivering high above the churning ocean, Helen tugged off her jacket. How could she have ignored the fact that Jamie was nothing more than a well-dressed thug?

And now a murderer who wanted her dead?

She'd called her boss and said she would be out sick for a while. Since then, she'd spent most of the time fleeing from phone booth to phone booth, always checking over her shoulder, always calling the only person she could trust.

Her mother.

Jamie could have tapped her mother's phone, but she had to take the risk. She couldn't put her mother through the worry of not hearing from her only child.

The wind sprayed cold saltwater up into Helen's face as she recalled their most agonizing conversation.

"Go to the police, Helen." Her mother had tried to be firm, but her voice quivered.

"No, I can't trust them. Not after what Jamie said."

"Come home, then."

"No!" This call was risky enough. She'd have to keep it short.

"Helen, you can go to the police. Tell them everything."

"No, Momma!" She gripped the receiver. "I—I can't. I'm... I just don't have it in me."

"You do!" Not for a long time had her mother sounded so stern. What a pair they'd become since her father died. Weak and foolish. Hadn't she been weak and foolish enough with Scott Jackson?

"I wish I was stronger, I really do...." Still gripping

the receiver, Helen used her bent wrist to swipe away her tears. "I'm sorry..."

Her mother sighed. "Where are you?"

"Safe for now, Momma," she'd answered, peering out of the phone booth to the highway gas station nearby. If only she could tell her where she was. "Listen, Momma, I'm going to have to leave for a while."

"Leave? Where will you go?"

Helen shut her eyes. She had to be strong, but the effect took so much out of her. Finally, she blurted out, "I'm going to make it look like I've killed myself."

Her mother burst into tears. "Don't! You're all I have, sweetheart. I need you."

"I'm not going to die, Momma. I'm just going to make it look that way."

They'd hung up shortly after and with the help of several disjointed phone calls over the next few nights, she'd made her plans.

Relenting, her mother had suggested this cove. Long before Helen was born, she'd been a housekeeper for the childless couple who lived there. Her mother said the cove was quiet, but she'd heard the log home was still occupied. Perhaps the homeowner could discover the proof that Helen had killed herself.

Helen scanned the empty cove, thankful she'd taken her mother's advice. Though the log house stood as cold and dark as it had earlier when she'd checked it out, it was obvious someone lived there. Even the mailbox had been emptied each day.

She let her jacket fall onto her soaking shoes. After a week on the run, always reliving the horror of Tony's murder, she ached with fatigue. But she couldn't stop now. The tide would turn soon. Whoever lived in the log home had to find her favorite shoes, the beloved necklace she'd dropped into one of them. On the wet sand, left by the receding tide, they'd find the expensive sweater Jamie had given her.

She peeled off the sweater and dug her fingernails through the soft, loose knit, ripping it apart, venting her frustration and fear on the warm, pastel weave.

A tired shiver rippled through her, slowing her movements for a brief minute.

Focus! Only a little longer, then you'll be warm.

Hidden in a plastic bag not far away were her mother's old clothes and a dirty wig purchased at a yard sale. They'd warm her up. And she'd be free. She flung the sweater over the cliff.

Now, if she could get down to the next ledge, she'd leave part of her bra down there, too.

"Stop!"

She whirled.

And froze, a gasp jammed in her throat.

Oh, mercy. Him! The dirty cop!

Jamie had sent his latest henchman, his pet cop, to turn her fake suicide into something horribly real.

Her world went black.

Nick cursed, catching the woman before she fell and turned her damned stupid suicide attempt into an accidental death.

He'd had his share of lousy timings, of things that went wrong at the worst possible moments—all cops did—but this took the cake.

The woman slumped into his arms. He hooked his right arm under her knees and scooped her up. She was a real lightweight, maybe ninety pounds. Especially wearing nothing but a bra and tight jeans.

Her round, full breasts peaked, pushing hard through the

sheerest bra he'd ever seen. He had to cover her. There was no way he could trek back down to his home with those things pointing up at him.

Bending his knees while trying to keep her level, he managed to lay her out on the wet outcropping. He ripped off his jacket to cover her torso, all the while praying he didn't slip and somehow end up mashing her breasts into his face.

He could try to dress her in his jacket, but if she came to and saw him fooling with her…well, he didn't want that to happen. As an afterthought, he threw her wet jacket on top of his and lifted her up again.

He spun around and plowed through the trees, wanting her as far from the edge of the cliff as possible. Within minutes, he reached his house.

The woman was still unconscious when he laid her on the porch chaise he hadn't yet bothered to put away for the winter. After he unlocked his front door, he scooped her up again and carried her inside.

The cold, still air hit his wet face, and blinking in the semidark, he stumbled over his rubber boots. With a curse, he kicked them aside, before carrying the woman to the couch. Her head lolled toward him when he laid her down, and with his shoulder, he shoved it the other way. Satisfied she wouldn't roll off, he headed straight for the woodstove.

Once the kindling caught, he stalked over to shut the front door and kick off his shoes. After hesitating a moment, he stooped to straighten them. May as well try to keep the place neat, since he'd be pacing the floor like a caged tiger for the next few weeks.

He looked around, his gaze landing on his crystal chess set as it caught the dancing firelight. He would probably hate his house and everything in it by the time the police department decided what to do with him.

But for now, this place held a small measure of comfort, offering the familiar scents of the home his uncle had built for his aunt.

A whimpering moan interrupted his thoughts. The woman. He hurried to the bathroom to grab a towel. Returning, he found her gaping up at him in unmasked fear, frozen like a mouse caught in a cat's stare.

"It ain't hell, sweetheart, and it sure ain't Heaven. You're still alive." He stood over her, gripping the towel.

She paled worse than before and for a fleeting moment, he expected her to faint again.

Instead, she continued to stare at him in mute horror.

"What's your name?"

She said nothing.

"Your name!" he demanded. What was wrong with her?

It took her a moment to answer. "Helen," she whispered.

"I'm Nick. Dry yourself off." He dropped the cool, dry towel on top of the jackets and walked toward the stairs. "I'll go find you something dry, since you've decided you don't like your pretty little sweater." He stopped and stared at her, his fingers digging into the banister as she pulled the towel up to her bare shoulders. "And forget trying to run for the cliff again. I didn't bring your shoes and I know I can catch you. Easily."

Her throat bobbed in the dim light of the late afternoon. He rolled his eyes. Flighty ladies weren't his area of expertise. He dealt better with the hardened women who walked the streets. The kind who fought like animals and swore like their sailor boyfriends. Nick had no time for little ladies who couldn't take their pampered lives anymore and tore at their fancy sweaters in kittenish fury.

Leaving their firm, rounded breasts sheathed only in transparent lace.

Sweat beaded on his forehead. He had to get her dressed. Now. Ignoring the psychological training that had taught him not to leave her alone, he galloped upstairs to his loft bedroom and grabbed only a sweatshirt. His sweatpants would probably fall right off her.

He found her sitting half-naked on his couch, her slim legs stretching up to the rounded bottom he'd cupped moments ago.

Whoa, Thorndike. ''Here,'' he growled, thrusting the sweatshirt at her. ''Put this on.''

Her dark blue eyes focusing on his face, she accepted his sweatshirt and mumbled something resembling a thank-you.

A loud crack of thunder tore through the house. He glanced out the window, surprised he'd missed the flicker of lightning. When he returned his attention to the woman, he found her hugging his sweatshirt to those damn full breasts, her eyes still like saucers.

''You ought to be scared, sweetheart. You nearly died out there.'' He suppressed a shudder, himself. Her death would have been brutal, too, being mauled by the waves and jagged rocks. And if they didn't finish her off, the frigid Bay of Fundy water would. Then her body would have washed up on shore like DiPetri's had a few miles east of here.

''Couldn't you have found an easier way to do it?''

She blinked, her arms tight around his sweater. ''Do what?''

''To end it all. Kill yourself.''

Another bolt of lightning hit, the blue-white flash reflecting briefly in her huge, dark eyes. She didn't answer.

"Pills would have been easier. Surely you have a whole medicine cabinet full."

The selfish thought snapped back at him and he swore loudly. His usual cutting sarcasm worked great when he had to deal with hardened criminals, but this woman was sick. She needed help, not alternatives to throwing herself off his cliff.

A few seconds later, thunder growled through the house. Through him. "Get dressed."

The woman struggled with the sweater he'd handed her. Impatient, he bent down to help her, his knuckles accidentally brushing against her shoulder. Her skin wasn't as cool as he'd expected, but warm, smooth like the feel of one of his silk shirts on a summer's night.

He yanked his hands away from her.

As soon as the storm ended, she was going to a crisis center. The women there would be better at helping her.

Way better than he could be.

Chapter 2

Helen jerked awake, her arms flying out in front of her to stop…

Who? Jamie?

Or Nick Thorndike?

Where was he?

Not in the living room, unless he hid somewhere in the shadows. The only available light radiated from a low woodstove fire to her right, its crackle breaking through the insistent drumming of the steady rain outside.

Someone, presumably Nick, had thrown a blanket over her. Comfortable for the first time in a week, she savored the warmth that soothed her aching body.

No. Nick was dangerous. Jamie's latest henchman. She thrust away the blanket, just as distant lightning pierced the living room again to prove she was alone. When the thunder reached her, she sat up. Was Nick asleep, or since she'd been found, was he plotting to return her to Jamie?

Apprehension shivered through her and she rubbed her

arms. Maybe he'd left, gone to meet Jamie, to bring him here?

She had to leave, now. Even this late in the evening, she could still disappear and make it look like suicide. Jamie would give up looking for her then. She stood and the couch groaned, echoing her own protesting joints.

She went as still as she could, praying that only she could hear her heart pounding loud enough to wake the dead. After a tense minute, her gaze settled on her coat as it hung from a chair by the fire. She'd have to give up the warm sweater Nick had practically shoved over her head. Too bad. With aching muscles, she peeled it off.

"Where are you going?"

Startled by the commanding voice, she spun around. Nick stood a few feet away. Again, lightning flickered outside and for a half a second gave her a full, stark view of him.

He wore nothing but a pair of rumpled boxer shorts, the wide elastic resting just below his navel. Dusted with dark hair, his thighs spoke of hard exercise. The slanted lightning etched out his strong, sculpted chest, defining the flat nipples that lay in perfect symmetry. His unsmiling, angular features were a far cry from her first sighting of him at Jamie's cigar bar, when his easy good looks were smooth, polished like the top of Jamie's mahogany desk.

"Where are you going?" he repcated, a tired huskiness seeping into his tone.

Her stomach flipped. She'd like nothing better than to wrench her feet free, but they seemed glued to the floor. Her hands shook and his sweatshirt dropped like a stone.

Nick's fingers tapped on lean hips. Was that the remains of a bruise on one knuckle? Tony's bloodied and swollen face had taken a nasty beating just moments before she'd walked in on him and Jamie. Nick had given that beating.

Fear and attraction, the deadly mix, swirled and swayed within her, the longing stealing her breath.

It didn't seem possible that the same man to offer her dry clothes could also be responsible for pounding Tony into a bloodied pulp, but hadn't she already proved, several times in fact, that she was no judge of men?

Her knees threatened to buckle. "I have to leave," she whispered through the semidark. He looked half-asleep and she hoped against hope that maybe she'd awoken him. Maybe he hadn't called Jamie. And, she prayed, maybe he didn't even recognize her?

Over a roll of thunder, she heard something on the front porch bang against the house. Wind flung sheets of rain against the door, attacking it like a barrage of tiny machine guns. Jarring the tattered nerves she'd only just managed to fortify with a deep breath.

"You want to leave in this weather?" He stepped toward her, scanning her half-naked frame with guarded concern. "Do you think that's wise?"

She couldn't look into his face. She didn't want to see any hint of kindness in his eyes. He was a friend of Jamie's. He wasn't kind.

The same primitive heat she'd felt at Jamie's smoky party pushed aside the fear. On some basic, organic level, Nick attracted her like no other man had. She glanced down at herself. Tight jeans and a thin bra that clung to her breasts as if for dear life. Merciful heavens, she should cover herself and get out. "I—I have my coat. I'll be fine outside."

"I can't let you go."

She watched him close in, the strength she'd possessed a moment ago evaporating like water on a hot stove. Nick took her elbow and led her to the couch. "You should put that sweater back on."

She couldn't. All she could manage was to collapse against the cushions and feel the appalling tears of frustration well up in her eyes.

If only she was stronger. But she'd used up all her strength to reach the cliff. And she'd failed there, too.

Exhaustion pounded at her. A week's worth of running had drained her of even the energy to slip on Nick's sweater again. Let him see her half-naked. She didn't care anymore.

"Get dressed." He threw the sweater at her. "I'm taking you to the crisis center in Saint John."

She snapped her head up, ignoring the wind battering the house and moaning an even sadder tone than she felt herself. No, the center for abused women was out of the question. Calling on the fact she'd had the strength to carry out a dangerous plan, she lifted her chin. "No, you're not."

Nick blinked in disbelief. "Why the hell not?"

Because crisis centers and safe houses weren't safe enough for her. No doubt Jamie was already discreetly checking them out. He had connections at the police station, didn't he?

"How do you know where the center is?" Maybe if she could get Nick to admit he was a police officer, she could remind him of why he became one in the first place....

He shrugged. To her horror, she knew he wasn't about to admit he knew where the center was. Or that he was a police officer at all. "I'd drop you off at the hospital. They'd know who to call. Aren't there pamphlets and such in the women's washroom?"

She shut her eyes. Another failure. "I can't go to the center. Please don't take me there."

The couch sagged and she opened her eyes in time to

see Nick settle beside her. He threw the afghan heaped between them onto the back cushion.

He seemed to acquiesce. "Look, running outside in this weather won't help you, but the women at the crisis center will."

He reached for her arm, but held back, his hand hovering above her tingling skin. His voice softened, the warm timbre sliding over her like a hot, silken bath. "I promise I won't take you anywhere you don't want to go. But I think you should go into Saint John and find someone to help you, okay? Someone you can trust?"

She stared into his dark brown eyes. Flickers of light from the woodstove danced in them, giving him a devilish look so contradictory to his voice. God help her, she felt the stirring attraction again, deep inside of her. In a few seconds, the unwanted urges would lambaste her at full, hot force, and his kind words would do nothing to help her fight back.

Why must he sound so compassionate? Didn't he know the thin thread holding together her courage and self-discipline was already stretched taut?

"I can't go there." Please, she begged silently. Please don't touch me....

He parted his smooth lips. The action softened his tired features into a gentle look so different from the cop who didn't mind lining his own pockets with what she now realized was Jamie's illegal wealth. Right now, he was nothing like the man who didn't care what laws he broke, as long as he got rich.

"In the morning." His voice was marked with a quiet concern she wanted to believe was real.

She sagged away from him, afraid that the heat smoldering inside her would burst into flame. Oh, how good a genuine compassion would be. How good it would feel to trust him...and fall into his arms...and forget what had happened.

Swallowing, she glanced down Nick's frame. Firelight delivered a golden sheen to his chiseled muscles, a sheen that was surely as warm to the touch as it was to her eyes. A ragged scar puckered the smooth, inward dip near his shoulder. Over the smell of the wood fire, she caught his personal scent—musk, sharpened with the faint tang of citrus. The delicious fragrance hiked up her heart rate.

Even as she inhaled deeply, she steeled herself against the attraction. Not now, not when failure lured her into that bland void of giving up. "I won't go to the crisis center. Just let me leave. I won't be a bother...."

He glanced out the window, in time for another series of distant lightning strikes. Seconds later, thunder crashed against the house, rebounding on her drum-tight nerves. His mouth turned grim as he shook his head. "Not until the storm's over. I'm sorry."

He sounded sorry. He really did. But as much as she ached to believe him, she couldn't. She had only a few minutes before she'd lose all confidence. Standing up, she shoved down the attraction and forced her fear to give her strength. "You can't keep me here."

Quick as the lightning outside, he pulled her back down. She landed with a thud, teetering toward his big frame enough for him to steady her with his warm hand. His voice turned sharp. "Don't be foolish. You just tried to kill yourself, woman, and you think I'm going to let you walk out of here?"

She went rigid. Immediately, he loosened his hold on her, but still kept his fingers wrapped around her elbow. As the silent moments passed, his thumb caressed the smooth skin of her inner arm. Such an intimate gesture, hard to fortify herself against the pleasure of it.

''Sorry.'' His thumb continued to work its magic. ''I didn't mean to hurt you. Look, you're a whole lot safer here than out there. I won't hurt you. I promise. I'm a—''

He cut off his own words. Was he about to admit he was a cop? She held her breath, hoping for the chance to remind him of his calling. Instead, he brushed his fingers up and down her elbow, adding to the electricity already surging into her shoulder and beyond.

As if to taunt her with her own vulnerability, her breasts tingled. When his gaze dropped to the sheer cups, her nipples budded hard. Damn them for showing the tender underbelly of her response to this man.

She tried to shake off the attraction. Everything about this situation screamed bad news in her head, and yet her body ached to the bone from a week of running. It wanted comfort. It needed the comfort only a man could provide.

Why Nick? The man who could deliver her to Jamie?

But who had promised she'd be safe, in a way she could believe was genuine.

This attraction was strictly physical, until now, when she sensed a contradictory sincerity in him. Maybe she wanted to believe he wasn't all bad, simply to justify this crazy attraction.

Nick's hand trailed up her arm, stroking her bare shoulder before brushing his knuckles up her neck. She shut her eyes. Her lips parted and a soft moan escaped, foreign even to her own ears. Heat surged into her breasts, filling them to overflowing before pouring its molten honey into the empty mold of her womanhood.

Dear heaven, she wasn't strong enough to resist this attraction. Not with Nick so close. It didn't matter to her body that he could easily do to her what he'd done to Tony DiPetri. Or worse, kill her. Her betraying body simply didn't care. All it wanted was the fleeting pleasure of his touch.

And her mind, the only sane part of her, gave up and shut down in absolute exhaustion.

Her skin was so silky. Nick battled the urge to pull his hand away, but his fingers were already addicted to the satin they found.

Here, on his couch, during the storm that had stolen the electricity, the same storm he was determined to ignore, he fought the temptation of her skin.

She was warm. Despite the rain outside, the woodstove kept the house toasty dry. He'd banked the fire nicely after Helen had fallen asleep. Then he'd dropped onto the cot in his study under the stairs and lay there, his mind full of his suspension and murder...and her.

Now, as his bruised knuckles brushed up her neck to her tender ear, he realized how little time his undercover work had allowed for recreation. The abstinence hadn't bothered him before. He'd accepted the fact he was a loner ages ago.

He couldn't even remember when he'd last made love to a woman. And adding to the building frustration was the knowledge that his suspension would leave him with plenty of vacant time to linger on his past self-denial.

She leaned her head toward his hand, her moist, generous lips parting just as her eyelids drifted shut. Her groan danced over his wrist. Each and every hair on his arms stood erect, anticipating the pure pleasure that would course through him, straight to his groin.

He toyed with her bra strap, afraid to inhale in case with it would come the reality of this terrible mistake. He didn't want to listen to his conscience. He needed this brief encounter. More than anything.

With his suspension, his life would be impotent. At least he could be of use here, giving them both a taste of pleasure.

He slid his fingers under the strap and with a gentle tug, pulled her close. With careful precision, he angled his head to touch his lips to hers.

She moaned and softened against him. He slid his other hand around her waist and drew her even closer. Hard nipples scraped against his bare chest as he ran his hand just under the waistband of her jeans.

She welcomed his tongue into her mouth. A growl rumbling deep in his chest vocalized the need to plunge himself into her.

When his hands found the clasp of her bra, he released it and peeled the thin material away. He brushed his palms over her nipples, evoking another moan from her.

Her head tilted back, exposing a tender throat. Delicious.

He stopped a second before another guttural expletive rose inside of him. She was giving herself to him. Freely. This beautiful, desperate woman…who had just tried to commit suicide.

His nostrils flared, drawing in warmth and musk and the unique scent of a woman in need of a man.

Lightning forked jaggedly, illuminating her expression and branding it in his mind. Eyes shut and her face slackened with pleasure, she looked as she had when she'd fainted out on the cliff.

The curse he'd held back spilled out of his mouth.

What the hell was happening? In his frustration and anger at his world, he was taking advantage of a sick, helpless woman, who, only hours earlier, had been ready to end her life.

What was he thinking?

He hadn't been thinking. He'd been caught up with urges he'd denied his body for too long. He'd let the impotent anger of his failure at work take over what was left of his good sense. Then he'd twisted the logic to suit himself, believing she needed him to make love to her.

No damn way. He wasn't doing her any favors. He was adding to her problems. Adding to his own as well, considering he should be acting more like a police officer and less like a sex-starved teenager.

He was no better than that scum Jamie Cooms. Making love to this woman was no different than Cooms taking advantage of the poor addicts he sold drugs to.

His heart hammering in his throat, he pushed himself away. Breath burst from his lungs, hot and hard like his body. He should tell her to leave, except wouldn't she finish off what she'd started on the cliff?

But he couldn't finish what he'd started here.

Gently shoving her down, Nick settled in beside her, closest to the back of the couch, while evidence of his arousal thrust into her back. He pulled the afghan over both of them.

"Go to sleep." His words sounded so harsh and cold, and he touched his lips contritely to the back of her hacked off hair and wondered again who had done such a terrible thing to her.

Because he was no better than that bastard.

A distant ringing drilled into Nick's subconscious, stopping and starting until he shook his head and opened his gritty eyes.

He was alone on the couch, clutching one of the sofa's throw pillows, staring at the far wall of his living room while sunlight streamed in an eastern window.

The ringing rattled his nerves again. The phone. He staggered upright and reached for it.

"Yeah?"

"Good morning."

His partner, Mark Rowlands. Make that his ex-partner. Nick glanced at his watch. Seven-thirty. He drew in a sharp breath and threw a hasty glance around the room.

Where was she?

"I said good morning."

Shaking his head, he answered, "It's my day off, jerk. I'm suspended, remember?"

Mark fell silent and Nick regretted his outburst. But Mark should know his style. Work alone, live alone. Do his own thing.

"The chief wants you to clear out your desk and your locker. He needs them for the auxiliary officer he's called in. He's really pissed on this one, Nick. Saint John's chief called him, saying his mayor's not pleased they've spent thousands on an undercover operation that's shot to hell."

"Sorry." He barely paid attention. The sweatshirt he'd offered the woman lay neatly folded on the arm of the couch. Still holding the cordless phone to his ear, he peeked into his study. Where was she?

The cliff.

He swore into the phone. "I gotta go. Clean out my locker, will you?"

"Want me to come over and cook your breakfast, too?"

"Look, I'll call you back, okay?" Panic surged inside him. "I have to do something. Quick!"

He hung up and roared into his study to throw on the pants he'd peeled off the night before. Tearing shirtless and sockless into the living room, he grabbed his jacket. When he glanced down at the floor of the hall closet, he discovered his rubber boots were gone. Damn.

He wasted precious seconds struggling to shove his feet into his sneakers, but within the minute, he was out the door and around the house.

The edge of the cliff was empty. He tore into the woods, sprinting at top speed toward the tip of the cove. Wet branches slapped at him. Panting, he sucked in the smell of the forest after a cleansing rain.

He skidded to a stop at the cliff. In front of him were her sneakers and socks.

Please God, let her be safe.

Holding his breath, he peered over the edge. Caught on a jagged rock was the sweater he'd seen her tear in two.

His gaze darted back and forth, but he saw nothing else. No rubber boots, nothing. He pivoted and slammed into the thicket to his right, scanning all the time for signs she'd cut through the dense woods to the curve of the cliff facing directly into the Bay of Fundy. When he reached the drop-off, he stooped and leaned over. He could see the entire sunny coastline for miles.

No one.

Where *is* she?

Another expletive rising in him, he returned to the end of the trail. The ledge below him was untouched. No footprints in the wet sand that filled and smoothed the shallow crevices.

Wait. Last night the tide was low and now the water surged across the stretch of empty sand. In a few hours, the tide would be high again.

He scrubbed his face. Nothing was making sense. If she'd thrown herself off last night, as the tide was going out, she'd have been left on the beach. Not the most efficient way to die.

He'd seen his share of suicidal people and this woman didn't fit the profile anymore. Those who were determined to kill themselves were very efficient at it. So where had she gone?

He climbed down to the next ledge and peered over it to the ragged cliff below. Nothing, again. Did she have a change of heart and head for the crisis center? He doubted it, despite his asinine attempts of persuasion last night.

Muttering, he climbed back up to the top ledge. Her shoes and the socks shoved inside of them were sodden with rain. He picked them up and drained out the water. Each sock dropped to the rocks.

And so did something shiny.

A tiny set of vanity army dog tags on a delicate gold chain. Lifting the necklace up, he tilted his hand away from the brilliant sun to read the inscription.

Helen Eastman. Cyprus. 1985.

He frowned. Her name was Helen and if he judged her age right, someone in the military had done a United Nations tour of Cyprus while she was in her early teens. Her father, perhaps?

He shoved the necklace into his pocket and scanned the shoreline again, knowing the information wouldn't help him find her right now.

How had she managed to slip away from him? He'd always prided himself on being a light sleeper, but sometime in the night, she'd replaced her warm body with a throw pillow and disappeared without waking him.

Well, there was nothing he could do out here. He carried her belongings back to his house, where he threw the wet socks over the clothesline and propped up the shoes beside the woodstove. Then he phoned Mark.

''Can you run a check for me?'' he asked.

''Is it about Cooms? You're not allowed to work on this case, Nick,'' Mark warned.

"This has nothing to do with the case. It's a woman who might be missing. Her name is Helen Eastman."

"Where does she live?"

Nick grimaced. "Try Saint John. I think she might be hiding from an abusive boyfriend or husband."

There was a distinct, reluctant pause, but finally Mark answered. "Okay. I'll call you back."

After he changed into clean clothes, he spent the morning pacing the floor, stopping only to make coffee for himself. He resisted the constant urge to call Mark back, knowing that when the chief was p.o.'d, he was wise to lay low. Dennis Hunt's hot temper didn't cool easily.

A banging at his front door made him spin around. Helen? He stalked over and threw it open, halfway disappointed when his partner stepped into view and over the threshold. Mark wore a grim look, made all the sterner by his dark uniform. He dumped a green garbage bag on the floor. "Your stuff."

His insides tight, Nick thanked him. Then he asked, "Did you find out anything about Helen Eastman?" He couldn't breathe. He should have stayed awake all night and as soon as the storm let up, he should have driven her into the crisis center himself. What a fool he'd been.

Mark shut the door. "I asked you if this had anything to do with Cooms. You lied to me, Nick."

"No, I didn't."

Mark pulled a faxed photograph out of his jacket. "Is this the woman you're talking about?"

He took the thin paper. It was Helen all right. He recognized the soft, pouty lips. Luscious lips. And her hair had been as glorious as he suspected. Long, dark waves danced around her shoulders as she looked away from her companion—Jamie Cooms.

With a wash of cold dread, he glanced up at Mark. ''Where did you get this?''

''Saint John just got their hands on it.''

He gripped the fax, obviously a photocopy of a single snapshot. ''Are the Saint John police now snapping photos of their suspects like old friends?''

Mark smiled wryly. ''Only the special cases.'' He sobered. ''Did Cooms ever mention a girlfriend?''

''Yeah, he did. He'd had a string of them, but this latest one was new. He'd just started to date her. I hadn't been able to get a name.''

He rubbed his jaw. Helen Eastman wasn't the kind of woman Cooms usually favored. The guy preferred thin, cultured blondes. He looked back up at Mark. ''He didn't trust his buddies with his women, so I didn't expect to meet her. And that cigar bar party was a bust, remember? Cooms left as soon as he arrived, and didn't come back until much later.'' A frigid line of ice water trickled down his spine. The night of the party, he'd caught only the briefest glimpse of Cooms with a dark-haired woman, a millisecond before they turned and left. Someone said later that his girlfriend had taken ill.

He'd come so close, damn it.

''I don't know what happened at the party. You haven't kept me up to date.'' Mark's tone was cutting. ''This Eastman woman's landlord, a guy named Chester Ellis, called the Saint John police this morning, saying Eastman hadn't been around for a week. Ellis let them into her apartment and they found the photo shoved under some papers on top of the refrigerator. When the constables recognized Cooms, they handed the case over to the Major Crimes Unit.''

Nick's hands started to shake. ''When was she last seen?''

"A week ago. They've got an eyewitness who saw her running from Cooms's office a few minutes after you left." Mark paused before his voice dropped. "Around the same time the coroner figures Tony DiPetri was shot."

Nick dropped to the arm of the couch, feeling his sweatshirt under him. He put out a hand to touch the back cushion, hoping to restore the reserve he'd always enjoyed. DiPetri's needless murder had eaten at him all last week because he'd been there, with Cooms, moments before the man's death. Bloodying his knuckles on DiPetri's face to prove himself to Cooms.

Mark leaned over him. "Do you realize Helen Eastman could be our only witness?"

He nodded. Oh, yeah, did he ever realize that.

"Did you tell her who you were?"

"No."

"Did she recognize you?"

She must have. That was why she was gone this morning.

Mark kept talking. "This is a stupid question, but did you tell her you were undercover? Because if you did, there's a lot of officers out there who need to know—"

"Damn it, no!" He took a deep breath. "You know I would never do that."

"Do you realize that she might be willing to testify against Cooms and every suspect involved, if she's really on the run?"

"Yeah, yeah," he snapped. Helen, the woman here last night, the woman who made him feel alive for such a short, tender time....

"Nick, where is she?"

He blinked Mark back into focus. "I don't know."

''Blast it, Nick, how can you not know? You just called me about her. Where is she?''

He swallowed. ''I think she may have committed suicide.''

Chapter 3

"Don't screw with me, Nick. Where is she?" Mark grabbed him by the shirt and hauled him up to glare in his face.

He let Mark vent his anger because he felt pretty much the same way.

But Mark tightened his grip. "This is our first break in a murder investigation, not to mention the op. You might not care about it, but I sure as hell would like to see this whole thing wrapped up. I've put too much time into it and into figuring out your moves, since you never bothered to keep me informed."

Enough of this crap. Nick threw Mark off, easily, as he was the bigger of the two. "Look, I want Cooms behind bars as much as you do," he snapped. "And I'm not screwing with you, either."

"Then why did you say she's killed herself?"

"I didn't say she's killed herself. I said it may be a possibility, but frankly, I'm not sure." He blasted out a frustrated sigh. ‘‘I caught her yesterday up at the edge of the cliff, ready to throw herself off. Or so I thought. I didn’t even know who she was. When I called out to her, she took one look at me and fainted.’’

‘‘What happened then?’’

He threw out his hand to indicate his living room. ‘‘I brought her in here. By that time, the weather was too miserable to take her into Saint John. The storm turned out to be a real kicker, so I figured I’d drop her off at the crisis center today.’’

He paused, reluctant to expand on the actual events of last night. ‘‘When I woke up, she was gone.’’

‘‘You went to bed and left her alone?’’ Mark let out a laugh of disbelief. ‘‘Why?’’

He knew what Mark was suggesting. No police officer would leave a suicidal woman alone. If she’d been in custody, she’d have been checked every five minutes.

But Helen hadn’t been in a cell and Nick wasn’t about to explain how he managed to keep his arms around her most of the night. It was bad enough he’d fallen into so sound a sleep, he didn’t even remember her slipping a pillow into his arms and fleeing.

Mark’s cell phone rang abruptly. Shortly after he answered it, he frowned, thanked the caller and hung up. He stared at Nick. ‘‘Go on.’’

Nick was instantly suspicious. ‘‘That was about Helen, wasn’t it?’’

Mark paused, and Nick knew his straitlaced ex-partner too well. ‘‘Mark, that woman tried to throw herself off my cliff. She could exonerate me, for pete’s sake. Give me a break.’’

Mark lifted his eyebrows and shook his head. ‘‘All right. Here’s an interesting piece of info. Saint John just ran her name through the computer. She’s got a lousy credit rating. Five years ago, she emptied her overdraft protection and moved down here."

Nick blinked. What for? Did it have anything to do with Cooms's drug business? He felt his jaw tighten as the possibilities flickered through his mind. "What else?"

Mark's gaze danced around him, lighting on his own phone, still held tight in his hand. He pursed his lips. "She's...Nick, you know I'm breaking all the rules here. I'm sorry."

"So why the hell did you tell me about her bank account?"

"Old habit, I guess. Look, Nick, she stole from her bank and got caught. We don't need to guess why, considering Cooms has been—"

"Shut up." He didn't want to hear anymore. Not while he considered Helen might be dead, and he could have stopped her.

Both men fell into an uneasy silence, until Mark, shoving his fingers through his hair, glanced over to the living room. Nick followed his gaze when Mark focused on Helen's shoes, tipped over in front of the fire.

"Those hers?"

He nodded. "Looks like she's taken my rubber boots."

"She wears sneakers? Not the kind of woman I could see with Cooms."

"I thought the same thing." Cooms didn't seem the type to date a coltish thing like Helen. Odd.

"Did you go back up to the cliff?" Mark asked.

He bristled. "Of course. There's no sign that she returned there. So I brought her shoes and socks back with me. And this." He pulled out her necklace. "This is where I got her full name. When I suspected she may not have thrown herself off the cliff this morning, I came back here and called you."

''Any idea where she might go?''

Nick shook his head. They hadn't done much talking. The kind of getting-to-know-you stuff they'd done didn't include words. He looked up at Mark, keeping his glance quick so his ex-partner wouldn't catch the guilt lingering there. ''Did anyone check her bank accounts here?''

''I imagine Major Crimes in Saint John will. Why?''

He stood and stretched out his aching muscles. No jogging yesterday or today, and he felt stiff already. ''If she witnessed Cooms shoot DiPetri, then she's been on the run for a week. She'd need money. Does she have any family here?''

''The landlord said she has a mother, but we haven't located her yet.''

''Call me when you do?''

Mark's face clouded over with warning. Nick crushed the urge to snap at him. Finally, Mark spoke, his voice low. ''This isn't your case, anymore.''

''Don't you think the mother would like to know what's happened to her daughter?''

''The mother didn't file the missing persons report.'' Mark wore a cocky look which Nick considered punching off his face. But why bother? He was madder at himself than anyone else and with good reason.

''Well, I know my mother would like the man who stopped me from committing suicide to drop by and say hello. But if you don't want to tell me, I still have some friends in Saint John who could find out for me.''

Mark's mouth went tight. ''Don't bother them. I'll call you with the address. But frankly, Nick, if the woman hasn't missed her daughter yet, I'd say she doesn't care too much.''

He didn't answer. Rather, he furrowed his brows together. Yeah, what kind of a mother was she?

"Nick?"

He looked up at Mark. "What?"

"Do us both a favor, okay? Stay off the case. I know you like to run the show, but frankly, it backfired on you this time. Don't let this case ruin your career."

He snorted. "I don't have a career anymore."

Mark smiled, ever so briefly. "If we can find Helen Eastman, you might. Providing she isn't dead." He turned and walked out the front door.

Nick sagged as the police cruiser disappeared down the driveway. Mark had been the best partner he'd ever had. Not that there were many to choose from. His first partner, fresh out of the academy, was the worst. He froze during an armed standoff, leaving Nick to talk the scared kid into dropping his weapon, or take him down.

Except the boy hadn't put down his weapon and Nick had glanced toward the crowd and caught the mother's eye. He couldn't take the kid down in front of her, so he aimed for the legs. Meanwhile, the boy had aimed for Nick's heart, but got him in the shoulder.

He and the suspect ended up at the local emergency room, while a doctor sewed up two flesh wounds. The boy's was in the thigh. Nick took one in the shoulder.

Had the bullet entered three short inches up and to the right, he'd have taken the shot in the neck.

He rotated his left arm, feeling the scar tighten over the muscle. He hated partners, but he had to say, Mark was his best. A bit by-the-book, but all right.

And right about Helen. If they could find her and she was willing and able to testify against Jamie Cooms, his career might be salvageable.

He scrubbed his day-old beard, contemplating the shower he needed badly. Though not while Helen was out there somewhere, alone. Did she have enough money? Was she considering suicide again? Had she already?

An icy chill danced down his spine. How could he look her mother in the eye and tell her he'd let her walk out of his house to kill herself?

He stopped in midthought. Her mother hadn't missed her. But no gentle thing like Helen Eastman would go a week without calling her mother. Sure she was on the run, trying to hide, afraid but gutsy enough to walk out on the cliff—

Holy cow. The sweater, rent in two.

The neatly placed shoes, the necklace that was so precious, she'd tucked it safely into her shoe. The hair, hacked off to better fit under a wig.

The reluctance to peer over the cliff…

Ramming his feet into his sneakers again, he threw open the front door. Outside, he searched the soft, wet ground, finding Mark's thick-soled prints beside his own.

And there! His boot prints, barely indented!

Careful not to disturb them, he followed them into the trees, traveling to the start of a neglected path that wasn't far from the one leading to the cliff. If his childhood memories were correct, this path led to a small bog.

Her trail of broken branches was easy to follow and he plunged into the woods. The thin trees, their lower limbs dead wood, snapped at his jeans like angry dogs.

Hope seized him when he reached the small bog. The spongy earth was forgiving to intruders, but someone had recently flipped back a wide section of rich green peat moss, revealing the black acidic soil beneath.

His rubber boots stood beside the hole. So did a clear plastic bag with her jeans, bra and panties inside it.

Bingo!

The sun hit his back as he hunched down. Indian summers were always hot after a good storm.

Sheltered from the bay wind, he carefully spread out the plastic bag. Inside it, a few strands of blond hair glinted in the sun. The color and shine told him it was from some kind of cheap PVC wig.

Relief swamped him and he sank to his knees on the soft peat. She hadn't killed herself, nor had she ever intended to. She wanted to fake her death and disappear. A bit amateurish, but hell, he didn't care.

And like the good daughter she must be, he'd wager she'd told her mother. That was why Mrs. Eastman didn't report her missing. At least not until after the suicide was to take place when she could "suggest" where Helen might have gone.

Time to pay the mother a visit.

Helen sank into the back seat of the bus and slowly let out the breath she felt she'd been holding for a week.

Only one other time had she fully relaxed, let out her breath in a swirl of pleasure....

No. She refused to think of that insane moment.

An elderly man and his young grandson came down the aisle toward her. She watched, waiting with another bated breath for some suspicious behavior. But the pair ignored her and settled down in the seats close to the lavatory.

Returning to Saint John had been a big risk, but she needed the ordered chaos of a major depot. Dressed in her disguise, she had driven straight through to the east end bus station. She'd parked her car in the long-term lot and boarded the first bus. Now it rumbled out of the city depot, headed for its next stop, Lower Cove.

Lower Cove. Helen sank deeper in her seat. She should never have chosen that cove in which to fake her suicide, but Momma's suggestion had made sense at the time. If her "death" had to be discovered, it may as well be somewhere Momma knew. Her mother could say she'd told her about the place many times. It would be more convincing that way.

Giving in to the idea was the least she could do for her mother.

She shivered. She'd have been in Maine by now, maybe through it and on her way up to Quebec, if Nick hadn't pulled her off the cliff.

Last night's events still tumbled about in her head. An impossible set of odds had put him living in the very house her mother had spoken of so often. Him, the dirty cop. The man who'd carried her back to his home, who'd taken care of her, instead of finishing off what she had pretended to start.

He who, a few hours later, had practically made love to her.

Heat smoldered where he'd touched her and she shoved away the need. He was a dirty cop, wasn't he? Jamie had boasted about him, invited him to his cigar bar. And she'd seen him moments before Tony's murder.

But he hadn't taken her to Jamie. He'd seemed to care about her well-being.

She rubbed her forehead. Maybe he'd called but the weather delayed Jamie from coming to get her.

And then, to wile away the time, he'd tried to make love to her. She'd even reveled in the idea because her body demanded a break after a week of nonstop running.

Sick of herself, she closed her eyes and let the bus carry her into Lower Cove.

The depot here doubled as the coffee shop in a small strip mall near the highway. The driver grabbed the mike and announced a ten-minute break.

She had to get off the hot and stifling bus. The nausea of a few moments ago waned, but she still needed some cool autumn air. Fumbling with her purse and keeping her head low, she made her way off the bus.

Inside the women's washroom, she leaned against the cubicle door and swallowed. Please don't get sick, she begged her body. She didn't want to lose the small breakfast she'd eaten, especially when money was so tight.

Someone entered the washroom. Hastily, Helen straightened and finished her business. The bus wouldn't wait for her.

She threw open the door and hurried out.

A man stood there.

One of Jamie's men.

Connie Eastman's modest bungalow was at the western end of the city, on the road leading to the small peninsula used as a nature park. Fog had rolled over the whole city and by nine that morning, was as thick as the day-old coffee the chief preferred.

Nick drove along the road at a dead crawl, counting the indistinct houses until he reached the right one, but only knowing for certain when he pulled into the driveway to get close enough to read the number.

As he shut off the engine, his cell phone rang. Settling back into his seat, he answered it.

''Nick?'' Mark asked.

''Yeah?''

''News for you. Good or bad, it changes everything.''

Shock numbed him when his partner gave the details. Nick had a million questions to ask, but stopped when a slight figure, an older version of Helen, peered out the front window like a ghost. Connie Eastman.

"Can I call you back?" Nick quickly rang off and climbed out of his SUV.

He pulled up the collar of his jacket as he walked to the door. He rang the bell, a damp, disturbing cold slowly replacing the numbness Mark's call had created. A call he still wasn't sure how to take.

Finally, the front door opened and a blast of warmth hit his face. Mrs. Eastman appeared, wiping her hands on a tea towel.

"Mrs. Eastman? I'm Nick Thorndike. I called earlier."

"Oh, yes." She hesitated a moment, and pursed her lips.

"Please, Mrs. Eastman, I need to speak with you." She had been cool on the phone, but now she acted down right cold to him. "May I come in?"

With another hesitation, she opened the door wider. "Come in."

Politely, he slipped out of his damp shoes and followed her into the immaculate living room. The rich smell of sweet baking filled his nostrils.

Seeing him inhale the delicious scent, she said, "I'm baking for the senior center's card party." She extended her hand toward a chair. "Sit down."

She perched herself on the edge of another easy chair. "I've already had other policemen come by to ask questions."

Really? Interesting. "When?"

"Yesterday. I can't imagine how I can help you. Have you found my daughter yet?"

Nick studied her. No signs of overworrying, no tracks of salty tears. She was even baking for a social. With nothing but mild concern in her blue eyes.

She knew where Helen was, all right. He'd stake what was left of his career on it. "No, I haven't found her," he said, finally. "But I should tell you I'm no longer with the police force."

She stiffened. "Are you a private investigator?"

"No."

She folded her arms. "What are you, then?"

He took a deep breath. If he wanted her to be honest with him, he'd have to be honest with her, to a point. He handed her one of his cards. Printed on it were his pager and cell phone numbers. "Suspended."

She leaned forward and put the card on the side table. "I beg your pardon?"

"I said," he answered, louder than he'd muttered a moment before. "I *was* a police officer. I'm currently on suspension."

"Why?" She peered at him with surprise in her candid eyes.

"That's not important. What's important is finding your daughter."

Mrs. Eastman stared at the tea towel she'd scrunched into a tight ball. "Yes. Of course."

Enough of these courtesy games. He undid his jacket and leaned forward on the seat he'd chosen, the one closest to both the kitchen and front door, yet still had a view of the hall, on the off chance Helen would appear from a bedroom.

"How long has your daughter been seeing Jamie Cooms?"

"On and off for a couple of months. I should have said something, but didn't want to make waves, and she'd—" She stopped and her sudden frown melted away.

"She'd what?"

"She'd…she'd hinted she was ready to quit seeing him." She looked around the room, blinking. "I know she would have tried to do it with as little fuss as possible, but I didn't know she'd..."

"I know she didn't commit suicide, Mrs. Eastman."

The older woman's startled gaze flew to his face. "How do you know that?"

"I stopped her."

"Stopped her?" she echoed.

He gritted his teeth, ordering himself to be patient. If he was undercover, working on an act, this conversation would be a piece of cake. But now, as Nicholas Thorndike, he was nothing but a suspended cop trying to find the woman he'd tried to save. The woman who could save his career. There wasn't any act to follow, no smooth personality to cultivate. His career was at stake, sure, but more importantly, he needed to see a woman safe and everyone involved in this drug smuggling op behind bars.

"Yeah, I saved her life. When I got home yesterday, I saw her on top of a nearby cliff. I raced up and grabbed her before she could throw herself to her death, though she was more likely to slip. It was raining out. And with those sharp rocks below, ready to gouge out a person's guts..."

Mrs. Eastman flinched, her face showing how his brutal description disturbed her. She swallowed to retrieve her composure. "When you got home?"

"Yeah. My house is the only one in the cove."

"Lower Cove?"

Why was she repeating everything he said? He let out an impatient sigh. "That's right."

Leaning forward, she searched his face. "The log home?"

She knew his house? With a frown he nodded.

"You're Abigail Saunders's nephew?"

More surprised than annoyed with her question, he answered, "You knew my aunt?"

"A long time ago. Before you were born, I imagine. I got my first job out of high school working as her housekeeper." She looked again at her hands. "Your aunt introduced me to my late husband."

Her voice dropped at the mention of her husband. Helen's father was dead? He cleared his throat. "Was your husband in the military?"

"Why, yes! Did Helen tell you that?"

"No." He wished he hadn't given the necklace to Mark. He could offer it to her now, earn her trust a little more. "I saw your daughter's necklace."

Connie Eastman paled. Blinking, she dared a hasty glimpse to the mantel of a natural gas fireplace. He spotted a photo there and stood. "Is this your husband? Did he give her the necklace?"

"Yes," she answered slowly.

He retrieved the photo. A man, dressed in combat fatigues and a blue UN beret, hugged a teenaged Helen in front of what looked like military housing. He set the photo down.

"Was she wearing the necklace?" Connie Eastman's voice wavered.

"No, she wasn't. Found it in her shoe."

Mrs. Eastman relaxed somewhat. "Do you have it now?"

"I gave it to the police when I called them."

Again, the flare of fear. This time, though, he could see something click in her head. Her mouth pursed until tight little lines radiated from her lips. Her stare went cold.

It didn't take a cop to realize she wasn't going to tell him anything more. With a sigh, he tried anyway. "Do you know where your daughter is, Mrs. Eastman?"

She blinked and stood. "Excuse me, I have cookies in the oven...."

He stood, too, and in one stride, he caught her arm. "I found where she hid her disguise. Where was she headed?"

Mrs. Eastman threw off his light grip and bustled into the kitchen. "I told the other policemen I don't know where she is. I told them—" She cut off her sentence.

"What did you tell them, Mrs. Eastman?"

She bent down and snatched a tray of cookies out of the oven. At the entrance to the kitchen, he felt the steamy sweet scent bombard him, a strong contradiction to the cold tension Connie Eastman cast through the room. "I told them the same thing I told you, Mr. Thorndike."

"Did they ask why you didn't report your daughter missing?"

She whirled around, her hands still in her oven mitts. "They did, and I told them she doesn't call me every day! Not since she started to see Jamie Cooms. Now, please leave my home, Mr. Thorndike, before I call the real police and ask them to remove you."

The real police. The words stung him. He pivoted, preparing to leave.

The phone rang. Mrs. Eastman hurried over to answer it.

"Hello?" A pause, followed by a low gasp as she threw Nick a sharp glance. "I can't talk. I'm busy..."

He stopped. Despite the warmth of the house and the comforting scent of chocolate chip cookies, he went cold.

Mrs. Eastman leaned over the counter, cupping her hand over her mouth.

Damn, it was Helen! He strode over and grabbed the receiver, knowing there would be time later to apologize. "Helen!"

Helen gasped on the other end. ''Where's Momma?''

''Helen, don't hang up. It's Nick. Where are you?''

A stifled sob answered him. His heart tightened, blocking a sharp curse before it rose to his lips. ''It's okay. Where are you? I'll come get you.''

''Put my mother back on.'' Her voice was a hiccuped whisper.

''Not until you tell me where you are.''

Another sob escaped and with a million things whirling through his mind, he considered handing over the phone. He couldn't. Even if Helen told her mother where she was, he knew Mrs. Eastman would never tell him.

He let out a controlled exhale. ''Your mother's safe. She's baking cookies. Now tell me where you are.''

''I—I'm at the strip mall in Lower Cove.''

''Which store?''

''I'll be behind the building. I can't...''

What the hell was she doing at the strip mall? Then he remembered. The bus stopped there. ''Can't what? Are you all right?''

A heavy, painful pause lingered between them. Nick held his breath until he could wait no longer. ''Are you all right? Answer me.''

Her voice hovered on the edge of tears. ''N-no. Can I speak with my mother, now?''

''Are you hurt? Call 9-1-1.''

''No! I'm fine! My mother?''

''Then stay where you are. I'll be there in twenty minutes.'' He hung up before she could protest further.

He hadn't reached the front door before Helen's mother caught him. ''Where is she?''

''In Lower Cove.''

Her fingers dug into his arm and her eyes, the same

dark blue as Helen's, widened with anxiety. "What's wrong with her? What have you done to her?"

He shrugged off her hand and grabbed his shoes. "I didn't do anything but save her life, Mrs. Eastman. Trust me, okay?"

"Why should I trust you? You're a suspended cop who—" She shut her mouth.

Nick gritted his teeth. What the hell had Helen said about him? Moreover, what could he say in his own defense? Nothing. "I'm going to get your daughter."

"I'm coming, too."

"Mrs. Eastman, I think it's best for you just to stay here and keep your doors locked."

She ignored him, throwing on her coat as she slipped into sensible, all-weather shoes. That done, she turned to him. "You don't know my daughter like I do, Mr. Thorndike. And you don't know me. I've been giving this a lot of thought, lately. I sent her to that cove because I wasn't strong enough to help her the way I should have. How can I expect my daughter to be strong, when I'm not myself?"

"Your daughter's stronger than she thinks. She was strong enough to run from Jamie Cooms. And she tried to fake her own suicide to throw him off her tail, right?"

"Yes, but—" she said, her voice hesitant.

He looked up from his shoes. "But what, Mrs. Eastman?"

Connie Eastman's jaw tightened. She didn't answer him, but he could imagine what lingered on her lips. But if Nick Thorndike knew where Helen was, Jamie Cooms would know, too.

There were days when he hated his job.

He finished lacing up his shoes. He didn't want Connie Eastman's help, but when he straightened, the woman looked at least six inches taller. He was on the verge of telling her again to stay put, but he stopped. Helen would welcome her mother. She needed her mother a hell of a lot more than she needed him. "All right. Let's go."

He didn't say a word to his pale, silent companion as he put the city in his rearview mirror. The fog still hadn't lifted and when he reached the highway, his headlights cut the thick soup with two wide beams of yellow light.

He wished to hell his heart would stop racing like a jackrabbit. It was too distracting. He was a police officer. He should be able to control himself, think rationally, do what had to be done without his heart going into overdrive.

Lower Cove's only strip mall finally appeared through the lifting fog. He roared into the quiet parking lot, pulling up to a stop at the far end, beside a bar that wouldn't open for another four hours.

He threw open his door a second before Helen shot out from behind the brick building.

Reaching him, she balled her fists and flayed his chest with them. "You bastard! You leave my mother alone!"

Stunned momentarily, Nick grabbed her wrists and propelled her against the wall of the building. He heard her mother rush up behind him and cry out her name.

But Helen wasn't listening. "Let her go! Run, Momma, run!" She yanked one hand free and with her fist, smashed his jaw in a surprisingly painful punch.

What the hell? "Damn it, woman, cut it out! I didn't kidnap your mother, all right? I went to her house to find out where you were!"

"Leave us alone! Can all of you just let me go? I won't tell anyone. I promise."

Nick cursed under his breath. She *did* know who he was. Rather, whom he played in his undercover role. Wonderful. She knew he was buddy-buddy with Cooms. And then she'd witnessed Cooms murder his best friend, Tony.

Nick swore again. Right after she'd seen him leaving the office with bloodied knuckles, he bet.

He fought down nausea as he took in her outfit. Her coat was torn, her hair, once pinned up to accommodate a wig, stuck out in disarray. A bruise darkened her right cheek, the one that bore trails of dried tears.

He resisted the urge to haul her into his arms. No, she needed her mother. He leaned in close to her, catching the lingering scent of the coffee shop in her disheveled hair. "I'll let you go, but don't hit me anymore. You're a lot tougher than you realize. Okay?"

She nodded and he slowly lowered her arms. Once free, she raced over to her mother. Rubbing his sore jaw, he waited for them to finish hugging.

"What happened to you, Helen?" he asked.

She turned and straightened her clothes. "I went to the washroom when the bus stopped for a break. When I got out of the cubicle, one of Jamie's boys was there."

"Are you sure?"

Her eyes flared. "I know when a man is standing in the women's washroom!"

"I mean, you knew who he was?"

"His name is Clive something. I think he works as a deliveryman for Jamie, but I haven't seen him in weeks. Big, ugly man."

He nodded. Yeah, he knew the guy. Clive Darlington. A nasty thug with a string of priors he'd managed to pay off with hefty fines, until the last time when a disgusted judge had thrown him in jail. Nick had made it his business to keep tabs on the man. Darlington had been freed yesterday afternoon after serving thirty days for petty larceny.

The facts he'd learned today from Mark also fell into place. They didn't look good. "What happened then?"

She swallowed. "Clive had locked the door and when I came out of the cubicle, he grabbed me. I kicked him in the groin and managed to unlock the door…." She shivered and glanced around.

"But not before he did that to you?" Nick touched her face, brushing his fingers below the growing bruise.

She flinched slightly, but nodded just the same. "I was lucky my wig wasn't properly attached. He grabbed it and it slipped off. Then I ran through the coffee shop kitchen and out the back door. I hid behind the Dumpster. He came looking for me, but something must have scared him off." Fresh tears filled her eyes and her voice broke. "Jamie wants me dead, you know that! Please, Nick, just leave me alone! You were once a good cop, weren't you? Can't you remember? Can't you let me go, just this once?"

Nick hauled her in close, ignoring her mother's short cry. He grabbed her head and nestled it against his jacket front. Stroking her messy hair, he whispered, "It's all right. Cooms won't hurt you again."

She lifted her head and peered at him through watery eyes. "How can you say that after what he did to Tony?"

He cupped her face, not really wanting to tell her why Mark had called him. But she deserved to know. "They found Jamie Cooms floating in the Saint John River this morning. The tide was pushing his body upstream, past the Reversing Falls. He'd been dead for about two or three days."

Relief flooded over her expression and behind him, her mother sighed.

The wind picked up and scattered a few pieces of litter around the corner. Behind the mall, on the nearby highway, a large tractor-trailer raced past, its Jake brake pounding in his ears.

For a moment, he let mother and daughter enjoy the relief. Neither of them realized the nightmare wasn't over.

While incarcerated, Clive Darlington hadn't been in contact with Cooms. In the past thirty days, he'd only spoken to a handful of Corrections officers, a few policemen and his mother. A guard had kept him informed on who visited him.

The shiver rippled through him again and he clung tighter to Helen. Jamie Cooms hadn't ordered the grab on Helen.

Someone else had.

Chapter 4

"I'll take you to the station," Nick said.

"No!" Helen shut her eyes, sagging away from Nick and against the cold, damp wall. Her nightmare was over. Jamie was dead. Why couldn't they all forget it? Nick could go back to being a crooked cop and no one would be any the wiser. They both knew she had no evidence against him. It would be her word against his and no one would listen to a woman who had tried to fake her own suicide. Nick could easily twist the facts to make it look like she'd actually tried to kill herself.

"Don't argue. You were assaulted and you should report it." He tried to grab her hand, but she was quicker.

She whipped over beside her mother and glared at him. When a noise caught her attention, she shot one glance to her right.

Oh, mercy. Another cop. A cruiser had just pulled in front of the coffee shop at the other end of the strip mall. She threw another glance at Nick, who caught her defeated expression and stepped out from beside the building. He muttered something she didn't catch.

The officer climbed out and looked across the parking lot, his gaze connecting with hers. Nick growled out something else and latched on to her elbow. Her mother made a protesting noise and reached for her, but Helen held up her hand. "It's okay, Momma."

"Over here," Nick said, steering her out of her mother's earshot and back to the wall. "Listen to me. Clive Darlington just got out of jail. He hasn't been in contact with Cooms for thirty days."

Helen blinked up at him. A look of concern creased his face. His eyes glimmered with an intensity that nearly matched the other night when she'd made a fool of herself in his arms, enjoying the pleasure only this crooked cop could offer.

She reddened and looked away, too tired to try to push Nick away. "So that explains why Clive hasn't been around lately. So what?"

"Jamie Cooms probably died two or three days ago. He hadn't spoken to Darlington for a month."

The truth sank into her fogged brain, leaving her limp. "Oh, my God."

Nick turned her so her expression was hidden from her mother. "You're still in danger," he whispered. "Someone out there wants you dead. Maybe the same someone who put a bullet in Cooms's chest."

An invisible band tightened around her lungs. Jamie had killed Tony, a life-long friend. Then someone had killed Jamie. And someone had ordered that slow-witted Darlington to kill her.

Where did Nick stand in all of this? Did he want to be the one who finished her off? Was this some sick "good cop/bad cop" routine he was pulling here?

She rubbed her temples. ''What do you care? Why is it so important to you?'' She was insane to ask the questions, but here, with that policeman just around the corner, what could he do? She already knew he wasn't carrying a weapon. She'd have felt it when she wrapped her arms around him just a moment ago.

Nick frowned, his eyes not focusing on her, but rather expressing some inner turmoil. The lie she expected didn't come.

It was too late for a conscience, she wanted to spit out to him. Two men were dead. ''If I report this assault, will you leave me alone?''

''I can't promise you that.''

She squared her jaw. ''Then send my mother home. Put her in a taxi—'' Oh, dear. She didn't have enough money for a cup of coffee, let alone a taxi fare into the city. ''Pay her fare to my aunt's house, will you? She lives in Saint John, too. Then I'll go to the police.'' She waited a moment. ''Deal?''

''Where does your aunt live?''

''In a senior's complex. It has a security guard out front. It's safe.''

Nick nodded. ''Okay.''

She smiled at her mother. ''I'd feel better if you went to Aunt June's for a few days, Momma.''

Her mother glanced toward the parking lot, then at Helen. ''Come with me.''

Helen shook her head. ''Her place is too small for both of us. And everyone will notice me. You go over there all the time, so no one will pay any attention.''

''Where are you going?''

Helen paused. Her bus had already left and she had no cash on her. Apart from the outside chance she could trade in her bus ticket for another one to take her to Quebec, she was pretty much out of options. Momma didn't have any money, either, and Helen refused to give her anything more to worry about.

"She's coming home with me," Nick said by her side.

"What?" She snapped her head over, but the look on his face hit her hard, unrelentingly, right in her chest. His words were authoritative, direct and assumed there would be no argument.

But his eyes... They weren't what she expected. Hot, plaintive...in need of something. Her insides tightened. Did he want her? Why?

And why did her traitorous body answer in a way it shouldn't have? This kind of immediate reaction hadn't been there for the other men in her life. Mind you, the other men in her life hadn't pinned her to a couch and immersed themselves in the solitary task of giving her pleasure.

"Nick..." Helen's feeble words of protest faded when a police officer appeared behind her mother.

"Ladies." The officer touched his cap. "Nick? Problem?"

Nick didn't smile. "Hello, Chief. No. There's no problem at all. This lady claims she was assaulted in the women's washroom. I was talking her into giving a statement at the station."

Helen wanted to protest, but the burly, ruddy-faced police officer looked at her, taking in her rumpled and torn clothes and bruised jaw. His eyes narrowed and he looked grim. "Do you need to see a doctor first, Ma'am?"

She shook her head, focusing on the nametag instead of the man's face. Dennis Hunt.

"Then it's best you get down to the station as soon as possible," Chief Hunt said.

"You won't catch him," she warned. "He's long gone."

"Let's talk about it at the station." He turned to Nick. "I know you're under suspension, but why don't you bring her in?" His eyes went dark. "As a civilian, that is."

After he sent Connie Eastman to her sister's, Nick drove Helen to the police station. Once stopped, he shoved the gear shift of his truck into park and glanced across at Helen, hoping his own apprehension didn't show on his face. Not that he didn't want her to file a report.

No, he wanted to get the bastard who'd brutalized her. But he didn't want the chief to take down the details. He wasn't sure what the chief knew about the Cooms's case and if he learned Helen was involved, he'd guess Nick was still investigating. Then any chances of him returning to the force would slide down the drain.

Thankfully, the chief had returned to his office with no intentions of handling the statement personally. Nick let out a silent sigh of relief.

Helen gave her disjointed version of what happened to another officer, the station's rookie. Nick tried to listen in, tried to focus on the facts, but his mind kept wandering as he weighed the options of telling Helen why he cared about her. But would she believe him? To her, he was a crooked cop. A suspended crooked cop.

Mind you, that assumption kept a nice, prominent barrier between them. One that could clearly stop him from doing something stupid like finishing what he'd started on his couch.

But it wasn't just that and he knew it. He didn't do the partnership thing very well. Not in his work life, and certainly not in his private life. He rolled his shoulder. It still ached after all these years. No, if you wanted things done, you did them yourself. And only by yourself.

So why was he taking her home with him?

The front door opened and he looked up in time to see Mark walk in. Still in uniform, he threw his briefcase on his desk and gave Nick a grim look when the other officer gave him a brief run down of what had happened, using all the proper jargon needed to keep Helen baffled.

Mark nodded. "Ms. Eastman, while you're here, I need to ask you a few questions about Jamie Cooms. And you, too, Nick."

Nick frowned, sneaking a glance across the room into the chief's office. He sat working at his desk, ignoring them. But Nick knew he was the one who had called Mark in. He turned back to his ex-partner. "Are you still on the case?"

"Loaned out until they wrap this up." His voice low, Mark met Nick's eyes with a challenge. "I may as well start with you while Ms. Eastman is busy."

In the coffee room for the next hour, after Mark had consulted with the young rookie, Nick went over the barest facts of where he was when Cooms was murdered. In return, Mark would only tell him the approximate time of death.

He knew what that meant. He was no longer a cop on the inside. He was a suspect. Along with Helen.

"So." Mark frowned at the statement. "You scooped this woman up and took her back to your house and never asked her name?"

Nick stood, irritated. "You know what happened, Mark. She was out cold and when she came to, I asked her name. She only told me her first name—Helen. She was terrified. And we were stuck there until the storm ended. I fell asleep and when I woke up, she was gone."

Mark leaned back in his chair. ‘‘Do you think she knows who you are?’’

‘‘Of course she does!’’ he snapped, driving his fingers into his hair before dragging them down his face. ‘‘To her, I'm a cop on the take.’’ He frowned. ‘‘She didn't tell that rookie that?’’

‘‘No.’’

Nick focused his gaze out the window at the passing highway traffic. She had her chance, and yet she didn't report him. Why?

‘‘In that case,’’ Mark said, throwing down his pen. ‘‘I don't want you to tell her any different.’’

Fine by me, Nick thought.

‘‘Because,’’ Mark continued, seeing the need to explain, ‘‘she may not know about the operation. I think she may have suspected Cooms of some illegal activities, but she didn't say so. All she knew about him was that he owned warehouses and other income property. So don't tell her any different.’’

Nick nodded. There were other officers out there whose very lives depended on anonymity. He wouldn't put them at risk. ‘‘What did you ask her about Cooms?’’

Mark shut off the recorder he'd been using. He always complained he could write fast enough. ‘‘She told me pretty much what we already knew.’’

Nick felt himself sag. Fatigue was taking its toll on him. All he wanted to do right now was crash on his couch.

He mentally pulled himself from that idea. It was a bad one. Too many recent memories there.

He stared at Mark. ‘‘Anything new on the money she ‘borrowed’?’’

‘‘You know I can't tell you, Nick.’’

Of course. Mark followed the rules. Helen wasn't a suspect, she was a victim. Mark would protect her privacy as much as he could. Wearily, Nick nodded.

Mark interviewed Helen in much less time. Nick had just begun to pace the floor when she was allowed to leave the small room. Why so short a time?

"You can go, too," Mark said, looking at Nick. "You're taking her home with you?"

Nick ignored the speculation in his ex-partner's eyes. Helen peeked up at him, too, and their gazes locked. He'd known then, as he knew now, what she was thinking. And if he didn't tear his gaze immediately away, his body would remind him that he hadn't given it satisfaction yet.

Too late, the tightening in his groin taunted.

He forced himself to look at Mark. "Just until she gets sorted out." There was still the rest of the investigation to consider. Cooms couldn't have worked alone. He was smart and obviously in charge, but there were too many drugs, too much laundered money involved. And someone else had been keeping the police several steps behind Cooms for the past few years. If that someone wanted Helen dead, too, that meant she knew something.

And that something could salvage his career.

As soon as they were outside, she turned to him. "Don't feel you have to take care of me. I'm fine."

He took her arm. "You're still coming home with me." He had the barrier of the crooked cop routine between them, banking on it to make sure they both kept their distance.

He hoped.

"I'll be fine, Nick."

"Do you think you'll be safer on a bus to the States, or wherever you were headed? Cooms didn't order Darlington to find you, but someone did. They found you pretty easily. And what about money? It wouldn't take a rocket scientist to check out which cash machine you used. Tracking your movements wouldn't be hard, trust me.''

Helen swallowed.

''Or would you rather go to your aunt June's and endanger the whole damn building full of seniors?''

''No!'' Her eyes widened.

''Then you have no other choice, do you?'' He steered her toward his SUV.

''Why would anyone want me dead now? I don't know anything. I only saw Jamie kill Tony. Nothing more.''

Nick turned to her and as if just realizing she'd spoken out loud, she bent her head down and hurried toward his truck.

Disturbed, he unlocked the passenger door and walked around to the other side. She'd asked a good question. If she'd bought drugs and not paid for them, yeah, someone would pressure her to pay. But she sure as hell wasn't fitting that profile.

As he climbed in, she said, ''Nick, take me to that crisis center.''

He twisted in his seat. ''And you figure you'll be safer there?''

She wrung her hands in her lap, a habit he noticed she shared with her mother. ''Yes.''

''You're wrong. Sure, they have the best security systems and sure their windows are bulletproof, but you'll be safer at my house.''

A shadow of fear skimmed over her face. ''Will I?''

It was a direct reference to his association with Cooms. For the first time, she was practically admitting she knew who he was. Or was it a reference to what he'd done with her on the couch?

His reasons for keeping silent rang in his mind. The

main one, the one becoming a mantra, rang the loudest. Trust no one.

He could lie. It was his job. It kept him alive during undercover operations. But staring at her, seeing her innocence, feeling the way her fear struck a long, resonant chord deep inside of him, he realized this was the hardest lie he'd ever made. He reached across the seat and brushed his knuckles along her cheek, careful to avoid her bruise. "Yes, you're safer with me."

Tears filled her eyes. And slowly, as if she didn't really want to, she shook her head. Her small mouth opened, almost forming a soft word, but relaxed back into that kissable, parted-lip pout.

He couldn't believe he could ache so much with need. Merely looking at her was driving him to the point where he wanted nothing but her.

Her mouth had looked like that last night. And if he hadn't pulled back, he'd have devoured it then and there, all the while filling her with his full length, satisfying himself with her perfect, responsive body.

"I think you'd better take me to the shelter, Nick."

He jerked his hand away from her cheek. Ramming the gear shift into reverse, he backed out of the parking spot, avoiding checking the rearview because turning around meant he'd have to face her again.

What did he want, anyway? Her? His job back? He wanted to kill whoever attacked her. He wanted vindication that there were, as he suspected, more drugs, more money laundering and more corruption than they could now prove.

But what he really wanted was Helen. He'd be a fool if he believed she didn't fascinate him. Her slight body, her innocence and the fear she exuded whenever she looked at him.

There might be that perfect barrier of duty and secrecy to hold him back, and she might be saying to herself that barrier of a crooked cop and a woman's shelter were all she needed to stay away from him…

But he wasn't sure even those barriers were strong enough.

As they pulled in front of the large, old home that housed the women's shelter, Helen peered out the windshield of Nick's truck and again wished her father was still alive. He would have protected her. He would have stopped her from dating Jamie that very first time and prevented all this ensuing insanity from starting.

But her father had been dead for five years. And she'd jumped into an awful relationship immediately after. She was still paying for that one, literally. Mercy, the police would know all the humiliating details, she bet. She'd filed a complaint. For all the good it had done. And then she'd left the province.

And just when she'd finally relaxed, she met Jamie.

"The volunteers at the shelter won't let me in," Nick softly interrupted her thoughts as he killed the engine. "I'm not here as a police officer and the shelter has a strict policy on male visitors. For good reasons, too."

She nodded, wondering briefly if he was going to expand on his police business. Like why was he suspended?

But he didn't and frankly, a part of her was glad for it. Through quirks of fate, she'd relied on a crooked cop and she kept telling herself she was better off without the details of his life. Safer, too, she added.

Trouble was, in the dim light of the afternoon that threatened another bout of rain, she couldn't deny that a part of her refused to believe that she was better off.

"Helen?"

She turned to him, seeing again the perfect good looks that had made him stand out across that cigar party, months earlier. A rugged, almost Latin handsomeness.

"Call me if you need anything," he said. "I'll try to get one of the female officers to come by and check on you, all right?"

Again, numbly, she nodded.

Nick knew he had only a minute before the porch lights flicked on and the volunteer he'd called came out to escort Helen into the house.

He wanted to kiss her and the chances of her letting him were pretty damn good right now, too. She'd looked at him just a moment ago as if he could grant her every wish and they were all centered on him.

But if that volunteer got to the door in the next minute, his chances would dwindle rapidly.

Besides husbands, boyfriends were the most likely cause for a woman to seek shelter and the volunteers would do their utmost to keep him away from Helen.

He straightened. Hey, he wasn't her boyfriend. He was nothing but a suspended cop who was just doing a good deed. That was all.

When—and if—he did have a relationship, he wouldn't just be a boyfriend.

As an undercover cop, he'd been too wrapped up with each investigation to deal with another person in his life. It was no different now. Especially now, with Helen. She'd drained her overdraft and got caught. What the hell had she done with the money?

It didn't matter. He was suspended with nothing to offer a woman.

Suspended. Nothing to offer. How ideal.

''I should go inside,'' Helen whispered across the warm interior of the truck.

''Wait.'' He leaned over and tunneled his fingers through her short, blunt hair. He cupped the roundness above the nape of her neck and hauled her in close. She blinked at him, that same mix of fear and need that both angered and aroused him.

Damn, he wished things were different. He wished he was leaning over her in their bed and starting to make love for the umpteenth time and she was as trusting as he was aching.

But things weren't different and all he could do right now was touch his lips to hers. She responded, opening to him. He could feel her tongue greet his, gingerly. Meeting her warm moisture sent hot arrows of pleasure through him, making him hard with possibilities.

He was not denied the kiss, after all.

The porch light flashed on. Helen pulled back, giving him one of her haunting looks before throwing open her door.

''Thank you. For everything.''

He watched her slip in past the volunteer, who threw a cool look directly at the windshield, before shutting and no doubt locking the door.

The porch light flicked off, plunging Nick into the cool semidarkness of late afternoon. He leaned back against the headrest.

Sending Helen there was for the best, he told himself. Any thoughts of a big bed were only caused by his libido reacting to her absolute femininity, or some institutional need to fit in with the rest of humanity. If and when he found a woman, she would be his partner. Only after she'd earned his trust.

Helen hadn't done that yet.

With a sigh, he backed out of the driveway and drove down the street. A restless itch tickled him and he didn't want to go home. There was nothing to do there, except stare at the couch and play a mental game of What-If.

Pushing down the signal arm, Nick changed lanes and headed for the Saint John police station.

The men he'd worked with deserved an apology. They'd put in plenty of overtime on the investigation, even before DiPetri's murder. And he imagined that Cooms's own death had now added to their workload.

He pulled into the back parking lot and luckily found an empty space. As in most cities, parking was always a matter of good timing. Then he strode into the building.

"Hey, Nick."

He turned around at the front door to find Mark walking down a hallway with several files.

"What are you doing here?" he asked.

Mark shook his head. "Just tidying up some paperwork from when I was acting chief. Really useless stuff, like chief of police meetings and next year's canine training schedule."

Mark had been acting chief of the Lower Cove police for a week last month when the chief took his wife on a Caribbean holiday. Nick was glad Mark had been stuck with the duty and not him. Training schedules and meetings often brought the chief into Saint John. But being undercover had effectively removed Nick from that boring duty.

"Mark," he began, "About Helen Eastman—"

Mark's expression turned dark. "Nick, you're off the case."

"I'm a concerned citizen."

"Jeez, Nick, let us do our job." Mark shot a glance over his shoulder. "Listen, we've issued a warrant for

Clive Darlington's arrest. If he's in Saint John, he'll get picked up."

"Thanks." Relief drained through Nick. He ached to ask what else Mark might know about Helen, but he knew his ex-partner. He'd walk the straight, thin line between rules and loyalty.

"Nick?" Mark's voice dropped even further. "Hell, I shouldn't say anything, and you didn't hear it from me, but Helen Eastman's money problems aren't related to Cooms."

"What are they related to?"

An officer walked past and Mark straightened. "A con artist. Old case. She must have been looking for a bit of security. You know, with her father dying and all. But it backfired on her. Did you only come here to ask about her?"

"Not quite." He tried to sift through the details, absorb the fact that Mark had just stepped way across the thin line he liked to walk. Finally, shifting his weight, he added, "I figured I owed the guys an apology for screwing up their case. Or do you think they want to see me?"

Mark lifted his eyebrows in surprise. "With Cooms dead, all they want to see is the shooter delivered to them complete with a written confession. If you don't have that, I suggest you keep it brief."

In other words, they're too busy to be bothered. Nick watched Mark leave, wondering if the staff here had already received Helen's assault file.

Mark would make sure they knew. He was the one who went by the book, not Nick.

Changing his mind about the apology, he turned on his heel and left the station.

Helen ran her fingers through her new haircut, courtesy of one of the volunteers, as she paced the deserted living room. The repair job lifted her spirits somewhat, but outside, the dreary afternoon waned into a dreary evening. So much for the sunny weather this morning.

Edgily, she approached the window. She shouldn't be doing this, peering through the gauzy sheers expectantly. Who know if Clive Darlington was out there, waiting for her to appear. Perhaps waiting with a rifle.

But why?

If Jamie hadn't ordered Clive to find her, who had? Nick had said she was still in danger. If she could trust him. And if she couldn't, why did he bring her here?

Shivering, she moved back to the center of the room. She should call her mother, let her know she was safe, but the volunteers had asked her to restrict her calls.

She wandered out into the hallway. The voices of the other women filtered down to her from the kitchen as she glanced through the open door to her left and into the small, empty office.

Just one call. She'd feel so much better if she heard her mother's voice. Glancing quickly over her shoulder, she slipped into the room and silently shut the door.

Within seconds, her aunt's phone was ringing.

"Hello?"

"Aunt June, it's me, Helen."

There was both tension and relief in the older woman's voice. "Where are you? I've tried to call you all day!"

"I'm at a women's shelter. Is Momma there?"

"No, dear. That's why I've been trying to get you. She popped out this morning, saying she was going to return to her house for a change of clothes and some food. She hasn't come back yet."

Helen sank down into the chair, cold flooding into her. "When did she leave?"

''About eleven this morning. She was very upset. I think that's why she forgot her things.''

Tears sprang into her eyes and she hastily brushed them away. No need for panic, yet. ''Did you call her house?''

''All day. No answer!''

The room began to spin and Helen grabbed the arm of the chair for support. Her mother missing? *Please, Lord, no.*

''Shall I call the police?'' her aunt asked.

Helen snapped out of her fear. ''No!''

Afraid she would have to explain her situation to her aunt, she backed off from the fear and anger that threatened to bubble up. ''No, not yet. They won't do anything for forty-eight hours, anyway.'' She drew in a strengthening breath. ''I'm sure she's running around doing some errands and has let time slip away. I'll go over to the house myself and see if she left a note or something, okay?''

Satisfied for the moment, June agreed. ''Call me when you get there.''

Hanging up, Helen flew around the desk. Out in the hall, she knew she had only this chance to leave. The volunteers were there to protect the women, sometimes even from themselves and she knew they would try to stop her from leaving.

Helen grabbed her coat from the front closet and stole outside.

Afraid she had triggered the alarm, she dashed down to an adjacent street and hailed a cab. Here's hoping the change she found at the bottom of her pocket was enough to pay the fare.

The cab dropped her off in the empty driveway of her mother's home, taking every last cent she had, before backing away. Her mother's car was nowhere around. By now, dusk and a faint drizzle chilled the neighborhood.

Smeared into the wet pavement was the reflection of the single streetlight down the road. Neighbors were probably all tucked into their warm homes with hot suppers and blaring TVs.

She walked up to the front door, slowing her pace as she stared at the house.

The front door was wide open. Oh, God, please, no!

Gingerly, Helen slipped in, warring with herself the wisdom of calling out to her mother, or just running away to a neighbor's to call the police.

She listened. Nothing. The air was damp and still and cold over her tongue as she barely inhaled.

Apart from the open door, nothing looked different. Her mother's shoes were lined up in military precision by the closet. The carpet was clean, no muddied bootprints.

She tiptoed into the living room. The same eerie stillness greeted her. Nothing seemed out of place, and yet, something was wrong. She could feel it.

Each room of the bungalow was empty. Helen checked the closet in the spare room where her mother kept a set of small suitcases. They were all there. She checked the cookie jar. There was about ten dollars in cash in it. She set the lid gently back in place, cringing as the clink echoed in the still kitchen. At least she knew where the money was, in case she needed it.

She found a fully thawed roast in the refrigerator. Odd. Her mother would have taken it to her aunt's apartment to cook.

If she'd come back here.

Fighting back her alarm, Helen headed for the phone. There was only one person she could call. But she didn't know his number.

Instead, she called the Lower Cove Police Department.

''Chief Hunt,'' a voice answered.

"I'm looking for Nick Thorndike."

The chief paused. "He's not available right now. Can I help you?"

She remembered the burly, humorless man and decided to take a chance. "Could you please pass on a message for me?"

"How about I give you his pager number? You can leave your message there." He rattled off a number, leaving her to scramble for a pen and paper, hoping she wrote the number down correctly.

After paging Nick, Helen sank into the nearest chair. This was too much. She willed herself to stay calm, running through a mental list of all the places her mother might go. But nothing viable came up.

The phone rang, making Helen jump. She grabbed it quickly, hating the way the ring blasted through the air.

"Hello?"

"It's Nick. What's wrong? Why are you at your mother's place?"

"How did you know I was here?"

"Reverse directory. What's wrong?"

She bit back tears. She hated herself for being weak, for not knowing what to do and most of all she hated herself for liking the way Nick's rich voice trickled heat down her spine to warm her cold body. "My mother's missing. When I called Aunt June, she told me Momma had come here this morning to pack some things up and she hadn't returned yet. I came straight here and the front door was open and the place is empty...."

Nick barked in her ear. "Helen, don't tell me you just walked in and called me?"

"Yes."

He swore again.

"There's no one here. And Momma never came back.

She left all of her suitcases and a roast in the fridge and money in the cookie jar, but the front door was wide open!'' She took a shaky breath. ''It feels like someone was here.''

''Is the front door still open?''

Helen shut her eyes to her own foolishness. ''Yes.''

As if hearing her contrition, Nick turned calm, soothing. ''It's all right. Go and close it and lock it. Don't hang up. Just go do that right now and come back to the phone.''

She did as he said. When she returned, Nick's warm voice sounded approving, coaxing. ''That's good. Now, I'm coming out to get you, okay? I'll be about twenty minutes, so why don't you make yourself a cup of tea and relax? But don't open the door or answer the phone. Not to anyone.''

''Okay.''

''You'll be fine, Helen. I'm leaving now.''

''Thank you.'' She wet her dry lips and wished she could somehow crawl through the telephone wires to him. He was crooked and couldn't be trusted, her head told her sternly, but her heart ached to hear his voice, and her body ached to feel him grip her again.

And she wanted so badly to trust him.

Chapter 5

Nick roared into the driveway. The house ahead of him was cold and dark, unwelcoming. He leapt out of the truck and strode up to the door. Pounding on it, he called out, "It's me, Nick."

A moment later, Helen threw open the door. He plowed in and dragged her into his arms, ignoring the way she stiffened briefly. He released her as quickly as he'd hugged her. "Let me check this place out."

He did a thorough search, every room, every nook, every dark corner of the basement, even. Only when he was satisfied they were alone, did he let out a long breath.

"Why did the women at the shelter let you go?" he asked when they returned to the living room.

"They didn't. I slipped out." Seeing his darkening expression, she blurted out hurriedly, "I couldn't stay there, not allowed to make a call or anything while my mother was missing!"

Of course not. Relenting, he said, "Phone the shelter

and tell them you've gone to check on a relative and will be back as soon as possible. They'll be worried about you.''

Nodding, Helen went into the kitchen to make the call. When she came back, she glanced warily around the room, anywhere but at him, he noticed.

''Is there anything missing here that you might notice?'' he said to mask his irritation.

She scanned the living room, then the kitchen and finally her mother's neat little bedroom. ''No. But it feels different. I can't explain it, but it's like someone was here. Looking at things.'' She shivered, rubbing her arms. ''It's a creepy feeling.''

At the sound of her wavering voice, Nick strode across the carpet and pulled her into his arms. There, looking down on her as she rested her head on his chest, he noticed someone had fixed her massacre of a haircut. Giving into the temptation, he touched the soft waves, then plunged his fingers into the silky thickness and shut his own eyes.

She clung to him with an intensity that brought to mind the other night. Automatically, Nick's body went rigid.

He broke the embrace. What the hell was he thinking, taking her in his arms, not once, but twice, like they were old and familiar lovers? They weren't. One short-lived mistake on his couch didn't make them lovers. It didn't make them anything. It was just that she constantly carried this aura of needing someone.

It wasn't him. No way.

He shook away the mental image of her on his couch. ''Did you call your mother's friends?''

''She would have told Aunt June if she was going to see them. She's very good that way.''

''Look, we can't do anything about your mother tonight.

The police won't either. But we can try to figure out what someone would want here."

"There isn't anything here that anyone would want. My mother threw out a lot of stuff when she moved here. I got some of it, but most of it was just old junk." She looked around the room remorsefully. "We never had very much."

"Did you ever leave anything here?"

She shook her head. "I may have forgotten a jacket or something, but not recently."

"When did your mother move here?"

"After my father died. We had to move out of the married quarters on the base he'd been posted at in Ontario. She bought this place with his insurance money to be closer to her sister. They grew up in Saint John."

"What about your brothers and sisters?"

"I'm an only child."

Nick watched her straighten her shoulders. He forced his police training to take over, to somehow prevent him from hauling her back into his arms again. "You were close to your father?"

She nodded, walking over to the mantel and picking up the small photo there. "Momma was sick a lot, nothing serious, but she ended up having a hysterectomy. She relied on Dad a lot. It was hard when he died and we had to move away. We'd spent most of his career, nearly all my life, at that base. We had to start again."

She paused, as if wanting to add something. But it never came.

"Why don't you live with her?"

Helen clenched and unclenched her fingers. There was another unusual pause. "I lived at home in Ontario, because I had a good job on the base. When Momma said she wanted to move back to Saint John, I decided to move out. So I managed to get a job as a receptionist for Globatech, the company that builds specialized equipment for the government.''

Globatech. A fairly new company, it had secured a forgivable loan from the federal government, as long as it employed several hundred people in the city. Everyone knew that. It had been in the news enough. He could see the flashy symbol in his mind, but it wasn't from the outside of their corporate headquarters, as seen in the news clips. It was from somewhere else he couldn't place.

Should her job there mean something to the investigation? Globatech wasn't on his mental list of companies Jamie Cooms dealt with.

Nick gave Helen a pondering look. ''How did you meet Cooms?''

She paced the living room. ''He came to a meeting one day and I was the one who directed him around. Globatech uses a language all its own and it's hard to navigate through the labs without help. Jamie came back several times and then asked me out.''

Nick felt his mouth tighten to a thin line and made the pretense of taking the photo she still held and replacing it, in order to hide his expression. ''What kind of business did he have with Globatech?''

She shot him a confused look. ''Real estate. They rented some of his warehouse space down by the docks. Nothing big, I don't think. After the original agreement was signed, he never came back to Globatech. Not ever.''

''So, why did you date him?'' Damn, he didn't want to ask that question, but it came out in full force, as if it had a will of its own.

Helen looked away, blinking, with her mouth a thin, contrite line. ''He was nice to me. Mostly, I spent my weekends with my mother. I was lonely, she was lonely..." She trailed off. Then she added, "It was nothing serious. He even said there wouldn't be any commitment until I was ready. He was good at guessing how I felt. What I wanted to hear, too."

Oh, yeah, that fit Cooms very well. "And you never suspected Cooms of anything illegal?"

"No!" Her eyebrows shot up. She seemed to want to say more, and when he waited patiently, she continued, "Well, only once. He mentioned he was paying off some politicians and some...well, he was drunk at the time, so I didn't say anything about it later. I figured it was either he was boasting or that maybe all businessmen get kickbacks." She threw up her hands. "We hear about it on the news all the time!"

Bingo. Nick leaned forward, but stopped when her eyes widened and her mouth softened. He ached to ask her more about Cooms, about the corruption. Instead, stupidly, he knew, he asked, "Any other boyfriends?"

"The only other man I see regularly is my landlord." She shook her head. "He keeps an eye on me. Like he's doing me a favor. He's harmless."

"Have you been back to your apartment?"

"Not since..." She shuddered. "Not for over a week." She looked up at him, and he knew she was gauging his reaction to her words. "Do you think someone has been through my place, too?"

Meeting those dark blue eyes directly, he wished he could pigeonhole her personality as easily as he had others like Cooms. He couldn't, though, and that fact irritated the hell out of him.

Her mother's home had been broken into and she was upset, but now, as she faced the possibility that her own place had suffered the same fate, she remained controlled, but wary. Of him? He didn't like the suspicion he saw in her eyes as she looked at him. But what could he expect?

"It's hard to say why someone broke in here." He scanned the room again. "It wasn't for the electronics. They're still here. But if it had anything to do with Cooms, it's logical to assume they'd also go through your apartment to find whatever they're looking for."

Fear flickered past her expression, the first time since he'd mentioned her apartment. "But what are they after? Do you know?"

He hated himself and all the training drilled into him for so long. It was all he could do to resist telling her the truth. She was better off thinking he was involved with Cooms. It kept her wary of him. It kept him from accidentally jeopardizing the lives of all the undercover operatives involved.

Did that also mean he didn't believe her innocence?

Helen took a step forward. He'd already decided to stamp her with the timid stamp, but he'd seen her when she felt her mother was being threatened. She had turned combative damn quick. Now, she wore a similar, albeit milder look. "Whatever they're after, I don't have it." Her words were thick with warning.

If he could go to her apartment by himself, he would, but not knowing what to look for would make it futile. He hated to do this. "Get your coat. We'll go check out your apartment."

He watched her disappear into the kitchen. Along with the noise of her coat scraping a kitchen chair along the floor, he heard a distinct chink of a ceramic lid being lifted and dropped into place again.

Helen followed Nick to his SUV, far slower than she should have. He'd asked her why she didn't live with her mother. A valid question, though the answer still hurt. How could she tell him she'd felt so lost after her father's death, she'd foolishly become involved with a man who'd stolen from her? Scott Jackson had drained her bank account and her overdraft protection. In order to stop the blasted bank from pressuring her own mother, she'd had to move out and pay it all back in high interest installments. When Jamie had entered her life, she'd been more than wary, but he'd been good at saying what she'd wanted to hear. *No commitments. Let's just keep each other company for a while.*

She climbed into the SUV. Not since her father died had she struggled so much with uncertainty. No. She had to be strong. She could be strong. Even while Nick had somehow insinuated himself in to her life.

She couldn't let him get any closer. He'd been paid off by Jamie. She knew that. Jamie had let slip that dangerous tidbit on more than one occasion.

And Momma was missing. Her heart seemed to squeeze shut when she considered her mother's safety. Where could she be? Could she trust Nick to help her? Like she'd trusted Scott, then Jamie?

Too late, she realized that she hadn't called Aunt June. As soon as they got to her place she would. At least she could put one person at ease, even though partially, using what Aunt June might consider a lie.

Helen directed Nick to her place, in as few words as possible. Talking took too much emotion. Too much effort.

They reached the large Victorian house within a few minutes. No sooner had she climbed out, than her landlord, Chester Ellis, zipped out of his ground-floor apartment. Helen rented the second-floor apartment from him, while the attic, now a studio apartment, was rented to a quiet university student.

"Helen!" Chester called out, jogging up to them. Chester wore his usual padded plaid shirt, his thin chest barely making a dent against the suspenders that held up his work pants.

"Hello, Chester."

Chester threw a suspicious glance at Nick as he rounded the front of the truck. "I'm so glad you're safe. You know, I called the police because you hadn't been back for a week."

Helen smiled thinly. Chester meant well and she suspected he was halfway in love with her, despite there being at least a twenty year age difference. He always kept a look out for her, though, and she appreciated that.

"I was away unexpectedly. I—I'm not staying, but I've just…come to…"

"To pick up some things," Nick finished for her.

Chester backed up, hurt lingering on his narrow face. But Helen knew from past experience that Chester wasn't going to let her get away that quickly. "I had to let the police into your apartment, Helen. I was worried and I knew you…" His voice trailed away as he shrugged.

She turned at the porch steps and looked at him. "Knew I'd what?"

"Um, that you'd have a picture of yourself in there, so I—the police—found a picture of you on top of your fridge. I let them have it. That way the police could keep an eye out for you." His face reddened.

Helen caught Nick's skeptical glare and offered a stronger smile at Chester. "It's okay. You did the right thing."

Striding past the older man, Nick steered her up to the door. "Do you have your key?"

''Here!'' Chester interjected, pulling on a tractable wire case on his empty belt loop. Keys jangled in his hand as he scrambled to find the right one.

''Thank you,'' Nick said, putting himself between Helen and her landlord. ''We'll let ourselves out.''

Up in her apartment, she shut the door behind Nick and surveyed her tiny living room.

''Is that guy always like that?'' Nick asked.

She nodded. ''He's single and I think he's a bit lonely.''

Nick said nothing, but it wasn't hard for her to sense his disapproval. Too bad. She wasn't looking for Nick's opinion.

''Let's check out each room, shall we?'' he said.

They moved from room to room. Everything seemed to be in place, nothing obviously missing, except the photograph. But it could take hours, maybe even days, to find if something had been taken. Nick stayed at her heels, his body heat bombarding her in every tiny room of her apartment. She stayed only a minute in her bedroom.

Back in the living room, she sank down on the couch.

Nick remained standing. ''This Chester, what does he do for a living?''

Helen leaned back and shut her eyes. ''Nothing. He's retired and rents these apartments to augment his pension. He's harmless, Nick.''

She heard him grunt, but couldn't care less if he agreed or not. All she wanted to do was close out the nightmare this past week had been. Her apartment was fine, safer than her mother's house, more comfortable than the shelter.

She opened her eyes. ''I'm not going back to the shelter, Nick.''

He was standing near the TV, peering out one of the

long, old-fashioned windows to the driveway below. "Yes, you are."

She moved in front of the TV. "Nothing has been touched here. Chester's always home and I have a good lock on the door. Look, Jamie is dead. He was why I ran away in the first place. You should be focusing on finding my mother. There must be something you can do. And I should stay here in case she calls."

Nick let out an impatient noise. "We can report it, but the police will ask you to wait. Unless she needs care or medicine."

"No. She's healthy." She swallowed. "Maybe she'll call."

"Neither of us believe she's out shopping. Helen, Cooms was murdered and Clive Darlington, who is out there somewhere, is wanted for assaulting you. He would know where you live because that sort of information is readily available. Plus he worked for Cooms." He peered into her face. "You don't believe you're safe here any more than I do."

So he saw through her thinly veiled need to keep her distance. She shoved her glance from his sturdy, long-legged frame down to her TV stand.

Her tapes were mixed up, not in the neat line they usually were in.

"Did you hear me, Helen?"

She dropped to her knees in front of the stand.

"What's wrong?" he asked.

"My tapes. Someone has been through them."

Nick bent down. "Chester?"

"No." She glanced up at him and acquiesced. "At least I can't see any reason for it. I know what you're thinking. Yes, he's been in here before. I even caught him once when I came home early. He said he was checking out the radiators. But he's never shown any interest in my tapes.'' She reached out to touch them.

Nick caught her arm. ''Don't. I'll ask the Major Crimes Unit to check them for fingerprints.''

Helen pulled her arm away. The mere touch of his hand did things to her system. Her tired, bone-weary system.

Oh, no. She didn't want to feel that way again. Not the way she'd felt when she lay on his couch, while he covered her body with kisses and made her a slave to her half-starved emotions. She couldn't allow herself to be moved by a man who could be involved with whatever illegal activities Jamie pursued.

Or with her mother's disappearance.

She bit back a groan of fatigue as she stood.

''What's on these tapes?''

''My life. Before my father died, he had all our old eight-millimeter film put on video. My mother gave them to me after she bought her new house.'' She tried to rub away the ache growing in her forehead. ''No one would be interested in my home movies.''

''Your landlord might be, if you're the star.''

Helen turned away. ''I never encouraged his crush, all right? He's been in my apartment before because he's my landlord. If he wanted to rummage through my tapes, he could have done so anytime in the last few years. Why now?''

''When he reported you missing, he let the officers in here to borrow a photograph of you. How would he know where one was?''

Helen pulled a slight face, wondering if Nick would think she was taking offense to his suggestion that Chester was a suspect. Or a lover. He thought that of Jamie, too. She shuddered. ''One of Jamie's friends had snapped that picture. Jamie took the film. But he gave me the photo later on. I had no desire to frame it, so it ended up on my fridge. When it fell off once, I threw it up on top. Chester must have seen it at some time."

"And Cooms? Had he been here often?" Nick asked.

She turned to him, frowning. Was he holding his breath, waiting for her answer? Surely neither of them wanted her to elaborate on whether or not Cooms had been in her bedroom? Didn't he believe her when she said their dates were only casual? No way was she going to get involved again. He should trust her on that one. She said, "That's none of your business, Nick."

He blinked twice, and she grimaced. All right, maybe it was a legitimate question. "Actually, there was one evening that he showed up here with Chinese takeout and suggested we watch some of those tapes. I know. It seemed odd that he should be interested, but hey, it was only home videos, and I figured he'd get bored long before I would. So we started at tape number one. Me eating ice cream at six months old." She shook her head. "I fell asleep. It was hardly riveting stuff. I think Jamie got as far as the third tape before he nodded off."

Nick walked over to her phone and called the police station, reminding her to call Aunt June.

"They're sending someone over right now. Quiet night, I guess," he said, after hanging up.

Fifteen minutes later, the officer she'd given her statement to, a corporal named Mark Rowlands, showed up with another officer. Nick went downstairs to let them in, while she stood at the top, watching Chester peer curiously around the corner. Nick led the way up. "Long day for you," he commented to Mark.

Mark agreed. "And it's going to get longer. I've been assigned to help Saint John with the investigation. We're going to put in a lot of overtime on this case. I'll be lucky if I get home at all this week.'' He said hello to Helen when he reached the top of the stairs. ''Ms. Eastman, is there anything else you feel has been touched?''

She shook her head and moved to one side, while the men stooped down in front of the TV.

Later, as Mark and the other officer were finishing up, Nick asked, ''What did you find?''

''A couple of sets of prints on a few tapes.'' Mark straightened. ''The TV stand is clean and so are the doors. Ms. Eastman, I'll need you to give me a set of fingerprints for comparison.''

She sat down at the coffee table and offered her hand, her gaze darting from the officer holding her hand to Mark and finally to Nick. ''My mother is missing, too,'' she blurted out.

Mark's head snapped over to Nick. For a few seconds, no one said anything. Some other expression, she couldn't fathom it, flickered over Nick's brooding look. Distrust, maybe? Did he expect her to also blurt out the truth about him?

Mark turned back to her. ''How long has your mother been missing?''

''Since nearly noon today. She left my aunt June's to pack a few things at her home. I don't think she ever made it there.''

''Do you think she went shopping instead?''

Helen raised her eyebrows. ''Would your mother, if she had everything at her home?''

''Did she have her car? Do you know her license plate number?''

She threw Nick a look and bit her lip. Nick said, ''I sent her to her sister's house in a taxi. There wasn't a car in her own driveway when I arrived.''

Mark looked confused. Nick's glare darkened. ''Remember you gave me Connie Eastman's address? I went to see if she knew where Helen was. Then I came back to get Helen an hour ago."

"Why?" Mark asked.

Helen stole a glance at Nick, wondering if his earlier visit to her mother had caused the intrusive feeling she'd noticed when she searched the house.

Mark folded his arms, matching Nick's glare. "Why don't you just start again at the beginning?"

The room chilled several degrees. Nick's lips thinned. To Helen, it sounded as though Mark was trying to trip Nick up. Were they on to him?

"I went there this afternoon," she explained to Mark, surprised by her desire to defend Nick. "I called Aunt June and she told me Momma left just before noon to go home. Yes, she has a car. And I know the license plate number." She told him.

Mark scribbled it down. "We'll see what we can do. Usually we have to wait forty-eight hours, though."

So long? Momma could be anywhere, out there...in any kind of danger.

After her prints were recorded, as the other officer handed her an alcohol wipe to clean her fingertips, Mark said, "You may want to look at each of these tapes again, in case some have been tampered with."

"What do you mean, tampered with?"

Nick and Mark exchanged quick, obvious looks. They both knew what it could mean, but they weren't going to share that information with her.

"Do you think that someone might have taped over them?" Nick asked, as if pretending the quick exchange never happened. "Or switched labels?" He was rubbing his arms. Was he cold? Even at this distance, she could see goose bumps.

"Just a long shot. They could have been looking for something completely different." Mark shrugged before smiling at Helen. "I saw the titles. Can't be that bad to check them over again."

"Ugh. Speak for yourself." She pulled a face. "My life on eighteen tapes. Do you know how boring they'll be?"

The other officer's head flicked up from the fingerprint case. Mark frowned. "Eighteen? There are only seventeen tapes."

Helen leaned away from the men. "There must be some mistake. I've got eighteen tapes. One for each year of my childhood. No more, no less."

Nick bent down and quickly counted the tapes. He turned to Helen. "There are only seventeen." He peered down at the tapes again to read the titles. "One for each year? There's no thirteenth year."

She stood. "Are you sure?" She came close and studied the titles. Her thirteenth one was gone. "Why would someone want a tape of me when I was thirteen?"

"What's on it?"

She crossed her arms to warm herself. Someone took a tape of her at her most awkward stage? That was worse than stealing baby pictures. "Just my family." She thought a moment. "We went to Wonderland in Ontario that year. And some Christmas and birthday parties. Nothing more, really." She looked at Nick, wondering if he believed her, his expression was so unreadable.

"Well," Mark said, shutting his notebook. "That's all we can do for tonight. Look around, you may have misplaced the tape. If you think of anything that might help us, let us know."

Helen hesitated, but then nodded briefly, not knowing what to do anymore. Mark didn't believe her. He figured she was wasting their time, and as the latest girlfriend of a murdered crook, she was automatically under suspicion.

She listened as Nick saw them to the door. Didn't they know that Nick was the crook?

Icy nausea washed over her. What a fool she'd been. She should have told them about seeing Nick that afternoon at Jamie's office. She should have blurted it right out like she'd done with her mother's disappearance. Mark and his partner were the ones with the guns, not Nick. They would have protected her.

Not if she was a suspect herself, though.

She shut her eyes and slumped against the well-worn windowsill and listened to the officers leave. As if they would believe her. What would Nick do if she did blurt it out? It wasn't hard to tell he was a volatile man. Announcing that he was in league with Jamie might set him off. She might be signing Mark's death warrant. Or her own.

And now Nick knew she had no place left to hide.

''Get some things together while I put your tapes in a bag. You can look at them later.'' Nick had watched Mark carefully examine all the tapes as he searched for some sign of tampering. Since Mark hadn't taken any of them, they must be clean. But if someone had handled them, they could have recorded something of importance on one of them. Sure it was a long shot, but worth checking out. Someone had rifled through them.

Turning to Helen, he could see she was on the edge of collapsing. She had to get moving, do something, however mindless it might be, or she'd end up in hospital.

He didn't want to take her back to the shelter, but where could she go? Someone had been here and at her mother's house.

Helen shuffled past him and automatically, Nick drew

in a deep breath, remembering the way she smelled that night on the couch. Had it only been last night? It didn't seem possible. Tonight, she smelled slightly of warm soap. Nothing erotic and yet the strong memory weaved itself into his conscious thought.

He resisted the aching urge to catch her and hold her. Strength didn't drain from one person to another by way of an embrace. Besides, how strong was he, himself? He'd screwed up a vital undercover investigation and then the same day, tried to make love to the woman who was the key to the entire operation, whether she knew it or not. Now, a day later, the very scent of her warped his perspective of this investigation and if he wasn't careful, he'd jeopardize what had been salvaged of the whole operation.

"Where are your plastic bags?" he asked her gruffly.

She turned at the door to her bedroom. Her eyes were clouded, like her fear and pain were simply too much to bear. "Um. In the second drawer in the kitchen."

He found some neatly folded grocery bags where she'd said and pulled one out. Back in the living room, he dumped the tapes into it. Would she bother to look at them? There was only the slimmest chance that they held anything but childhood memories. And in her state of mind, right now, Helen might not be able to watch them without breaking down.

He should watch them, instead. Excuse me? No, thanks. That kind of work had a bit too much of an intimate feel to it.

They'd been intimate enough.

Hefting up the bulging bag, he turned around in time to see her return. She carried a small overnight bag.

She'd changed as well, from the old baggy clothes to a pair of beige slacks and a lightweight sweater.

"Got everything?" he asked.

''Yes.'' She grabbed a coat from the tiny closet at the top of the stairs. They said nothing on their way to the shelter. Nick pulled to the curb on the other side of the street, his seat belt keeping him firmly in place. No, he wasn't going to kiss her again.

''What are you going to do now?'' she asked, cutting into the silence with her urgent whisper.

''Go home. It's getting late.'' Not really, but this time of year, it could be either nine at night or well after midnight. It all looked the same. He turned to her. ''They'll find Clive Darlington, don't worry. It won't take much to get him talking. He's got a list of priors as long as this street and knows that unless he plea bargains, he'll be looking at ten years behind bars without parole.''

''Thank you.'' Then, her face still grim, she said, ''Don't forget my mother.''

''I won't. Look at those tapes and call me.'' He wanted to sound gruff, professional, but he wasn't sure it was working.

''What am I supposed to look for?''

''I don't know. Blank spaces, snow on the tape. Anything out of the ordinary.'' He doubted she would buy the fact that the tapes were making the hair rise on his arms, a sure sign that something was amiss.

''All right.'' She shifted her gaze away from his face as she shoved open the door. She seemed detached, distant.

She still didn't trust him, damn it. He touched her arm as gently as he could. ''Helen, trust me. Please?''

Wide, wary eyes met his, blinking him into focus. ''Jamie said that to me once when he bought me a new VCR. And later, he told me he wanted to see me dead.'' She swung away from him, and climbed out hastily. Without looking back, she slammed the door and headed across the street.

Nick pulled a face. There was no way he could tell her the truth and set her mind at ease, but to be equated with that scum Cooms ate like acid in his stomach. He glanced down at the floor of the truck.

The tapes. She'd forgotten them. He grabbed the bag and threw open his door, fumbling with his seat belt as he called out, "Helen!"

She was halfway across the street when she turned.

"The tapes." He held up the bag as he walked toward her. It had recently rained and the pavement between them was shiny and slick. The harbor air smelled cool and moist.

An engine gunned to life, slicing the quiet dark of the street like a hot knife through butter.

Nick turned.

Dark early model sedan. Tinted windows, no headlights.

He registered all the details in a millisecond. Then, seeing the reflections of the streetlights whip past the hood and windshield of the car, he registered the horrible, immediate danger they were in.

Someone was going to run them over.

Chapter 6

Helen heard Nick's cry at the same time she felt him slam into her. The scream of an overrevved engine drowned out her gasp as she and Nick toppled into the narrow space between two parked cars. The bag of videotapes swung past her to slide under the rear car.

She hit a bumper and twirled as the rubber strip chafed against her cotton pants. There was a sickening, all-too-close scrape of metal on metal and she collapsed into the wet corner where pavement met curb. The car in front of her rocked dangerously as it absorbed the collision.

Nick fell on top of her, his legs and arms splaying out so as not to hurt her. Over his panting breath, she heard the sound of a car backing up and then the angry scream of peeling rubber.

Nick leaped up and raced out to the road. Still slumped on the short step of the curb, she turned to see him staring at the disappearing car.

''What happened?'' It was a woman's voice and Helen

lifted her head to blink against the high wattage porch light. Hurrying across the short lawn was the volunteer from the shelter.

"A hit-and-run," Nick answered curtly.

The woman gasped. Helen scrambled to her feet. She rubbed her thigh where it had connected with the bumper. Thankfully, it was the only place that hurt.

"Helen!" The woman hurried over. "Are you all right?"

"I'm fine. Thanks to Nick. I didn't even see the car." She tried to smile for him, but gave up after the first wobbly attempt.

Nick remained grim. "You didn't see the car because it didn't have its headlights on."

She swallowed. That meant this hit-and-run was a deliberate attempt on her life.

"Call 9-1-1," Nick ordered the volunteer. "The police will want to have a look at this car." He walked over to the car they'd hid behind and bent down. Helen followed him.

The rear door was scraped and dented, with long, dark scratches marring its gleaming white exterior.

The volunteer took Helen's arm and steered her into the shelter. Helen straightened. She could walk by herself. "I think they should impound that car for evidence."

"I only hope they catch that guy." The volunteer offered a small smile. "That's my car."

Inside, an hour later, Helen finished her second cup of herbal tea. She'd already spoken to Mark again, but her statement was useless. She hadn't seen the car that tried to hit her.

Nick spent most of the time outside and Helen could only guess he was helping Mark. The volunteer also stayed outside, coming in periodically to report on the photographer's arrival, or when an investigator chipped samples of the hit-and-run vehicle's paint from her car, or other important things that seemed to sail over Helen's disoriented head.

Finally, Nick strode into the shelter. Helen was surprised he was allowed to do so, but under the circumstances…

"Let's go," he told her.

She pulled her jacket close around herself and folded her arms. "Where?"

No place was safe. Not her own home, not her mother's.

"My house."

Helen swept the room with a cautious glance. They were alone, no volunteer to quietly remind her of the many women who had returned to their boyfriends, their lovers, the men they feared and who had forced them to hide. Such reunions rarely worked out to the woman's benefit.

Mercy, where had everyone gone?

She stood, finding some miraculous shard of strength she hadn't realized she had. "Why should I go to your place, Nick? Answer me that." Her voice dropped. "For all I know, you're the one arranging all of this crap. It wouldn't take a rocket scientist to figure out where I live. And you knew where this shelter was—"

"I'm a cop, remember," he snapped.

Anger boiled up inside of her, but she only glared at him. "We both know what you are, Nick. You want me to trust you? You may think I'm stupid to get involved with Jamie, but I'm not so stupid to trust a cop who says he's one thing but really isn't that at all."

She watched some indefinable emotion crawl over his face. Pain? No, it was more like frustration. He should be frustrated if he was trying to convince her that he meant well. Crooked cops don't mean well.

Nick drew in a seething breath. "Yes, you were foolish to get involved with Cooms. And to stay involved with him. You knew what he was like."

"No, I didn't know at first. To me, he was merely the man who'd rented out a warehouse to Globatech. He was kind to me at first." She shook her head. "Our relationship was supposed to be casual. For a while, it was. But I don't do relationships. I put in an honest day's work and I visit my mother regularly. And speaking of her, it's time we started looking for her more actively. Surely we can suspect foul play by now! Mark will and can help, you know. *He* is the cop. One of the good guys."

She wanted to threaten him. She wanted to warn him that if he didn't help her find her mother, she would tell Mark the truth about him. But her bravado had limits, especially as she watched his expression move from frustration to fury.

The chair felt good when she sank back down into it.

Nick leaned forward, his knuckles hard and white on the clean, bare kitchen table. "What do you think Mark should do to find your mother? He just told me she's not at any of the hospitals and she didn't leave the country. Is there something you haven't told us that might help us find her?"

His eyes glittered menacingly and she dropped her gaze to her fingers as they clenched each other.

"I'd say Mark has his hands pretty full right now, Helen. Maybe you'd like to go home with him, since you don't trust me." His voice turned sarcastic as he slapped his forehead. "Sorry, I forgot. Mark isn't going home tonight. He's got two homicides and a hit-and-run on his hands and he's not even a member of the Saint John Police

Department. So you can imagine how much overtime all those other officers are putting in.''

She blinked up at him. ''If Mark Rowlands is a member of the Lower Cove police, why is he involved with a Saint John homicide?''

Nick shifted back, surprise hitting his chiseled features. There was a distinct pause before he spoke, and Helen listened to the quiet ticking of the clock on the wall above her while she waited for his answer.

He pushed himself to standing—no, towering over her. ''DiPetri's body washed up on shore just inside our town limits. The tide must have dragged it out. Mark's the investigating officer and is—'' he hesitated ''—loaned out for it.''

''But I already told him what I saw.'' She didn't want to talk about that horrid day. She still couldn't get out of her mind the image of the gun pointed at the back of poor Tony's head. Shuddering, she peered up at Nick, feeling her strength slowly replaced by a bone-aching fatigue. ''Jamie killed Tony. That's the end of that investigation, as I see it.''

Nick sighed impatiently. ''The file isn't closed yet. And Cooms has been murdered now, too. The two police forces have to pool their knowledge to sort out this whole blasted mess.''

''Does that mean I'm a suspect, too?'' Her voice, barely a breathy whisper, cracked at the end of her question. She ached suddenly, her heart tightening.

Again, the silence rang out as she waited for his answer. ''Not as far as I know,'' he answered, finally.

She scraped together the last of her bravado. ''Then Mark could ask one of the policewomen to come home with me.''

Nick's expression softened, but only slightly. If she

hadn't been close enough to smell the remains of his aftershave and see the tiny lines that radiated out from his eyes, she would have missed that softening in his expression. "Helen, I know you don't trust me, but I'm going to ask you to, okay? The police here have their hands full. Not just with Cooms and the mess he made, but don't forget, the city goes on and other crime will continue. Please, trust me just this once. Will you come home with me? I promise you'll be safe and first thing in the morning, we'll put more pressure on those searching for your mother."

She blinked again at him, this time to stop the tears from forming. Her insides melted from a heat deep inside of her. It was a good thing she was sitting down. Her knees turned to warm jelly, her body betraying her with a wash of needful desire. Nick looked sincere. Mercy, he looked like he cared so much.

"Helen?"

She blinked him back into focus.

"Will you come home with me?"

He should have asked if she really trusted him. Yes, she did. She may be crazy, but she did trust him. Hadn't he just saved her life?

Before the trust could seep away like her bravado had, she nodded to him.

It seemed like nearly the entire evening had passed before she was allowed to leave. Not only had Mark and that other officer shown up, but also when Nick finally led her outside, she discovered several extra police cruisers parked outside.

"Why are there so many police?"

Nick took her arm after they weaved their way through

the parked cars. "It's because of the women's shelter being so close. The police don't want to take any chances."

Several officers looked up with unabashed interest. Embarrassed, she dropped her head. How did it look to them? she wondered. They saw her as Jamie Cooms's girlfriend, a woman who'd fled without reporting a murder. She'd been so weak.

Nick helped her into the truck before closing the door and walking toward Mark. The officer glanced her way as Nick approached.

Should she have told Mark this time that she'd seen Nick on several occasions with Jamie? Tears blurred her eyes. She trusted Nick, didn't she? That was why she was going home with him. He'd help her find her mother, wouldn't he?

Was she crazy to trust him? First, she'd been betrayed by Scott Jackson, who still wandered free, no doubt having spent all her money. Then by Jamie, the man who'd agreed to keep things casual, until she witnessed his horrible crime.

Was the third time a charm? Or did bad things really come in threes?

A dull ache throbbed behind her eyes. She needed to eat and sleep. She couldn't help her mother in this state and Momma definitely needed her help, wherever she was.

Nick returned to the truck. He twisted around in the seat as he fastened the belt. "I asked Mark to come by in the morning to discuss what's happening with your mother's disappearance."

Relief poured through her. "Thank you."

His face was dark in the shadow of the yellow streetlight behind them. Without saying another word, he started his truck and pulled away from the curb.

* * *

Nick couldn't believe how much the guilt ate at him. Never before had he been bothered by his lies. Or by his need to withhold information. Keeping information to himself was necessary to his job and therefore his life and the lives of several other undercover cops.

But tonight the lies bit at his insides like week-old coffee. He drove in gnawing silence, trying to concentrate on the slick city streets and glares of oncoming traffic. There was simply no other way around this. Though Nick believed Helen innocent of any involvement with Cooms's activities, that didn't give him license to tell her everything.

The road ahead darkened as they approached the stretch of highway that joined Saint John to Lower Cove. To his left, the utter blackness of the tidal flats made it feel like he was driving into oblivion. Thankfully, the landscape grew into low, scrubby hills as they closed in on his home.

He stole a glimpse at Helen beside him. At least Mark would drop by tomorrow to discuss the details of Connie Eastman's case. That would make Helen feel so much better, maybe even trust him. He had to be thankful for that.

His house was dark and undisturbed. He swung his truck around to face the rain-slickened rock, his headlights cutting through the misty night. All quiet.

"Home sweet home," he muttered half to himself.

Helen scrambled out and strode to the front door. Nick followed after he locked his truck. Inside his house, he threw off his coat and headed to the woodstove. It seemed like ages since he'd been home more than two days in a row. He'd been gone on his undercover work, renting a small condo in the city for his cover, and now, coming home should have felt good.

But it didn't. He had Helen here, a woman who could save his career. A woman whose body had tempted him nearly to the point of doing something so totally wrong, it still struck him hard in the chest.

And he was still suspended.

The paper he'd balled up and thrown into the stove caught fire in a blaze that roared up the stovepipe, puncturing the dark with flickering jabs of light. He turned around to find Helen slumped on the couch.

The same couch. Still, the image of her, her head thrown back, her body flexed, her female scent…

He jerked his head around to concentrate on the blaze. He'd told himself he wasn't doing her any favors making love to her, because he'd believed she was mentally ill and needed help.

Now? Oh, no. He still wasn't doing her any favors, but this time because of a list as long as his arm and growing longer each day. He simply couldn't afford to get involved with her, a victim, a witness, a lonely woman who missed her dead father and who was worried about her missing mother.

He couldn't fathom why she'd become involved with Cooms. Even only on a casual basis. The list went on.

Damn, he had to do something to take his mind off her.

"Hungry?" he asked, straightening.

She looked up as he turned on a lamp, seemingly surprised he was even there. A realization of something skittered over her face. She glanced around the room and swallowed. When she nodded, she set her mouth into a tight resolute line, as if steeling herself. The weariness had vanished from her eyes.

He'd take her nod as a yes, simply because if he didn't keep himself busy, he'd go crazy. Walking into the kitchen area of the home, he made a mental inventory of what food was there. He wasn't surprised when he found that there was nothing more than moldy cheese and half a bottle of flat ginger ale in his refrigerator.

His freezer held more promise. Nick pulled out a couple of frozen entrées, wondering when he'd bought them. They'd have to do, but next time he was out, he'd pick up some decent food.

"Can I help?"

Nick turned. Helen stood there, at the very edge of the breakfast bar that separated the kitchen from the living room. He held up the boxes. "No thanks. TV dinners are my specialty."

She smiled, however briefly, and he took it as a positive sign.

"You could set the table, if you like," he suggested.

"Sure." She gathered up the scattered papers he'd accumulated on the breakfast bar and tapped them into a neat pile, picking them up several times to get them perfect. Her hands shook and she glanced over at him. He offered her an encouraging nod and turned his attention back to the microwave.

Behind him, he could hear the papers crackle and flip to the floor. He glanced over his shoulder in time to see her quickly gather up the ones she'd dropped. She was incredibly nervous and he couldn't blame her one bit.

Don't embarrass her, he told himself, as he fiddled with the settings on the microwave. Don't make things worse.

After a moment's silence, he figured she was looking for cutlery and plates. "Knives and forks are under the knife stand," he said without turning around. He tore the shrink-wrapped plastic off the second microwave dinner.

What the hell were they supposed to do until the morning? The first, most obvious, most pleasing suggestion to hit his brain, he discarded immediately. What he should be doing was taking a statement from her. But she'd told

Mark everything that had happened when she'd walked in on Cooms and DiPetri.

Everything except his involvement. Why? he wondered. Did she know more than she was saying, something that connected her to Cooms in more depth than his fertile imagination conjured up?

She had to know more about Cooms's illegal activities, even if she didn't realize it. He'd been laundering money for years, smuggling drugs of every description into the country for even longer. She may have only been a casual girlfriend, but Cooms must have conducted *some* of his business in her presence. He'd have been cocky enough to do that. Maybe even while he held Helen in his arms...

Nick couldn't stop the gut-churning image of Cooms kissing Helen. Did she enjoy it? Did she allow him to grope her and take her to his bed?

Aw, hell, why was he looking for trouble? Forcing the thoughts out of his mind, he peered into the microwave.

And felt those tiny hairs on his arms rise up again. A warning as loud as the deafening silence that hit him square in the back.

Something was wrong.

Slowly, with precision borne of years of training, he turned, ready for anything.

Helen stood less than a yard from him, wielding his largest—and sharpest—knife.

Right at his heart.

Chapter 7

Helen could barely hold her hand still. Only thinking of her mother was she able to control the reflexive urge to shake.

"Put the knife down, Helen." Nick's words were calm, controlled, confident. Even his body language portrayed that cool efficiency. He held up his hands slightly and though his shoulders were slightly stooped, he kept his chin straightforward. His expression was relaxed, but his eyes were wary.

They locked stares. "Give me the knife," he said.

"No." She shook her head. "I can't. You know that. I can't trust you."

"You can trust me. Have I done anything to you, except save your life?"

Oh, yes, you have. Heat surged through her as she recalled his passionate onslaught the night they met.

"I'm sorry for that," he told her, reading her thoughts

as clearly as if she'd spoken aloud. "I never meant for anything to happen. It won't happen again."

"That's not why I've got this knife." She gritted her teeth to stop them from chattering with fear.

"Why, then?"

She took a step backward, shifting the knife to her left hand while she groped the breakfast bar behind her for the paper she'd found. "This fax. You were after me. You were using your connections with the police in Saint John to find me for Jamie. He wanted me dead. I saw him murder his best friend and that's why he sent you after me."

"That's not true."

"It is. And you were involved in that murder, too. I saw your bloodied knuckles that day. I know you beat up Tony just before Jamie shot him." She swallowed down the taste of her own fear. "I saw what you did to his face."

"It's not what you think."

"Yes, it is. And the only reason you haven't done anything yet is because Jamie is dead and you have to keep a low profile until his murderer is caught. Unless you had something to do with that, too." She glanced down at the fax through a blur of tears. The only picture she had with Jamie, taken at a restaurant he owned. She should have burned it. She'd been foolish to keep it.

She put the fax down and shifted the knife back to her right hand. "First up, I want you to tell me where my mother is."

Nick shook his head. "Put the knife down first and we can talk about it, okay?"

"No!" She gripped the knife tightly. The tendons in her wrist ached with the pressure. "You tell me where she is now, or I'll..."

"You'll what?" Nick dropped his hands and frowned. "I'm a hell of a lot bigger than you, Helen. I may take a few jabs and cuts, but it won't be hard for me to get that knife out of your hand.''

He was right, but she wasn't going to allow him to turn the tables on her. For once, she felt in control, a sensation she hadn't experienced for a long time. She shook her head. ''I can do more damage than a few cuts and jabs. Now, where is my mother?''

Nick sighed. ''I don't know. Not yet, anyway. And I haven't been stalking you. I want to help you.''

''Yeah, right. Why do you have a photocopy of my picture, then?''

He stepped toward her and she automatically backed up, her hip colliding with the edge of the breakfast bar.

''I called Mark the morning after the storm.'' He glanced at his watch. ''I asked him to see if anyone had reported you missing. You remember I found your necklace? That's how I knew your name.''

''So how did he get my picture?''

''He called Saint John for me. They'd already had a call from your landlord and had turned over your file to the Major Crimes Unit. Mark asked them to fax a copy of the photo they got from your apartment.''

''So you used the police to confirm who I was. What were you going to do then? Turn me over to Jamie, or kill me yourself? I know you beat up Tony.'' She wanted to call him a bastard, but held her tongue. Profanity didn't come easily to her.

''I didn't know who you were. When Mark told me, I could have kicked myself. I had a witness in my own house and I let her go.''

''I escaped.''

''From what, Helen? I wasn't holding you against your will. It was storming out.''

"You were." She shut her eyes. "We both know you wouldn't have let me go."

"Helen." His quiet voice cut through her failing courage. She opened her eyes, finding him closer, but at the same time, not intimidating. It was so confusing.

"Helen," he repeated. "I thought you were trying to kill yourself. Only after I found the strands of hair from your wig did I guess you weren't suicidal. After I learned who you were, I couldn't believe the coincidence. I had the one person who could prove my theories on Cooms and help us lock him up forever, and I'd let her slip away from me."

What was he talking about? She bit her lip, watching his attention drop to her mouth. Did she dare ask him to explain?

"I think you can also help me salvage my career."

She laughed. "Which career? The one you had as a cop, or the one getting you rich with Jamie's illegal activities?"

"Remember, I'm suspended."

"They caught up with you."

Nick shook his head, sagging slightly. Immediately, she tightened her grip on the knife. She wasn't going to drop her guard, like Tony had before he'd got himself beaten up and then murdered.

"No, Helen. I was suspended because I broke a couple of piddly rules. Rules designed to protect undercover cops."

She didn't understand. "What do you mean, undercover cops?"

The microwave beeped, but both of them ignored it. "I'm with a joint task force set up to combat major crime. We work with the Saint John Police Department. I've been doing undercover work for them. We've been trying to stop the flow of drugs into the city for years."

"You're lying." The knife in her hand had begun to shake. "Jamie didn't even smoke. And besides, if he was involved with drugs, he'd have made sure you got your share. To keep you incriminated."

"That's right."

Startled, she gaped at him.

"I did take my cut. And I turned it over to the Major Crimes Unit as evidence. Sixteen thousand dollars last month." Not taking his eyes off her, he motioned to the drawer nearest her. "There's a file in that drawer. Take it out and look at it. I have receipts for everything I've taken from Cooms. Go on, look at it."

She glimpsed out the corner of her eye at the drawer he indicated. Did she dare take a chance and open it?

"It's all there, Helen. Even the claim forms for the condo I rented. Take a look. I won't move."

Keeping the knife pointed at him, she yanked open the drawer. A blue folder lay across an assortment of other papers. She pulled it out and flicked it open.

Receipts, and plenty of them, held together with a large paper clip, were tucked into the left side of the folder. On the right were claim sheets, stamped Paid by the City of Saint John. She was used to skimming official documents. The one on top was for two months' rent on an uptown condo.

"Sorry my filing system isn't as good as what you might have at work. I'm a cop, not a secretary. But it's all there, Helen. All my receipts for everything Cooms ever gave me. Even the samples of the different grades of cocaine he told me he often hid in specially designed calling cards."

"Calling cards?"

"Yeah. Nice, good quality ones." He looked surprised. "Haven't you seen them?"

Helen's stomach turned over sickeningly. She'd seen those cards once, even commented on how thick they were and what pretty colors he had for them. Jamie had told her laughingly he only used the best imported cotton blend watercolor paper for them. And only for his best clients. And then he'd put them away.

"That receipt is on the bottom. Lift up the others," Nick told her. "The calling cards were ingenious. Peel off the top layer of paper and there it was, a sample of cocaine, spread thinly over the bottom paper. Different colored calling cards for different grades. He had them done up in South America."

She lifted up the receipts with her left hand and read the description on the last receipt. For personal cards. She swallowed the nausea. She'd touched those cards. She'd touched cocaine and never even knew it.

Feeling dizzy, she lowered the knife.

Nick was beside her before the next heartbeat, removing the knife from her hand and carefully slipping it back into its home in the knife stand.

"I'm sorry." She couldn't think of anything more to say. When she looked up at him, she found her vision blurring with hot tears.

He said something that sounded like a soft curse, but she wasn't sure. All she knew was that he was pulling her into a hard embrace and she was welcoming it with everything she had in her.

Slowly, Nick let out the breath he'd held for the past five minutes. He knew he could have easily wrestled the knife out of Helen's hand, but not without the risk of one or both of them getting cut. Helen didn't need that kind of stress.

He tilted his head down and his nose skimmed the top

of her dark hair. Her warm body molded itself to his, soft against his straight, hard frame, and he found himself clinging back with equal fervor.

All he had to do was tilt his head to one side, push his hand up to her chin and direct her face toward his. Once their lips were close enough, they'd kiss.

He wasn't sure if she would welcome his kisses. Once the relief was over and the truth settled into her, he knew she'd be angry. Women didn't like deception. After squeezing her hard one last time, he peeled her away from him and waited for the backlash.

''I suppose the only reason you didn't tell me was to protect yourself.''

He was right, sort of. Her words did have a slight sullenness to them, but not as much as he expected. ''It's not just me, Helen. Don't ask me anything more about the investigation. There are other players in it, whose very lives depend on keeping their identities secret.''

She blinked. ''I won't.'' She paused, throwing a quick glance up at him. ''Why were you suspended? What piddly rule did you break?''

He felt his jaw tighten. ''It was nothing. I'd rather not talk about it.'' Her trust was too new for him to tell the truth.

''But why did you tell me all of this, now?''

''How else would you let go of the knife?'' He shook his head, trying to sort out the jumble of mixed emotions he was feeling right now. Frustration, relief, worry. Attraction. All of it churning inside of him.

''I'm sure you could have talked me into putting the knife down, somehow. Isn't that what undercover cops are good at? B.S.-ing?''

Nick felt a small smile crack the corner of his mouth. ''Yeah. But you're not just a witness anymore. You're a witness needing protection and I can't protect you unless you trust me completely. I thought you had when you decided to come home with me."

Helen hugged herself. "I did a bit, but I was more interested in finding my mother. I couldn't let you out of my sight, in case you knew where she was."

She wanted to find her mother so she'd stuck close to him. He wanted to find Cooms's killer, so he'd stuck close to her. And unless he got down to forcing out some facts he was sure she had inside her head, neither of them would get what they wanted.

He turned back to the microwave. "Let's eat first. We can talk later."

"Talk about what?"

He reset the microwave and when the interior lit up, he turned. "I think you know a lot more than you realize. Someone wants you dead and someone had to have been helping Cooms launder money and distribute drugs."

"And that someone killed Cooms." It was hardly a question.

He heaved a sigh. "Don't jump to conclusions, yet. It's quite likely, but until we have the evidence, we have to keep an open mind or else the court will throw it out."

"Do you think it was me?"

"No." He really didn't. His gut told him no, and her alibi was obvious, damn it. Besides, he'd noticed that Cooms didn't do business with women. He'd told Nick once they were strictly for pleasure.

Thrusting the sickening thought of Cooms with Helen out of his mind once again, Nick busied himself with supper.

"Why don't you get those tapes out and we'll skim through them while we're eating?" he suggested curtly.

Helen grabbed the plastic bag of tapes and sorted them

out on the floor in front of his VCR. By the time he had supper on the breakfast bar, she'd started the first one.

"I'm warning you. They're boring even to me, and I'm the star," she said, carrying the remote control to the bar.

"Why don't we put them on fast forward?"

She clicked the appropriate button. Abruptly, she smiled. He looked up at the television. A tiny, crawling baby with tufts of the same dark hair he'd just nuzzled, jerked around a living room in happy, fast-forward action. "This is better. You forget, I'm an only child. My parents doted on me."

"Spoiled you?" He settled down in front of his meal.

Helen picked at her food. "No, but I always had their full attention. Especially my father, when he came home from work. I would run to him, see if he had brought me a treat of some kind."

"From the army? What kind of treat? A bayonet or two?"

Helen laughed, a soft, throaty sound that tickled up his spine. "Nope. From his box lunch if he had been out in the training area. He worked for Range Control. I'd get a fruit cup or juice box or pack of cookies. He'd always save something for me."

Nick watched a small toddler dashing for her father, then peering into the wide pockets of his combat shirt, her eyes expectant.

Helen focused on the tape. "This one's almost over." She turned to him. "Where are your parents?"

"Retired in Nova Scotia, pruning apple trees and playing with their hobby farm. I don't see them very often."

She watched his hooded expression for a moment and guessing correctly that he preferred not to discuss his family, she turned back to the television. The tape had already ended.

The next few tapes were the same, nothing seemed to be amiss with them. He may as well kill two birds with one stone and start asking the necessary questions. As she inserted the fifth tape, he asked, "How serious did you consider your relationship with Cooms?"

"I told you. Not very serious. Not at all."

She caught his skeptical look and explained, "You didn't know about me, did you? So how serious did you think it would be?"

"I knew you existed. No man who says women are only for pleasure goes without a girlfriend. Or two."

A flicker of distress danced over her features. As quickly as it came, it vanished. The stark light from the kitchen, the only light if you didn't count the TV, showed her tired face. But the emotion wasn't strong enough for him to guess what he'd seen.

"Jamie was the kind of man who acted on whims. At least he was that kind of man around me. He would show up at my apartment unexpectedly, or send flowers for no reason, or call me and tell me he was taking me to some restaurant for the evening. My schedule was always pretty loose, so I went along with it."

Nick stiffened. Cooms wasn't whimsical. He had been a calculating bastard who'd managed to charm people very easily. The sudden changes of plans Helen had just mentioned must have meant something. A meeting with a prospective client, a middle man for drugs, a possible businessman who could clean his money for him. Helen must know, without realizing it.

"Where would you go?"

"To his restaurants, mostly."

"Did he ever leave you alone?"

She shrugged. "Sure he did. He'd go into the kitchen or something to check the place out or order some special dish. But he was never gone long.'' She had resignation all over her face. It somehow reflected his own frustration. ''I know now he wasn't a model citizen and that he would have killed me without thinking twice, but...''

''But what?''

''But he was a good date. Polite most of the time. Attentive, though sometimes a bit too possessive, but,'' she said, shutting her eyes as if trying to purge the memories with a shake of her head, ''nice, without expecting anything back from me. Which was what I wanted.''

Nick felt his jaw tighten. ''Not expecting what?''

She opened her eyes, the look in her irises sad. ''Permanence.''

''And that was good?'' he gritted out.

''Yes, it was.'' She stood and after staring at the TV for a moment, she gathered up the empty dishes. ''I don't do relationships.''

The fifth tape ended. Damn, he'd barely watched it. He twisted around. ''Why don't you do relationships?''

She lifted her shoulders once and dropped the dishes into the sink. Wordlessly, she returned to the VCR and changed the tapes.

Nick tried another tactic. ''Why didn't you turn me in when you gave your statement to Mark about the assault?''

She turned, the fifth tape still in her hands. ''Because I was scared. Besides, would Mark have believed me? I was a murderer's girlfriend who hadn't reported what I'd seen, but rather took off and tried to fake my own suicide. Not exactly a credible witness.''

That was true. A good defense lawyer would have a heyday with her. And Mark liked to do things by the book. All the way. Though they'd been in a few difficult situations, their lives hadn't really been on the line. Mark wouldn't trust his instincts like Nick did.

Nick would rather a partner who did. But more than that, he'd rather not have a partner at all. By the book or simply freezing up like his first partner had, either way could get him killed. Sometimes it worked better if you bent the rules occasionally.

The next tape was running. A skinny, preadolescent Helen was having a birthday party, dancing around with her friends to music Nick couldn't hear because of the fast forward mode.

"Do you trust Mark Rowlands? Do you think he would have believed me if I had told him I thought you were being paid off? If you hadn't been on an undercover assignment?"

Nick glanced over at Helen as she walked toward the breakfast bar. "Mark would have listened to everything you said. He's a good cop and goes by the rules."

She watched him, her expression showing a large dose of skepticism. "But you aren't? You said you were suspended. Did you deliberately break the rules?"

Darkness seemed to take that moment to settle around the house. The cool kitchen lights strained to reach the entire downstairs. "You could say that."

"Did it have anything to do with the investigation?"

"Yes and no. I didn't fill out some forms I was supposed to." He couldn't think of anything else to say.

Helen sat down on the stool beside him. Those same fluorescent kitchen lights that couldn't warm his home lit up the walnut highlights in her hair. Her skin, smooth he knew from personal experience, glowed clean and clear. Even in the harsh light, her beauty shimmered.

"Who suspended you? The Saint John police?"

"My own chief."

"Sounds like a picky reason."

"The forms were for the force's protection." He really

didn't want to go into detail. Not when she was relaxed and ready to talk. Not when she sat close enough for him to smell her body heat. He swore to himself. There were other reasons for not telling her. Reasons, as a civilian, she wouldn't understand.

She was nodding. "Sometimes we have to do things we don't like, for our own protection."

The hairs on his arms tingled. She wasn't saying anything important here, was she? He scanned the room. The drapes were closed against the darkened sky. He knew his doors were locked, his alarm set. A part of him didn't believe that he was in danger here, so why the heck did he just get that telltale shiver?

"What's wrong? Are you cold?"

Nick looked at her. Cold? No way. He tried another tactic. "You said you didn't mind going out with Cooms because it was nothing serious."

"That's right."

She'd been an only child. The tape running now proved that. Christmas and loads of presents to unwrap. She'd had a stable upbringing. Then she'd dated a drug dealer because he was nice to her? Until he tried to kill her and she felt her only recourse was to fake a suicide. She had serious self-confidence problems.

She should trust her instincts. They were good.

But right now, the instinct that raised the hair on his arms was wrong. He'd always relied on it and this time, it was wrong.

His instinct, which was more important than anyone's rules and as good as his training, was wrong?

It couldn't be.

He snapped his attention back to Helen. "What did you say?"

"I asked you if you were cold."

"No, I'm fine." She wasn't telling him everything but did what she was hiding have anything to do with Cooms? Or her mother?

Or that mysterious con artist from her past?

"What about my mother?" Helen stood and stalked to the VCR, unaware, it seemed, that she had just read his mind. She waited a few minutes, watching the images of her opening a present. A moment later, the tape ended and she peered over her shoulder at him. "These tapes haven't been tampered with. But my mother's missing. We have to find her more than we have to look at these things." She jabbed the eject button. "She's out there somewhere. Unprotected."

Nick sighed. But Helen was safe *here,* working with him, trying to figure who wanted her dead, and maybe where her mother was.

Damn, he didn't do partnerships or protection very well.

Chapter 8

The next morning, as Nick had promised, Mark arrived. Helen had spent the night upstairs in Nick's bedroom, with Nick downstairs on the cot in his study.

She suppressed a yawn, as Nick let Mark inside. Neither of them had slept well. She'd listened to Nick pace the floor, run through the last of the tapes and knew he must have been hoping to drop off, bored stiff by her childhood.

Across the living room, Mark nodded to her. This morning, he was in uniform and looked as tired as Helen felt.

''Thanks for coming over,'' Nick said. ''Coffee?''

''Only if it's strong and black.'' Mark dropped his briefcase onto the breakfast bar and turned to Helen.

He said nothing and in a fleeting moment, she got the uncomfortable impression that he was checking her out. What for? she wondered. Automatically, she stole a glimpse at Nick and knew then. Did Mark think she and Nick were lovers? Was he searching for signs that they had spent the night in each other's arms?

She felt her face heat up, betraying the fact that she considered Nick, in some strange confusing way, to be her lover. Foolish notion. One night going a bit overboard didn't make them lovers.

Thankfully, Mark said nothing as he accepted a mug of steaming coffee. "So." He spoke after he'd taken a sip. "Let's start at the beginning, shall we? When was the last time you saw your mother?"

"When Nick put her in a taxi."

"The day you were assaulted?"

She nodded. "I asked him to send my mother to my aunt's house."

Mark asked the name of the taxi company and Nick supplied it. Then he asked for the addresses of her aunt June, her mother, the community center where she volunteered, even her friends.

"She got to my aunt's place okay," she added hastily. "I called my aunt from the shelter and that was when she told me Momma had gone back home to get some clothes, shortly after she arrived. But when I went to her house, the door was wide open and Momma hadn't been there!"

She tried to force down the fear that had tightened into a thick knot in her throat and had squeezed tears into her eyes. When she looked up, she found Nick watching her closely, his brows pressed together and expression hooded.

Mark continued to write down all she said, including her garbled description of her mother. "Why wouldn't she stop at her house on the way to your aunt's? Would she take her car?" he asked.

She clenched her hands together. "I don't know."

Mark said, "If you don't mind, I'd like to take a look around her house." He looked at Nick. "Did you check it out?"

Nick nodded. ''It didn't appear that anything had been taken, but Helen said it felt different.''

''Like someone had been there,'' she added. ''I can't explain it.''

When he'd finished writing, Mark chewed on the end of his pen, all the while studying her. Didn't he understand what she meant? She opened her mouth to speak, but Nick quickly interrupted her.

''Drink your coffee, then,'' he ordered both her and Mark. ''We're wasting time.''

Mark dropped his notes into his briefcase and clicked it shut. ''Did you look at your tapes yet?''

''There was nothing of importance on them,'' Nick said.

''That's right.'' Helen threw a quick look at him as she agreed. ''There wasn't anything unusual with them. Just my boring life.''

Mark made an agreeing noise, though his face remained expressionless. She couldn't help but wonder if he really believed her. Or was it Nick he didn't believe? After all, she hadn't stayed up to watch all of the tapes. She'd heard segments of them during the night, but what if there was something on them, and Nick wasn't telling Mark the truth?

Forget it. She trusted him. But still, she didn't dare glance at Nick again, with Mark watching their every move. It didn't take a psychic to sense there was a mutual distrust between the two men. It shimmered just beneath the surface.

Nick spoke. ''Anything on the vehicle that tried to run Helen down?''

A distinct silence lingered after his question. Finally, Mark said, ''Actually, something interesting did show up on it this morning.''

Helen stopped buttoning her coat. Nick glanced at her and then back at Mark. "What was it?" he asked.

"The license plate number says it had belonged to Clive Darlington."

"*Had* belonged? Did he sell it?" she asked.

Mark shook his head. "No. When he was incarcerated, all of his assets were seized and sold at a Crown assets auction, by order of the judge, to pay retribution and some outstanding fines. He had a lot of them. Anyway, there was an auction the next week and the car was bought by a man named William Townsend."

Helen gasped. Both men turned to her. "You know him?" Nick asked her.

"That was Jamie."

"How do you know?" Nick's frown looked as tight as Mark's and Helen knew she was in for a grilling.

"I found out one night when he was drunk."

The two men shared a single understanding look. Helen knew they'd communicated something important—trusting each other—in that one split second.

"His reason made sense, even though he'd been drinking. I didn't give it much thought at the time."

Nick turned to Mark. "Did you run the name through the system?"

Mark's expression turned cool. "Yes. A man called William Townsend did buy the car, and there is a driver's license issued to him. No photo, though. I don't have much more info than that. Yet."

It wasn't mandatory to have a driver's license with a photo in New Brunswick. Helen didn't spend the extra money for it, either. "But surely someone would have recognized Clive," she protested.

"I doubt it." Mark shook his head. "It's just a clerk who handles the paperwork and there were a lot of items sold that day." He faced Nick. "You heard of this alias before?"

Nick said, "No."

"Interesting." Mark walked to the door. "Meet you at your mother's place," he told Helen.

When he was gone, Helen turned to Nick as she finished doing up her jacket. "He doesn't believe me."

"Why would Jamie tell you about his alias?"

"And not you?" She yanked on the hem of the jacket. "Remember I told you he got drunk one night and told me he had a few politicians in his back pocket? Later, he was fumbling with his jacket and his wallet fell out. I saw the driver's license with William Townsend's name on it."

"Did you ask him about it?"

"Of course I did. He said it was for tax purposes. That way, if any of his businesses went under, they wouldn't be able to seize all of his assets."

Nick said nothing until he'd donned his own jacket. "That's not completely true, but it doesn't matter. Helen, weren't you the least bit suspicious?"

She swallowed, feeling foolish. "No. Jamie wasn't that important to me. He was just a boyfriend who was nice. I told you, I don't do permanent relationships. Or even semipermanent. If he wanted to evade taxes, well, to me he was just one of millions in the country. I...I was getting ready to break it off with him, anyway."

She looked into his eyes for something to tell her that he understood. In a way, he was like her. As an undercover cop living alone, he had no one permanent in his life, either. Did he?

But thick, dark lashes shielded Nick's eyes and his expression told her nothing. Maybe he'd never understand what it was like to be protected all your life, then lose it all one day when your father's heart gives out.

And then get involved with not only one, but two crooks. She pursed her lips as she walked past him. What lousy judgment she had.

Out in Nick's truck, Helen clicked on her seat belt and fell into a melancholy silence.

Nick slid in beside her. "I didn't mean to give you the impression that we think you're stupid."

She stared out the window. "But you do. It's all right. I know you don't understand." She twisted to face him. "I'm not a police officer. I'm not suspicious of everyone. And I made a mistake dating Jamie, okay? I may be naive, but I'm as tenacious as any of you cops. Now, let's go. My mother is still missing and I won't stop looking until I've found her."

A short smile almost relaxed Nick's hardened features. For a flash, Helen was sure he was going to chuckle or shoot a devastating smile at her. She hadn't seen one yet, but knew incomprehensibly that any smile Nick had would be a killer to women.

Instead, his features tightened again as he started his truck.

After they reached the highway, she asked, "Was there anything on those tapes? I know you watched them last night."

"Nothing except birthday parties and Christmas presents. And one time when you fell off your bike and skinned your knees."

Helen smiled. "I remember. My first day with my new bike."

"Your mother must have been filming you. It shows your father scooping you up."

"He always took care of us." She froze, her mouth falling open slightly. "Wait! I just remembered something.

Jamie bought me the VCR in my apartment. I mentioned it yesterday, too, but I just realized that it was a few days later, he asked to see my tapes.''

Nick frowned at her, as she leaned forward. ''I remember he said he bought it at Globatech, just after they began to rent one of his warehouses. At the time, I thought it was odd, because Globatech doesn't make VCRs.''

''Did you say anything?''

Helen shook her head. ''No. When he brought it to my apartment, Chester was there, talking about heating pipes and such and it took a while for him to finish looking at my radiators.''

''Why didn't you ask someone at your work about it?''

''Jamie asked me not to. He said that Globatech, like many other companies, just imports cheaper models and slaps their logos on them. It wasn't a good quality, top of the line one, he said, and asked me not to say anything, so as not to embarrass my bosses.''

''Still, it's a big present for just dating.''

''I thought he was just being nice to the company, thanking them for their patronage, that sort of thing. Besides, mine was on its last legs. It was my parents' old machine and I wasn't going to look a gift horse in the mouth. Remember, too, that Jamie acted like that with me. Spontaneously. And he didn't like to take no for an answer.''

''What does Globatech specialize in?''

''They're best known for highly specialized electronic equipment. I know they have a government contract, but what for, I'm not sure. They also do computer systems and networks for big offices. All their stuff is top of the line.''

''Except their VCRs.''

She blinked at him, aware of only the cold chill that

trickled down her back. "Yes. Except their VCRs," she repeated absently.

Nick's eyes became hard and dark like coal. "Then let's take a look at the thing, shall we?"

"What about my mother? Won't Mark be waiting at her house? We need to find her!"

Nick had been expecting her question ever since he took a left turn instead of a right as soon as they entered the city. "We won't be very long. I want to check out your VCR first."

He sensed her disapproval. "But you're suspended. Are you supposed to be investigating this?"

"No, I'm not supposed to be investigating anything." He gripped the steering wheel, refusing to elaborate on his words.

She fell silent, only after shooting a curious look that even now still lingered on him. Damn, she wasn't missing much.

Nick noticed Helen's landlord outside, already starting his fall cleanup. The day was good for it, with clear skies and just the barest of the constant breeze that blew over the city. Through his open window, Nick inhaled deeply, drawing in the scents of the fall and cooler temperatures.

And Helen's freshly shampooed hair.

He should never have insisted she stay at his house, he realized belatedly. How was he supposed to concentrate on this illegal investigation of his while she sat beside him, smelling like tangy sweet apples?

"Do you trust Mark? He doesn't seem to trust you."

He turned to her as he parked his truck in the driveway. Her mind wasn't on the investigation, anymore than his was. Only she wasn't thinking of hair.

"Mark's a good cop," he answered. "A bit of a straight arrow for my liking, but okay."

"That's not what I asked you." Helen undid her seat belt, but made no move to climb out.

"That's the only answer I have for you." With his terse words, he threw open the driver's door. He listened to Chester greet Helen, who managed to thwart his questions with a smile and a quick word on how they were pressed for time.

Up in her apartment, they both went straight to the VCR, Nick pulling it out until the cables in the back protested. Quickly, he unscrewed them and freed the machine.

"Where are Globatech products made?"

"Mostly in Canada, but a few are made in the United States and some components are made in Japan," Helen answered. "I know that because it's one of the founding tenets on the company. Quality products made at home."

Nick flipped the machine over and scraped back the corner of the label with his fingernail. Under the gentle pressure, the label peeled neatly away. A Spanish name appeared.

Nick squinted at the fine print on the upside down VCR. "This was made in Colombia."

Helen peered at the writing, leaning too close to him. "I don't understand. Globatech is very strict with its policies. The only reason we have some parts from Japan is their products or parts are classified and sealed units, used in special equipment. The owners would *never* buy from Colombia."

"This time they did."

"What does it say?"

"It says it's a fake."

"A fake? A knockoff?"

Nick nodded. ''Looks that way. I don't recognize the real name of it, but I bet it's not allowed in Canada.''

''Why not?''

''Probably doesn't meet Canadian Standards Association guidelines.''

Helen backed up to the corner of the couch and sank down on the arm. ''What are we going to do now? Take it with us?''

''No.'' He carefully replaced the label and returned the VCR to its place on the shelf, taking his time screwing in the cables again.

The hairs on his arms were tingling, too, telling him with absolute certainty that it was better if they kept quiet about this VCR. For the time being, anyway.

Helen watched him. ''Why didn't you know that Jamie had rented warehouse space to Globatech?''

Nick carefully finished his task. ''The investigation was just getting started. These things take time. And the investigation had been headed in a totally different direction, too.''

''But you were investigating drug smuggling, not a black market in electronics, right?''

''We figured Cooms was bringing in drugs somewhere along the coast, possibly on fishing boats.'' He looked up at Helen. ''Cooms smuggled drugs. He'd been doing it for years. But he had legitimate business interests, too. I bet if we checked out the rental agreement between Cooms and Globatech, it would be perfectly legal.''

''It would have to be. Like the federal government, the city also gave Globatech a forgivable loan, but one of the stipulations was that they could monitor their books. Globatech complied. In fact, the city has already been in once to look at them.''

Nick crossed his arms. Of course, not everything Cooms

did was illegal, but something about Globatech wasn't right. "We need to get into Globatech's warehouse."

"Not right now, we don't." Helen stood up. "Mark's waiting for us at my mother's house."

He'd nearly forgotten. Naturally, her mother took priority. "Let's go then, and later, we can figure out how I can get into the warehouse."

Helen held the door to the stairs open. "Why can't Mark just get a search warrant?"

"Because," Nick answered, glancing down the stairs to ensure they were alone, and that Chester wasn't at the bottom. "Mark needs to prove to the judge that it's related to the investigation and to do so, he'd have to tell how he discovered his suspicions. I know Mark. He wouldn't want to tell the judge it was because of a suspended police officer's illegal investigation. Mark won't lie, therefore he won't get a search warrant."

Outside, Chester's lawnmower roared to life. Helen stared at Nick, capturing his attention with dark blue eyes that had suddenly lost their sensuality. Now they were cool and dark. And even her full bottom lip seemed tighter as she leaned closer to him. "Because of the new security regulations, the warehouse is locked at all times, including during a normal workday. I have the keys to the warehouse in my desk, but we have to go to my mother's house first." She waited patiently for him to answer, her lips set.

Blackmail. Or bribery. A curse lingered on his tongue. He didn't want to ask for her help. He didn't want to have to drag her around with him, needing her, and needing to protect her at the same time.

Pushing away the thoughts of her pouty little mouth, her warm, scented body, he knew one inevitable thing.

He was screwed.

* * *

Helen couldn't help but feel a tiny bit pleased. Except now wasn't the time to gloat. Nor was it time to think about Nick's not-so-legal investigation, or the revelation that he didn't trust anyone but himself. Her mother was still missing and Mark was waiting to help her.

Nick followed her downstairs and Helen made a beeline for his truck, ignoring Chester. Once they found Momma, she'd help Nick. But not before.

With Nick focused on his driving, Helen let out a tiny sigh. Never before had she stood up like that to anyone and certainly never before had she blackmailed anyone. Even now, as the fact settled on her, she found herself tingling all over.

They found Mark waiting outside her mother's house. The look on his face said he wasn't pleased with the delay. Helen caught a glimpse of the two men staring each other down as Nick climbed out of the truck.

Mark spoke first. "While you were touring the city, I got a call." He turned to Helen and his voice immediately dropped its sarcasm. "They found your mother's car at a parking garage near the waterfront. I have to leave now if I want to check it out with the Saint John Police. I'd also like to go over the security tapes. I still want to have a look in your mother's house, but I can't now."

Helen nodded. Horror was spreading slowly through her, numbing her far more than the autumn sun could warm. Where could her mother be? In the trunk?

She glanced at Nick, finding his image swimming in her unshed tears. He said, "It's okay. Mark will check it all out. He has a description of your mother and will let us know what he finds out." His tone softened. "Do you have a spare set of her car keys?"

Helen swallowed the burning bile that had begun to rise. "Yes, I have a spare set somewhere." Her hands shaking, she dug through her purse to the bottom and pulled out the set.

Mark took them. When he reached the police cruiser, he pivoted and walked back to Nick. ''I forgot something. Saint John ran the list of Cooms's real estate over to the land registry office. Some of his properties were recent purchases.''

''How recent?'' Nick asked.

There was a pause as Mark stared pointedly at her. Was he reluctant to say anything in front of her? Why start to say that little bit in the first place, if he wasn't going to finish it?

''Only a few months ago, he bought a small building and lot just outside the city from Chester Ellis. It had been used for storage. Is Chester Ellis your landlord, Ms. Eastman?''

Helen nodded.

''What does he do for a living?''

''Nothing. He's retired—'' She cut off her own words.

Nick took a step closer to her. ''What?''

The numbness seeped from her belly, allowing the sun to warm her. ''He was a clerk at the Customs office downtown. I think he did a lot of his work down at the docks, too.'' Oh, dear. Why did she have to tell them that? Chester was innocent.

Nick looked at Mark, but Helen stopped any chance of them talking. ''He never goes anywhere,'' she burst out loudly, hoping it would somehow erase the doubt her words of a moment ago had caused. ''He'll be at home whenever you get around to talking to him. Meanwhile, my mother is still missing.''

Both men lifted their eyebrows at her forcefulness. ''I'll go then,'' Mark said, pocketing her keys and returning to his cruiser. A minute later, he was gone.

Nick surveyed the street and Helen followed his gaze. Several neighbors were taking advantage of the clear weather and like Chester, were doing yard work. But their automatic actions were a poor mask for their curiosity. "Let's go inside. You can leave your mother a note. Mark will call and we can ask him then when he can check this place out."

Helen unlocked the front door. The cool, quiet air inside caught in her throat. Momma loved the heat. She was always baking something, too.

Where could she be?

Trudging into the kitchen and sitting down, she said a silent prayer for her mother's safety, pleading with God to keep her alive.

Nick went straight into the living room.

She sighed and pulled her aching body out of the kitchen chair. She found him squatting on one knee over by the television. "What are you doing?"

"Do you know how many VCR tapes your mother uses?"

"Hardly any." Helen dropped to her knees and peered in at the few tapes that were stacked below the VCR. Two Billy Graham tapes and a senior's exercise tape she must have borrowed from someone. "My mother can play a tape, but she doesn't have a clue how to tape something. She says it's too complicated—"

A sharp noise behind them stalled her words. Nick was on his feet in a flash, stepping in front of Helen as she tried to pivot around.

"Stay here," he ordered.

"It came from the bedroom!" she cried softly. "Someone's here!"

Chapter 9

Nick silenced her with a quick wave of his arm. Helen watched him creep toward the hall, his hand feeling for the gun that wasn't there.

He didn't have a gun. He had no way to defend himself. Helen tore her gaze from him to the archway that led to the kitchen.

There were several knives on the counter, any one of them suitable weapons. Helen leaped up and hurried into the kitchen, snatching the largest knife she could find. Gripping it tightly, she stepped into the hallway.

Silence greeted her. Silence and no sign of Nick. Panic surged in her chest and she swallowed. Which bedroom did he duck into?

Then the scrape of her mother's closet doors.

And a soft, plaintive cry.

Helen blinked, her grip on the knife so tight, it ached.

"Helen!" Nick's voice was sharp, demanding.

"Thank God in Heaven!"

Her mother? Abruptly, Nick came out of her bedroom, his arm around her mother.

"Momma!" Helen rushed forward.

"Whoa!" Nick caught her before she reached her mother, twisting her arm up and out of harm's way. "You seem to have an affinity for knives, don't you?"

Helen relinquished the knife she'd forgotten she wielded. "Sorry, I knew you didn't have a gun, so I thought it might help protect us." She turned and threw her arms around her mother. "Momma! Are you all right?"

Her mother gripped her back and Helen could smell dust and mold in her clothing. "Yes, sweetie. I'm fine, now. I hid in the closet when I heard a car pull up."

"Where have you been?" Helen led her into the living room.

Connie Eastman sank into the faded couch and sighed. She looked worn and tired and very near tears. Helen's heart went out to her. She knew how her mother felt.

Had her mother felt this way when Helen had told her she'd planned to fake her own suicide and leave?

Connie rummaged in her dusty cardigan pocket for a crumpled tissue. "I came back here to get some things I needed plus that roast in the refrigerator."

"How did you get here?" Nick asked.

"I had my car. After you put me in a taxi, I asked the driver to bring me here instead. I picked up my car and drove to my sister's place, like you thought I should. But when I came back here to get some things, I realized that someone was following me."

"Why didn't you get your things when the taxi dropped you off?"

Connie paused. "I guess I wasn't thinking straight and when June said I should stay a few days, I realized I needed some clothes and that the roast would go bad if it wasn't used.''

''What did you do for the whole day and night?'' Helen asked, perching on the couch beside her mother and still holding her hand.

''I didn't stop. I just drove around all night. I didn't go back to June's apartment because I didn't want her in danger.''

Nick sat on her other side, his attention riveted on her. ''What happened next?''

''When I was sure no one was following me, I left my car in the parking garage and took a taxi here. But as soon as I got here, I heard someone pull into my driveway.'' She shuddered.

Immediately, Helen stood. ''I'll make some tea.''

''Thank you, sweetie.''

As she filled the kettle, Helen listened to her mother continue. ''I hid in the plumbing access hole and waited. But my hearing isn't as good as it used to be....'' Her mother trailed off.

Nick asked, ''What did the car that was following you look like?''

''It was an older car, one of those big ones with four doors.''

Her voice sounded doubtful, even to Helen, out in the kitchen. She hurriedly carried a tray in and set in on the coffee table. Handing her mother a steaming mug, she asked, ''What color was it?''

''Dark green, I think. It had tinted side windows, too.''

Helen exchanged looks with Nick. His expression was clear, telling her to keep quiet. Fortunately, her mother took the opportunity to sip her tea and she missed the silent warning.

''Mrs. Eastman?'' Nick leaned forward. ''How many videotapes do you have here?''

Stunned by the odd question, Connie looked up. She looked to Helen, who tried to keep her face passive. No need to upset her mother further, but at the same time, she knew she had to trust Nick to do his job.

Connie put her tea down on the tray. "Tapes? I don't know. Three or four, if you count the one Helen left here."

She looked across her mother's lap to find Nick staring at her. "I didn't leave any tapes here."

"It's the one when you were thirteen. I meant to ask you why you brought it here, but it slipped my mind."

An icy chill traveled down Helen's back. "I didn't bring that tape here."

Nick sat back, looking deep in thought. She knew his unspoken question. If she hadn't brought it here, who had? "When did you first notice it?"

"A few weeks ago. Maybe less. I meant to ask you about it, but, well, you got busy. Things happened after."

Busy trying to fake a suicide. Busy running for her life, trying to escape Jamie. Busy trying to purge the memory of watching Jamie kill his best friend.

Helen leaned forward and grabbed her mother's tea, taking a hard swallow of the scalding liquid and hoping it would wash away the chill and fear.

"Where's the tape now, Mrs. Eastman?"

Connie looked at Nick. "In my car. I meant to give it to Helen. What's all this about?"

"I'm not sure." Nick patted Connie's hand. "But I am going to find out. Have you got your car keys?"

"Yes, but Helen has a spare set."

"I gave them to the police when they found your car," Helen said, replacing the empty cup. "Why don't we take you to Aunt June's place? You'll be safer there."

She tried to coax her mother to stand, but Connie sat back instead. "Someone broke into my home and left a tape that they had taken from your apartment? I don't understand what's going on."

Helen took her mother's hand and pulled her up. "I don't either, but Nick and I will find out. It's better if you go to Aunt June's."

"And you? Who will protect you from whoever is behind this?" Connie turned to Nick. "Can I trust you to look after her?"

Nick's expression hardened. Helen waited, her breath stuck in her throat. Was he going to send her with her mother, feeling now she didn't need to help him with his investigation? If he didn't trust a well-trained officer like Mark, he certainly wouldn't trust her.

"She'll be fine," Nick said. "Let's get you to your sister's so you can rest. You must be exhausted."

Connie nodded, allowing herself to be led to the front door, only after retrieving her purse from her closet.

After Connie Eastman was safely ensconced at her sister's well-protected apartment building and they'd retrieved the missing videotape, Nick finally relaxed. As much as he could with Helen so close. He'd pushed aside the mix of churning emotions while they talked to her mother, but now those emotions threatened the dam he'd built.

"Thank you."

Nick straightened and looked over the interior of his truck to Helen as she buckled her seat belt. "For what?"

"For everything." She indicated her aunt's apartment building. "Bringing my mother here, taking care to see she's safe."

"It's nothing." He rammed the car key into the ignition and twisted it savagely.

Focus, Thorndike, focus.

Next stop was her workplace, where they could ''borrow'' the warehouse keys. Then he'd have to figure out where to leave Helen. Anyplace safe and far away from him.

Unaware of his thoughts, Helen toyed with the videotape. ''I wonder who took this. And why.''

''The first chance we get, we'll play it. What's on it might tell us. In the meantime, I want to have a look at that warehouse.''

''It's a normal workday. The shipping staff may be there.''

Nick drove toward the uptown area, past the circular Harbour Station and the enclosed pedway that connected the stadium to the downtown mall. Even though the tower of a fancy hotel blocked their view of the warehouses across the narrow harbor, the sun streamed into the truck. Nick turned left and headed to Globatech. ''Do you know any of the shipping staff?''

Helen shrugged. ''Sure. But by now they'd know I'm not at work. They won't keep quiet.''

Nick glanced at the time. ''It's just after one. What time do they take lunch?''

''Usually between twelve and one, splitting it up so the warehouse isn't empty. Let's go to my office first. Nothing will get done if I can't get the keys.''

Nick parked around the corner. Helen scrambled out and dug through her pocket for some change for the meter. She offered a short smile. ''No need to get a ticket. You may not be able to get it fixed.''

Very funny. Nick took her arm and led her into the building. Globatech rented the fourth floor.

As the elevator doors slid open at the correct floor, Helen peered out gingerly. ''I told my boss I was taking some sick days. He wasn't impressed. I doubt I'll have a job to come back to, especially if we get caught."

"We won't." He steered her out.

"Hello."

He turned to face the voice. Seated at a reception desk nearby was a young woman. "May I help you?" she asked.

Helen strode up. "Hello." She threw a cautious look over her shoulder to him. Judging from the woman's polite expression, she didn't recognize Helen. He took a step forward, but Helen took command of the situation.

"I'm looking for Mr. Parker."

The young woman smiled back, obviously hired to fill the void Helen left. "Everyone's in a staff meeting right now. Did you have an appointment?"

Helen smiled back. "No. I'm just a friend. It's not important. Perhaps I could leave a message?"

The woman handed her a piece of paper and a pen. When Helen flicked her foot, Nick stepped up to the desk. "I wonder if you could show me where the washrooms are?" He gave her his best smile, hoping his face didn't show his fatigue and strain.

"Certainly." She stood up and walked around the desk. He caught a glimpse of Helen's slight nod as she lifted the pen. The receptionist walked around the corner with him. He could only give Helen about ten seconds, maybe a few more, to "borrow" the keys.

"You seem familiar to me," he told the woman, stopping her in the middle of the corridor. "Did you work over at city hall last year?"

She shook her head. "No. I did work for some time at the university, though."

He nodded, devoting as much of his attention to her as possible, all the while keeping an ear out for Helen.

"That's it. I took a course on computer programming last year," he lied, his face relaxing into a polished smile. "I'm sure that's where I've seen you."

The woman smiled back. Adrenaline hit him hard. He'd forgotten the feeling of working undercover. The improvisation and need to remember every detail of every lie. Any slip could mean immediate danger. And yet, any lie that passed unnoticed was a powerful victory.

The rush felt good.

Nick gritted his teeth. Another emotion surged in just as quickly. Regret? Contrition? He shoved whatever it was away. Now wasn't the time to gain a conscience.

Helen appeared around the corner. "Ready?" she asked Nick. She smiled at the woman. "I put the note on your desk. Thank you."

Outside and around the corner, she flipped the key up in the air. "Child's play. And we're in luck. Mr. Parker doesn't hold staff meetings very often, but when he does, he gets really long-winded. And he likes everyone to be there."

Nick didn't share her optimism. "Why do you suppose he's holding the meeting now?"

"Probably to talk finances. Mr. Parker watches every cent the company makes. He probably wants everyone to tighten their belts."

The hairs on Nick's arms rose. He didn't like the timing of this meeting. Did it mean anything to the undercover op? What did it mean to the flow of drugs into the city? He had to warn Mark. Those working undercover might not know.

"The best news is that the warehouse will be empty," Helen chatted on as they strode to the car.

Nick unlocked the passenger door. "Good. I'll need it to be empty."

Helen's smile fell away. ''You're not going in there without me.''

''I am.'' Something wasn't right and he'd be damned if he was going to risk Helen.

''You need me, Nick, and we have an agreement.''

''Which is over now. Your mother's safe. You'll unlock the door, turn off the alarm and go sit in my truck. Doors locked, engine running.''

''No way.'' Helen glared at him. ''I know where everything is. I've worked at the warehouse when they've been shorthanded.''

''We don't even know what we're looking for,'' he muttered.

''All the more reason to have an extra pair of eyes. Oh, come on, Nick, we both know what's going on here. You suspect Globatech of smuggling drugs. That means the paperwork will have to be very creative in order to get past the city's reviewers and Canada Customs. I know the paperwork. It'll shorten our time.''

She leaned over as he pulled out of his parking space. He felt her hand settle on his arm, the warmth of it soaking in, relaxing the hairs and coaxing them to settle down and enjoy the sensation of her touch. ''You know I'm making sense here.''

''But you also want me to protect you, too,'' he said, trying to ignore her hand.

A frown skittered over her face. She blinked as she withdrew her hand. ''What I want is to be able to go back to my own life again.''

Without him. Those two words rose unbidden into his chest, squeezing his lungs until he was sure he would let out a strong hiss.

''You need me, Nick. Admit it.''

Yeah, he needed her. He needed her soft, pouting mouth

and warm blue eyes. He needed to feel her warm, soft body again.

Forget it! This wasn't why he was letting her tag along. The sooner they got to the bottom of this investigation, the sooner he could get his career back on track. The sooner they found out what Globatech had to do with Jamie Cooms, the sooner he could warn those undercover cops who were risking their lives right now.

It had nothing to do with Helen Eastman and her soft, trusting body.

Nick drove in silence to the warehouse and they climbed out of the truck.

Despite the clear day, the air was heavy with the smells of the port. Nick glanced casually around, finding the street relatively quiet.

"This key is for the back door," Helen told him as they circled around. The building was the last in the row, closest to the terminal where the ferry from Nova Scotia docked. A gull screamed at them overhead.

Helen quickly unlocked the narrow steel door and left Nick to shut it as she hurried inside to turn off the alarm.

"They left the lights on," she commented, coming back through the maze of shelving.

Nick looked up. "They're sodium lights. They take a long time to heat up. Where's the office?"

"Up here." She pointed to a flight of stairs that hugged the wall ahead of them. Up above was the balcony style office.

As soon as they entered, Nick went straight to the row of windows that stretched across the far wall. "Keep the lights off," he ordered. Keeping himself low, he peered through a section of window that opened outward.

Helen appeared beside him, and he hauled her down to keep her out of sight.

"Hurry up, will ya? I haven't got all day."

Helen gasped at the voice that filtered up to them. The whine of an electric forklift cut off any answer.

Nick stooped down farther and found himself face-to-face with Helen.

Her eyes were wide with fear and he knew in an instant that she recognized the voice.

"It's Clive!"

Chapter 10

Nick straightened and, hugging the window frame, peered down at the warehouse floor. Below, two men worked quickly, one driving the electric forklift as it carried in a large open tri-wall box. The other, a smaller man he hadn't seen before, moving smaller cartons out of the way.

"Okay, that's good."

Nick felt Helen's hand grip the back of his light jacket, but couldn't afford the sudden movement to look down at her.

"What's that name we're looking for?"

"Four small boxes. They should have the name W. Townsend on them."

The second man began to search. "Here's one," he said, pulling it out of the tri-wall.

The first man remained obscured by the forklift's safety cage. "There should be three more. Find them."

As Nick sank down beside Helen, she hissed, "That's Clive!"

He stared at her through the dim light of the office. The yellow sodium lights cast eerie shadows on her face. "Are you sure?" he mouthed. He knew Darlington by face only, not voice.

"Yes." Her words were barely above being mouthed. "And the other is Ron Mills. He works here."

Nick rested his head against the wall below the open window, listening as the two men hunted through the tri-wall. Helen shimmied closer. He could feel her body heat, smell the barest remains of her apple shampoo.

"Don't worry. Ron won't come up here. He suffers from vertigo and hates the view from the windows."

Nick shifted away, using the excuse of sneaking another peek out the window at the two men. Helen's words were welcoming news. He didn't really want to take on both men should they decide to come up to the office.

She'd been right. He needed her expertise. The words felt heavy in his stomach. So why did that revelation hit him so hard?

"Here's the last box," Ron Mills said.

Clive Darlington grabbed it and took it to a nearby bench. Sweeping the packaging equipment off it with his forearm, he dumped the boxes down.

"Hey, don't go wrecking the place! I have to clean up, you know."

"Not anymore." Darlington turned, pulling out a handgun from inside his jacket.

He fired it, the report splintering the still air. Helen jumped beside him, and Nick hauled her close, forcing her face into his side to stop her from witnessing another horrific act.

Then he watched Ron Mills drop like a stone.

Darlington ignored the fallen man. Instead, he sliced open the first box and snapped the cover off an exposed piece of electronic equipment.

He pulled out sandwich sized bags of snowy white powder.

Nick's stomach clenched. Cocaine. Cooms hadn't been smuggling it in on fishing boats as the chief had suggested. Maybe at first, but not now. It was coming in through Globatech.

Darlington grabbed his boxes and without even a glance down at the dying Mills, he stalked out the far exit.

As soon as the door slammed shut, Nick shoved Helen toward the nearest desk. "Call 9-1-1!"

"What happened?" she cried as he sprinted to the door.

"Darlington shot the other guy. Hurry!"

Helen's fingers shook as she struggled to punch out the simple numbers. When she was assured that an ambulance was on the way, she dashed downstairs to help Nick.

He'd dragged a first aid kit off the wall and had already donned latex gloves. One hand was pressed against a splotch of red on the man's shirt, while Nick's other hand searched for a gauze pad.

"Get me some bandages," he ordered as she knelt down beside him.

She did as he said. "He's still alive?"

"Just barely. Call 9-1-1?" He worked quickly to wrap the bandages around the man's chest.

"Yes." She slipped her fingers over the prone man's throat and found a thready pulse.

Then lost it.

"No pulse." She repositioned, but still couldn't find it.

Nick paused, but she shook her head frantically. ''I can't get a pulse!''

''Okay. Calm down. Do you know CPR?''

She nodded, immediately shifting to face the man's head and opening his airway.

Please Lord, don't let him die. Not another murder, please.

Not since her father had she been this close to a dying man. She blinked rapidly, all the while trying to quell the fear rising in her.

''Give him mouth to mouth, Helen. You can do it. Watch my rhythm. Every five compressions. Ready?''

She gave him another shaky nod.

''Now.'' She gave two hard blows. Immediately, Nick began chest compressions. She watched the bandages on his stomach stain more and more with bright red blood.

They worked together for what seemed like an age. Her back ached and her knees were on fire by the time they heard the wail of a siren.

''Go open the doors for them,'' Nick ordered.

She leapt up, adrenaline pumping through her tingling legs as she raced for the main loading dock door. She hit the overhead door button and then rushed over to the smaller door beside it. Already, the ambulance was backing into the warehouse.

''Here!'' she cried out, leading the EMT men toward Nick and Mills.

Nick gave a quick rundown of what happened and what he and Helen had done.

One of the men did an equally quick body survey and looked up. ''Good work. We have a pulse.''

She sagged against Nick, who caught her and wrapped a strong arm around her waist. She didn't care that he was covered in blood and had smeared her. Another screaming siren approached and she turned to see who it was.

''The police,'' she said, her voice low enough for only Nick to hear.

He let her go, forcing her to stand on her own wobbly legs. ''Now the you-know-what hits the fan.''

By the time they returned to Nick's house, every muscle in Helen's body ached, her eyes felt gritty and she wanted nothing but sleep. She'd even ignore the growl in her stomach for the promise of a good night's rest.

Ahead of her, Nick opened his front door and waited stoically as she dragged herself inside. It was dark and cold, the sun long since set. The last she'd heard of Ron Mills's condition was that he'd gone into surgery and that his wife had been called. The police and Mr. Parker both questioned her. She knew the outcome of one of the conversations, even though Mr. Parker didn't say it directly. She'd stolen the warehouse key and then broken into both the warehouse and its office. She certainly wasn't up for a promotion after this.

And police had been just as critical, asking her with incredulity about her reasons for breaking the law.

What Nick had said to the Saint John police, she didn't know.

He pushed her gently toward the couch. ''You're dead on your feet. Go lay down.''

She fell onto the soft cushions. ''I'm not usually this bad,'' she muttered as her eyes closed.

The next instant, Nick touched her. Like when they first met, she jerked awake, her heart starting to pound. ''What?''

''I've got something to eat. After, if you like, you can take a bath and hit the sack.''

She looked around, rubbing her eyes and yawning widely. The small clock on the wall told her she'd been asleep for over an hour. The living room was warm, thanks to a bright fire. Through the open curtains of the kitchen window, she spied the full moon rising over the cliff at the edge of the cove.

Her gaze settled on him. He'd showered and changed into fresh clothes.

The enticing aroma of fresh pizza wafted around her, and she swallowed hungrily. ''Any word on Ron Mills?'' she asked.

Nick opened the flat box. ''I called about ten minutes ago. He got through the operation okay, but is still in intensive care, heavily sedated.'' He indicated the food. ''I ordered a pizza for us. The last time I cooked, you tried to knife me.''

''Sorry about that.''

He smiled. ''I even got the delivery guy to pick up some groceries for us.''

She stood, stretching out the painful kinks in her protesting body. ''Smells good, but if you don't mind, I'd like to shower first.''

Their gazes locked. ''Sure.'' The single word rippled through her, its low growling tone possessing none of the succinct crispness she'd learned to associate with Nick. Maybe it was the heat in his eyes, seeing the flames from the stove dancing in his irises. Maybe it was the warmth of the room, the rich, spicy scent of hot pizza, or her own languid, half-asleep state.

Maybe this attraction was getting too hard to control,

even after the terrible circumstances of the day. ''Thanks,'' she murmured, before fleeing to the bathroom.

A few minutes later, they sat down, awkwardly, Helen felt, at the breakfast bar and began to devour the pizza.

Swallowing the last of her third piece, Helen straightened up and dared a glance at Nick. Something wasn't right here, and it had nothing to do with the thick, potent attraction she felt toward Nick.

No. Now that her stomach was full and a nap had restored some of her attention, she knew something was wrong. She studied Nick, finding him silent, but far from relaxed.

Some of the wavy tips of his hair were still damp from his own shower and over the aroma of cheese and tomato and oregano, she caught the citrusy tang of the aftershave he'd splashed on his clean-shaven face.

She swallowed. The urge to haul him into a tight embrace almost overpowered her. As if holding him could conquer the unsettled feelings inside of her.

But still something nagged at her. She stood. ''What's on your mind, Nick?''

He took the last piece of pizza and then rolled the empty box into a tight cylinder. ''Everything.'' He walked to the woodstove and threw the cardboard into the firebox. ''I want you to go to your aunt's and lie low. Don't leave the apartment, not even to go to the lounge downstairs.''

She felt her jaw drop. With a shake of her head, she stepped toward him. ''What? I can't do that.'' She stumbled over her words for a few seconds. ''I won't risk my mother or Aunt June. Why are you asking me that?''

He didn't meet her shocked stare. ''I don't want you following me around in the investigation anymore. It's dangerous enough for me, let alone a civilian. Frankly, I don't want to waste my time protecting you."

She bristled. "You don't have to protect me."

"I do. You know that."

"I don't need protection."

He whirled around. "You know you do! That's what you look for in a man, isn't it? What you got from your father all your life. Even what you looked for in Cooms, too."

His words stung, as if he'd slapped her face. It took a moment to recover. "You're wrong. It's not what I looked for in Jamie or Scott!"

"Scott? Who the hell is Scott?"

She stiffened. "No one. Just someone…an old boyfriend."

"I though you didn't have boyfriends?"

"I don't." Mercy, she should never have blurted out his name.

Nick's stare riveted to her, drilling in hard. "Who is Scott? What does he have to do with Cooms?"

"Nothing." She realized then that she had to tell him everything. "He doesn't have any part in your investigation." She sighed. "Look, after my father died, I got involved with this guy I'd met at the hospital. It turned out he was a con artist who preyed on women. But before I learned that, he emptied my bank account and my overdraft protection."

A rather peculiar light dawned on Nick's face, but she ignored it, feeling a bit shocked that the whole conversation wasn't as hard to bear as she first anticipated. "How much did he steal?" Nick asked.

"He stole almost ten thousand dollars. I'm still paying the bank back the overdraft protection amount. In fact, if

I'd been working now, I'd be making the final payment. I've been so looking forward to getting them off my back, too."

"Did Mark mention that when he interviewed you?"

"Yes. He knew all about the details. I guess he didn't tell you."

"Not all of it." Understanding brightened his face. "That's why you moved out of your mother's house, wasn't it? They'd begun to harass her, too."

She nodded. "Years before, when I first opened that account, we made it a joint account. So legally, she was responsible, too. And that bank knew she had insurance money, and that she'd pay it all back for me, too, but I stopped her. Don't let anyone tell you bank executives only want to help you." That last sentence dripped with derision.

"When we moved out of military housing, I moved into my own place and made arrangements to pay the money back. I made sure that they didn't know where she'd moved to. I didn't want to leave my mother alone, but I had to. My credit was ruined for seven years. I didn't want my mother's to be, too. She had her house to buy. She needed a new car, too."

"Why did you get involved with this guy?" His face slackened. "You were looking for comfort." His words, though, had no tone and she shut her eyes.

"Make up any excuse you want, but that's why I told Jamie I didn't want to get involved. I'd already learned from my mistakes. Jamie, however, knew all the right things to say."

She noticed Nick's jaw clench as he crossed his arms. He looked like he was trying to hold something inside of him. Something fighting to be released. ''See? You're still looking for someone to protect you.''

Hadn't he been listening to her? ''I can protect myself. I've learned that much.''

He made a short, disbelieving noise. ''Listen, sweetheart, don't mistake a bit of spunk for the ability to keep yourself safe.''

Anger roiled inside of her. She stalked across the few feet that separated them and grabbed his arm. ''I'm not mistaken about anything. Besides, Nick Thorndike, you couldn't protect me, because you're too busy pushing away those who give a damn just so they won't hurt you. You're too busy being an island and not getting involved with anyone.''

''Too late for that,'' he muttered. ''I'm already involved and I want to nip it in the bud.''

She held his gaze, determined to show him her courage, determined to show him how foolish he was acting. ''Nip it in the bud? Whatever we have between us, Nick, blossomed that night you tried to make love to me!''

''I came to my senses, didn't I?'' He turned away. ''And it didn't 'blossom' as you so delicately put it. If it had, believe me, we wouldn't be standing here arguing about it. We'd be upstairs keeping it well and truly alive.''

Helen moved closer, trying to recapture his attention, coming close enough to smell again the zest of his aftershave. ''You're already involved. You said that. You were when you took the undercover assignment and played up to Jamie. Long before you met me. And now we're involved with each other. You proved that on your couch over there.''

He grabbed her, but instead of hauling her into a tight embrace, he kept her at arm's length. ''That's what I'm trying to remedy here! I got involved with you and it was a big mistake. I did it only because I'd just been suspended and wasn't thinking straight.'' His voice rose. ''Now, will you listen? I can't do this job if I'm worrying about you all the time. Someone wants you dead. They've killed Cooms! Don't think for a minute it's just Darlington. He's working for someone, not plotting all of this himself. It's someone else. And I don't want to protect you, damn it!''

He stared hard at her and then, muttering some kind of curse, he clamped his lips down on hers, smothering her answer.

She slumped into him. He felt heavenly. His arms held her close and she wanted nothing more than to mold her body to his long, hard frame.

Was he right? Was she only looking for a white knight to protect her?

With a groan, Nick wrenched his mouth away from hers. ''I don't want to argue anymore.'' He scooped her up, causing her to gasp. She knew she was tiny, but no man had ever carried her anywhere.

Wrapping her arms tightly around him, she peered over his shoulder as he carried her upstairs. He lay her on his bed, the same bed in which she'd slept so lightly last night. The same bed she'd made up this morning.

The room was cool and lit only by the light from downstairs. Nick flipped on a small reading lamp at the far side, near a narrow window. He returned to the bed and drew her into his arms the second he sat down.

''See what you do to me? I'm trying to save your life, keep you safe for the real white knight. The one you deserve. But I can't. I'm not as strong as I figured I was.'' He swore softly, the brush of it barely reaching her face. ''When it comes to you, Helen, I'm not the white knight you should have. I'm a suspended cop who'll break the rules whenever he feels like it. That includes relationships. Because in my experience, they aren't worth the rules."

He leaned closer to her and in the gentle light of the tiny lamp, his face showed his anguish. "You said you don't do relationships, but you do. You're careful with your love and I don't want you to waste it on me."

She opened her mouth to speak, not even sure what she was going to say, but Nick stopped her words with a deep, firm kiss.

She pulled back. "Nick, we're two of a kind, more than you think. And if you don't want to admit that, or this attraction, that's okay."

His mouth trailed over her jaw, down to the soft underparts and into the tender hollow of her throat. She felt as well as heard his answer. "I admitted this attraction when I tried to make love to you on my couch. I've been keeping it at bay ever since."

She wanted to cry out to him, to beg him to never push it away again. His lips seared her skin, stealing her breath and forcing her body to arch instinctively toward him. His lips stopped at the neckline of her T-shirt. "Please..."

She had no idea why she said that word. It rolled from her lips with a sigh that told him more than anything else could. She had no doubt of that. And the T-shirt she'd pulled on after the shower felt constricting. She wanted to tear it off.

Nick's fingers freed the shirt hem and slipped under to brush against her skin. She had no bra on and the anticipation of his hands discovering that fact for themselves made her draw in and hold a deep, expectant breath.

Someone groaned when the tips of Nick's fingers bumped gently into the rounded bottom of her breast. Her, him, both? She wasn't sure who had made the noise. Nick lifted his mouth from the base of her throat and recaptured her lips.

There was no sense to this lovemaking. Someone wanted her dead, her family was in danger and the only man who could help her had just told her he wasn't the white knight she needed.

But still, as Nick's warm hand covered her breast and another hot sigh escaped from her slack mouth, Helen knew only one thing.

She didn't care. Not one bit.

Chapter 11

Nick couldn't believe how wrong it was to bring her up here. But like the night he had laid her down on his couch, after he'd been suspended, he wanted to shove the world away.

And experience Helen. Yeah, that was the word to use. Experience her. Her breasts felt heavy, smooth and warm under his hand, the nipple he'd just teased with his thumb puckered into a firm nub of desire. She'd just sighed against his cheek and the heat went straight to his groin. Tonight he would finish what he'd started on the couch, the night he'd found her. There were no impediments of mental instability, unless he counted the way she made him feel right now.

He could even forget how much danger they were in. Danger like someone wanting her dead, and by his association to her, wanting him dead, too.

Danger like falling for this tiny damsel in distress who

needed someone a heck of a lot less tainted by the harsh realities of life.

Someone who could give her a decent life.

Someone who knew how to trust.

Nick shoved the discouraging thoughts out of his head and slammed his mouth against hers. No more thinking.

Helen wrapped her slim arms around his neck, stroking the spot at the back where his hair swirled into a defiant ducktail. Then her fingers traced disorienting lines of heat across the skin of his neck, lingering a few teasing minutes at the scar on his shoulder. She brushed the short, jagged line briefly, sending heat surging through the cotton. He wanted to rip off his shirt and let her work that intoxicating magic on his back.

And he wanted to taste her, too. All of her.

He leaned her back against the pillows, but remained upright, targeting his hands at the hem of her soft T-shirt.

Helen shut her eyes. Her soft, pouty mouth parted as he lifted the shirt only until the bottom arcs of her breasts appeared.

He stopped, allowing his eyes to feast on the hint of the banquet underneath. He allowed his fingers to graze in and under and against the brushed silk feel of her skin.

Perfect.

In texture and sight.

Never in his life had he felt such wonder at a woman's body. In the past, now distant, he'd simply marveled at his bodily reaction, but now, Helen conjured up needs of total consummation, total desire to please her fully.

He shoved the hem up farther, letting the edge flick over her taut nipples. Helen lifted her arms and with his help, removed the shirt. He flung it behind him.

With willpower he hadn't thought he possessed, he resisted the urge to bury his face in her small cleavage.

Instead, he teased each wanting nub, filling his palms with her and letting Helen satisfy only a small, rationed portion of his need.

Sweat beaded on his forehead. Holy cow, how'd this room get so hot? He ached and his erection swelled hard against his jeans, making him throb with excruciating pleasure.

From the corner of his eye, he caught a glimpse of her soft smile. Those lips smoothed and widened, parting as she let out a tender laugh. ''Help yourself, Nick.''

He could hardly believe his ears. With a swipe of his arm across his forehead, he steeled himself. How was it possible for a half-scared woman like Helen to turn into such a wanton creature?

She lifted her hands and captured his head, guiding him down to her bosom. Automatically, he opened his mouth and filled it with one of her hardened nipples.

He suckled deeply, eliciting a deep, throaty moan from her, feeling her lithe body flex and gyrate under him.

He had to get out of his jeans. Now.

Tearing himself away from her, he stood. His member sprang free as he pushed the denim down over his hips.

Helen murmured softly. He didn't catch the word, but he recognized the appreciative tone.

He ripped off his shirt and took the moment to gaze at the woman on his bed. She still wore her own jeans. Good thing, for he'd have driven himself home, hard and fast, if she'd been laying there naked and waiting for him.

''Take off my pants,'' she whispered.

Leaning forward, he flicked the top button free. The scent of his soap on her warm, clean skin reached him, snaring his attention even more than he'd thought possible. His hands shaking, he pulled down the zipper. The low, raspy sound grated over him like the slow click of a weapon being cocked.

He threw off the thought of work, of killing and protection and all that led to this very moment. Nothing was going to ruin his time in bed with her.

Needing to still his nerves, he paused. His heart pounded in his ears and he clenched his hands into hard fists in an attempt to control the urges building in him.

Damn it, he didn't have the control. With a hard yank, he peeled her jeans down her legs until his sheer impatience caused them to break free of her ankles.

A thin pair of bikini panties was all that stood between him and paradise.

His hands shook worse than before.

Helen reached out and covered his fingers with her own. "Here." She guided her panties over her rounded hips, down those legs that seemed too long for such a petite woman, and flicked them over her feet.

Then she yanked him down to her.

Nick could smell her need. That musky, womanly scent he'd first inhaled on his couch. The memory still bombarded him. The merest hint of it swept it all back in waves of uncontrollable pleasure.

He bent down and kissed her soft, flat belly. Purposely moving upward, he found each nipple still tight and waiting, and replenished his need for them.

Abruptly, she wrapped her legs around him.

"Now, Nick! Please!"

She couldn't wait. He would have only been able to linger as long as she could, but it was impossible now. He shifted, the blunt end of his member bumping against her moist center.

Helen flexed her hips and like a powerful magnet, drew him into her. They rocked, each caught up in their own need, each giving over control of their senses to the other until they found their rhythm.

His controlled rhythm.

His arms ached. He wanted this to last, to give her slow, delicious pleasure, but Helen had different ideas. And he couldn't argue.

To hell with it. No more control, no more giving the physical pleasure without trying not to give himself.

He let out a cry and dizzily, he thrust again and again, gliding on liquid silk. And with every internal clench, she owned him a little more.

When she cried out herself, he opened his eyes. Her head was thrown back, her mouth relaxed into that soft pout which had become his undoing.

Then he climaxed.

A sliver of early morning light cut through the dark bedroom when Nick opened his eyes. Automatically, he turned to his right to find Helen curled beside him, still fast asleep.

Last night had been…well, mystical. But this morning, the rising sun brought back the truth with keen intensity. Someone wanted her dead. That person still felt Helen knew something she shouldn't know.

And he was still suspended.

He slipped away from Helen, glancing at the alarm clock as he rose. After eight. He'd slept in. Normally, he'd have been up for hours, even on his days off. As quietly as he could, he walked downstairs and straight for the phone.

He called the station.

"Hello, Sandra," he said to the woman who answered. Sandra was the clerk who came in several times a week.

She was a pleasant woman who seemed genuinely upset that Nick had been suspended.

"Nick! I've been thinking of you. How's things?"

"Okay." He paused, wondering if he should even be doing this. Then he took the cordless phone and walked into the kitchen to make coffee while he talked.

"Look, Sandra, would you do me a favor?"

"Sure."

"Is anyone in?"

There was a pause and he held his breath. Finally, the clerk spoke. "No. The chief just stepped out and Mark worked last night in the city. I know that because he was just coming in when I was leaving last night. We're a bit behind, so I'm working all week. The others did the night shift. What do you need?"

"Can you dig out Tony DiPetri's autopsy report?"

There was another pause. Nick busied himself shoveling scoops of ground coffee into the filter basket, just to keep his hands from shaking. Why the hell was he doing this?

Because he needed to know whether or not his beating on DiPetri had contributed to the man's death. What he was going to do with that information, he wasn't sure.

A noise caught his attention and he glanced out to the main room of his house, where he could see the last few steps of the stairs. Nothing but the wind. Helen was still asleep.

"Nick?"

He snapped his attention back to Sandra. "Yeah?"

"I have the file, but it's empty."

"Empty?"

"Yes." Sandra shuffled some papers around. "That's odd. It was here yesterday when I filed it. Let me check around for it."

Long, agonizing minutes ticked by. Finally, she returned. "I'm sorry. I can't find it anywhere."

"Can you call Saint John and see if they'll send you another copy of it?"

Sandra's voice sounded disturbed. "Yes, I think I will. In fact, I'll get them to fax it to me right away. I'll call you back." She hung up.

Nick put the phone down and turned on the coffeemaker. Why would that autopsy report be missing? Had Mark taken it to Saint John with him? If so, why? They would have a copy of it as well. There would be no need.

A creak on the stairs caught his attention. Seconds later, Helen appeared in the doorway. She wore the same clothes he'd peeled off her last night. Her hair was still mussed by sleep and a relaxed and dreamy expression lingered on her face.

"Mmm. Coffee smells good," she murmured. "Did the phone ring? I must have slept like a log not to hear it."

Nick stiffened. He thought about taking her back upstairs while the coffee brewed. He thought about the ways he could get her mind off his phone call. He didn't want her to know he was looking for some way to prove himself to her.

Oh, hell, that admission hurt. "I called the station." He drew in a deep breath. "So, why don't we look at that last tape while the coffee's brewing?"

Helen nodded, wondering why Nick changed the subject so quickly. She'd caught the words "autopsy" and "copy" while she'd been walking down the stairs. Was he looking for a copy of Jamie's autopsy? Would it help find whoever was trying to kill her?

She pivoted on the cool pine floor. She should trust Nick

to do his job, even the job from which he'd been suspended. She should let him keep them both safe.

No. She wasn't looking for that in a man.

Walking over to the video machine, she grabbed the tape and shoved it in. Behind her, Nick picked up the remote control and turned on the TV.

The tape started with January, as all the others had. Her parents had been particular about chronicling her life. This one began with a sleepy thirteen-year-old girl celebrating New Year's Eve with half an ounce of champagne in 7UP. Helen sank down on the couch, letting her mind drift back to last night. Nick had told her he wasn't her white knight, and as if to prove it, he'd taken her upstairs and made love to her.

But he'd hesitated as he'd leaned over her naked body. She'd forced him to finish what they'd started.

Then this morning, he was the knight back on his horse riding off to search out the dragon.

She let her head fall back to the soft cushion behind her neck. Across the room, Nick sat on the edge of another less comfortable chair, his whole attention focused on her at her most awkward. His hair fell into his eyes and he brushed it away as if it were a trivial annoyance.

Good heavens, did she really want a white knight? If so, she was looking in all the wrong places. Scott wasn't anywhere near one. Jamie had been kind to her, gentle even, sometimes, until she witnessed the other horrible side of him. Had she really wanted him to be her white knight?

No. She wasn't looking for a gallant savior. That would mean she wanted commitment.

Nick leaned forward, frowning at the TV. He was no white knight, either. No man who could fool Jamie could be a chivalrous Prince Valiant. Nick was a cop who'd been suspended.

She cut off her own thoughts. Why was he suspended? All he'd told her was that he broke some minor rules. Not filled in some forms or something.

"Nick?"

He turned his attention to her. "Yeah?"

"Why were you suspended? What exactly did you do? What forms didn't you fill out?"

He narrowed his eyes. "Did I say that?"

"Yes, I'm surprised you don't remember."

He glanced back to the TV. Helen could see out the corner of her eye that she was now celebrating a birthday, laughing with her school friends, blowing out fourteen flickering candles on the cake her mother had made.

She turned back to him. "Did you lie to me, Nick? It's okay. I understand. It's just that you say you're no white knight, but here you are, even before breakfast, right after we made love, searching for answers."

She heard Nick's heavy sigh. He stood up and walked into the kitchen. She listened to him as he poured out two mugs of coffee. When he returned, he handed her one.

"It wasn't a lie. Just not the complete truth."

She frowned at him as she accepted the steaming mug. He sat down on the couch beside her and while he was carefully placing his own mug on the coffee table in front of them, he glanced up at the video.

Piano recital. Helen knew it followed her birthday. It had followed her birthday for the last ten years' worth of videos. Playing softly from the TV were the slightly stilted strains of "Für Elise." She'd never managed to play that tune correctly.

Nick turned to her. "I didn't fill out some trivial forms, but that really wasn't what got me suspended." He stopped, as if waiting for the difficult moment to pass. "I laid a beating on Tony DiPetri about an hour before he died. Cooms had told me to do it."

A shiver danced down her spine, despite the heat rising up from the hot coffee. "Jamie and Tony were best friends once. Why did you do it?"

"I was undercover. Sometimes you do things you don't want to do. Sometimes you break the law." He shut his eyes.

"Why did Jamie want you to beat up Tony?"

"He said DiPetri had screwed up and needed to be reminded who was in charge."

"And you believed him?"

Nick opened his eyes and met her stare evenly. "Helen, I didn't believe anything Cooms said unless it had been proven to me. Cooms was testing me. He was pissed off at DiPetri and he knew damn well that he was going to put a bullet in the back of the man's head within an hour. He purposely got me involved. To strengthen my commitment."

The taste of coffee soured in the back of Helen's throat. She put the mug down, trying to focus on the reason she'd brought up this terrible subject. "And your chief found out that you'd broken the law and suspended you?"

Nick shrugged. "Whether I broke the law or not is debatable. But he interpreted it as such."

"Was that the autopsy report you were looking for this morning?" She quirked up her mouth. "I couldn't help but overhear. I'm sorry."

He paused before answering. "Yeah, it was. But it seems to have gone missing."

"Maybe it's gone to Saint John. They are the ones who are handling the undercover operation, after all."

"Maybe. Actually, we had a copy and Saint John had

one, and the coroner has the original. It's odd that ours would go missing."

She nodded. "Maybe the chief has them. After all, one of his own men is involved in the investigation. Surely, he's trying to help you. Or at least is interested."

He held up two fingers. "Two men were involved. Mark was doing some backup work for me. Checking stuff out, acting as liaison."

"Is that normal?"

"For Mark, yeah. He always gets stuck doing that stuff. He knows the regs inside and out. In fact, he was even in charge when the chief took his wife down to the Caribbean for a second honeymoon this summer. Too hot there for me. Anyway, Mark would make a good chief."

He sounded sad. Not bitterly so, but in a frustrated, despondent way. Not that she blamed him. He must feel pretty ineffectual right now. She ached to take him into a warm hug, but opted for a small smile, instead. "Your chief was just protecting your butt, you know, by suspending you."

Nick chuckled. "I wouldn't have used the word 'butt.'"

Helen smiled back, a small, watery smile. "It's as strong as I get, I'm afraid."

"That's okay." He reached out and flicked a short tendril of hair over her ear. Her heart squeezed tightly at his almost pained expression. He wouldn't have used that silly little word. Maybe he was right. He wasn't a white knight. Did that also mean he was wrong for her?

Nick's hand froze by her ear as he swore softly. Helen glanced up into his face, but his attention was focused on the TV.

She turned and faced it.

Gone was her awful piano recital. Taped over it was something she'd never seen before.

Chapter 12

Helen leaned forward, away from Nick's still hand. What was going on? The scene on the video was grainy, shot from high above and showed several people dressed in evening wear.

It stopped. Suddenly, the taped played the young Helen again, finishing the last few painful measures of ''Für Elise.''

Nick lunged for the remote control, hit rewind until he found the start of the taped-over section.

''What is it?'' she asked.

''It looks like a video clip from a surveillance camera. Taken at some kind of cocktail party. Do you recognize it?''

''I'm not sure.'' She studied the tape, shaking her head slowly. ''Wait! That's at one of Jamie's restaurants. In the back room, I think.''

''You're right. At the party I went to.'' Nick stared at

her, his handsome, even features tightened into a harsh frown.

Helen turned back to the TV. "No. Pause the tape." Nick did as she asked. "See, at the top corner? That's me!"

"So. You were there that night. I saw you."

She glanced at him. Another time, that revelation might have frightened her. But not now. Now she felt…a rush. Even the attraction that had terrified her once didn't seem to compare to the thought of him watching her. Her face heated up.

He looked away, at anything but her. "I only caught a glimpse of you. All I saw was long hair."

She touched her short mop in understanding. "No. It wasn't that night. I'm wearing the wrong dress. The night you saw me I had on my newest dress. The only formal thing I own. The night this was taped I was wearing a black dress I've had for years."

"When was this taken?"

Helen peered at the TV. "Shouldn't surveillance tapes show the time and date?"

"Normally, they do. I'm guessing this one is a private tape. Do you remember the date?"

"That dress is very light and I'm not wearing a wrap. It must have been during the early summer when we had that warm spell. I haven't worn it since."

"The date?" he hedged.

The tape ran on and Helen watched herself move back out of the line of the camera. Frustrated, she shook her head. Jamie had dragged her to several different parties. "Early June, I think."

"Do you recognize anyone there?"

"Of course." Helen scratched her head. "Umm, there's Tony. And Clive Darlington by the door. He was Jamie's shadow for a while. And I ran into my boss, Mr. Parker, there, too, that evening. If I remember correctly, he didn't stay long. I don't think I know the others' names. Just their faces.''

She shivered. There was something creepy about watching herself on a surveillance video. She looked so short compared to all those big, broad men that Jamie called his ''friends.'' There was a feel to the tape like there had been to that last tape of Princess Diana. Jerky, casual, yet tragic.

The piano recital abruptly returned. ''It was obviously Jamie who did this. But why would he tape this short section over the middle of my piano recital? Besides the obvious fact I was massacring one of Beethoven's finest pieces.''

Nick chuckled. ''I thought it was pretty good. But then again, I can't carry a tune in a bucket.'' He sobered. ''We can't assume Cooms taped it.''

''Why not? He was the only one who insisted on watching my tapes. And there couldn't be too many people who knew about the camera, either. Jamie could be quite secretive when he wanted to be. And it *is* his restaurant.''

Nick replayed the tape several more times, pausing it and peering at it at different points. After it ran through for the fourth time, he shut off the machine and headed for the phone.

''Who are you calling?''

''Mark.''

''Why? Did you see something I missed?''

Nick hit several buttons on his cordless phone before answering. He listened carefully to the quiet, insistent ringing. No answer. Mark should be in bed right now, after pulling the graveyard shift. He was a light sleeper and always answered the phone. Had something happened?

Had Ron Mills taken a turn for the worse while in intensive care? Or had he regained consciousness and was right now talking to the police?

He never felt so impotent in his life.

Furious, he slammed down the phone.

"At least this answers the question of why Jamie gave me the VCR."

He turned. She was beside him, a thoughtful expression marring her gentle features. Those pouty lips were pursed now, smooth and thinner, but no less kissable.

He shook away such distracting thoughts. "What do you mean?"

"Jamie gave me the VCR as an excuse to watch those tapes, which in itself was an excuse to find some boring section on one of them to hide that segment he'd videoed. He probably figured I wouldn't miss it."

He found it hard to keep with her train of thought. "Go on."

"Well, we both knew Jamie. He always considered himself smarter than everyone else. I wouldn't be surprised if he considered hiding the taped section in plain sight to be absolutely brilliant on his part. That segment of tape was important enough for him to steal the tape, probably after I fell asleep, record over it and return it."

"He didn't return it. He hid it in your mother's house."

"Don't you see? He must have felt it was too dangerous to leave it at my place. Maybe someone would have gone searching for it there. I hate the thought that he broke into my mother's house to hide it there, but he must have considered it necessary. I mean, I told several people he gave me a new VCR."

"A cheap knockoff."

Helen shrugged. "It worked."

"He gave you the VCR because it was of no use to him

anymore. He'd smuggled cocaine in it.'' Nick watched her swallow, regretting that he had to expose her to the truth.

''I guess,'' she said. ''But Jamie often killed two birds with one stone. And he liked to think himself quite intelligent and a step ahead of everyone else.''

''Which leads us back to why he bothered to keep this section of surveillance tape. These people, I bet, will all be ID'ed as known persons in the drug trade. And I'm not talking about the druggie on the street. But nobody's doing anything illegal here. Hardly blackmail stuff.''

He shook his head. Something wasn't adding up. Each and every hair on his arms was at full attention. Even the fine ones at the back of his neck stood up rigidly. Something was on that tape and he couldn't see it. The angle of the camera made ID'ing some of those people difficult, especially those who stood almost directly underneath it.

He looked down at the phone in his hand, feeling his stomach protest the delay in breakfast. And Mark wasn't around, either. Nick could use an extra pair of eyes here.

There was the autopsy report, too. He could call Sandra again to ask her if she'd received it yet, but he didn't want to put her in the position where she would risk her job, in case the chief was there.

Mark was his logical choice, but where was he?

Nick placed the phone on its cradle and walked into the kitchen. ''Let's scramble up some eggs. I'm tired of thinking on an empty stomach.''

''And then what?''

Nick threw open the refrigerator door. He didn't know what was next. But the tape needed to be taken into Saint John. Except something didn't feel right about that decision. Going into this investigation, Nick had known that the possibility existed of there being a crooked politician involved, or worse, a cop on the take. Was that why he hesitated?

But someone in Saint John should be able to recognize a few more people on that tape. "We go into the city," he finally said.

Helen didn't answer. He grabbed the carton of eggs and looked up at her. "Don't worry, I'm not dropping you off at your aunt's place. But I can't leave you here, either. We're going to take the tape into the station. Someone more familiar with the city's elite might be able to recognize a few people."

Helen relaxed. "Thank you. Maybe we could stop by the hospital to see how Ron Mills is."

"We'll call from the police station. I'm a bit reluctant to let you roam the streets. Remember, there's a hit-and-run suspect out there."

Helen took the eggs he was lifting out of the carton and began to break them into a bowl. "Do you think it was Clive?"

"I don't know. We'll see if the police have been in touch with his parole officer. Maybe he knows where Clive has been."

The sun chose that moment to break through the thinning layer of rising fog, lighting the kitchen as it did. Yeah, Nick decided. Darlington's parole officer may be able to help and surely one of the veteran cops could put names to some of those unfamiliar faces.

And Ron Mills must still be alive, or else Mark would have called.

But above all, Nick would find a copy of DiPetri's autopsy report.

The sun hit his face as he moved to dump his cold

coffee into the sink. Out of all those things he needed to do, the report seemed the most important, but he wasn't going to analyze why.

After parking in Saint John, he and Helen strode into the police station. Behind the reception desk, Nick spotted one of the officers who had responded to the shooting at the warehouse. ''Hey, Paul, how's things?''

Paul's face broke out into a wide grin and he walked out into the foyer. ''Hi, there, Nick. You look good. Get lucky last night? You sure look like you—''

The man's face fell when he spotted Helen and the rush of crimson surging up from her neck into her face. ''Jeez, sorry, miss,'' he stuttered out.

Nick tightened his jaw. He shouldn't have brought her here. He quickly steered her away from the embarrassed Paul. ''Sorry about that,'' he whispered into Helen's softly scented hair. ''Paul's mouth is…well, it's a guy thing, I guess.''

She nodded. ''It's okay. I wasn't expecting it, that's all.'' She still looked mortified.

Nick ran his hand through his hair. Had he really been thinking that Helen could fit into his life? The first time they meet a colleague and she looks like she wants to curl up and die. She wasn't cut out for this lifestyle. He grabbed her arm, hoping the contact with her skin would dismiss the sudden thought from his brain.

''Here,'' he said, taking her into a room filled with desks and various people. She looked around like a fawn on a busy highway, he noted. Damn, he didn't have the time to initiate her into his world.

What the hell had he been thinking of, making love to her last night, getting involved with her?

Falling for her.

The truth slammed into him, and he didn't even feel the bustle of another cop as the man steered a handcuffed youth past them.

He was falling for Helen?

How could that have happened?

''Sorry, Nick,'' the officer who gripped the youth's elbow called over his shoulder. ''Hey, who's minding your station? Seems all you guys are here.''

Snapping out of his own shock, he stared at the man. ''What?''

''Who's holding down the fort in Lower Cove? That cute clerk? You guys are overpaid if you can leave the station in her hands.'' Chuckling, the officer shoved his suspect out of the room.

Helen touched his arm. ''What's he talking about?''

Nick refused to look at her. ''Never mind him.''

''But he said all of Lower Cove's officers were here.''

''Look, Helen, he was being sarcastic. They're all jealous because we have better jobs than they do.'' He guided her to a vacant seat. ''Sit down here. I've got to find someone.''

He had to get away from her. He had to stop thinking of her as his lover, the woman he suddenly cared for more than he cared for himself. The very thought had rattled him. His chest felt tight still and the sudden need for fresh air made him glance wildly about.

He found Jones, a fellow undercover officer, in a back room. They'd done much of the preliminary set up work for the Cooms case together and Nick gave him a quick rundown of the tape. The guy had loads of computer smarts so Nick asked him to make some decent stills from the segment. To see if he could ID some of the people.

Warning him it might take a day or two, Jones took the tape.

After nodding, Nick asked about Ron Mills. Jones told him Mills was still in the ICU, still not talking to anyone.

Nick returned to the busy room, pausing at the doorway for a moment to stare at Helen. She peered around the office like a caged rabbit.

Again, the single thought hit him hard. What the hell was he doing falling for her, anyway? It didn't make an ounce of sense and certainly wouldn't work out. He'd only end up hurting her.

He strode up. "Let's get a coffee somewhere." He knew his tone was gruff and he didn't care that his grip on her arm was too tight. He was all wrong for her and maybe she'd realize all on her own that he wasn't Mr. Perfect.

Fifteen minutes later, they were seated in a small coffee shop in the upper concourse of a nearby indoor mall. He ordered coffee, bluntly told Helen where her tape was and sat to gulp down the scalding black liquid.

Helen dropped into the seat across from him. "So you suspect that someone on that tape is trying to kill me?"

Nick glanced around. Did she have to broadcast it? He slammed down his coffee. "Look, I just want to know who was there that night," he growled. "It may not give us an answer to who's after you."

Helen shot him a skeptical look. "And I'm the queen of England. You know someone is trying to kill me. You know Jamie taped a short surveillance segment over one of my tapes. You know my place and my mother's have been searched, but nothing taken. It's obvious that whoever was videoed is looking for evidence that could be used to blackmail them."

All right, so she was smart. "Speculation. You may know that, but *we* have to prove it. Leave the police work to the experts, okay? You don't even remember who was there at the party.''

Helen's features chilled. He didn't want her mad at him, but he didn't want her to feel the same way he felt. It would be futile. She wanted something in a man that he couldn't give. A little pain now, but the end result would be for the better.

''It wasn't as if I didn't remember all of those people.'' She glared at him. ''I didn't know them. Period. There must have been fifty people there and I had only met a handful of them. Besides, if we go by your suppositions, then we must assume those people are innocent. They were just partying, after all.'' Her tone turned sarcastic. ''Of course there weren't any drugs at the party. I didn't see any.''

Nick drained his coffee. ''All right. Those people knew full well why they were there and where the money for that party came from.''

''But I didn't.''

''Which only proves you should leave the police work to the experts.'' He stood. ''I shouldn't have brought you here. It's too dangerous. I'm taking you home.''

And he was going to lock her up in his bedroom and throw away the key. She was an innocent mixed up in a dangerous business. Like the night they met when he felt the urge to bury himself into her and forget the world, he knew he wasn't doing either of them any favors. He didn't want a relationship. And hadn't she said the same thing? Different reasons, but both valid.

Helen gaped at Nick's stiff-backed form as he stalked across the glassed-in catwalk that would lead them back to where they were parked.

She would not cry. She refused to. They were getting

so close to the answers. Soon they would find Clive and discover who was trying to kill her. She couldn't give up now and allow Nick to hide her away.

She stormed up to him, overtaking him with a surge of defiance. ''Take me back to the police station,'' she snapped as she passed him.

He grabbed her arm. ''What for?''

They were halfway across the glass catwalk. Below them was one of the busiest streets in the city center, the roar of traffic muffled by the glass and the sounds of the mall they'd just left. ''I'm going to take back my tape,'' she said. ''You may think I should just sit by and let the police do my work, but that's not what's going to happen. I don't trust the police.''

''You should.''

Helen pulled him to one side to allow a young mother with a stroller to walk by. ''Look, Jamie had told me he had some politicians in his back pocket. And he hinted about some dirty cops, too.''

''That was me, Helen. It was part of my cover.''

''I thought so at first, too. But then I thought, just one? That's not Jamie's style. And I don't believe he was always talking about you. Someone thinks I know all about Jamie's business and can ID them. Someone important. I'm going to find out who.''

''Don't be so foolish.'' Nick directed her off the catwalk and toward the stairs that would take them to his truck.

''I'm not being foolish. I'm doing what Jamie would do. Killing two birds with one stone.''

''And how do you figure that?''

''I'm proving to you I'm not looking for a white knight. Because no one like that exists. And I'm going to find and stop whoever is trying to kill me. If not for my sake, for my mother's. She can't even go home.''

Helen felt the last word tighten in her throat. The word stirred up warm memories that were hidden in boring filmed moments like her piano recital. All she wanted was to go home and be safe herself.

Like the way she'd felt last night.

Refusing to acknowledge that thought, she strode past the parking attendant of the garage where they'd parked. She could hear Nick swear as he followed her.

Outside, she found the sun had slipped behind a layer of mackerel clouds. The fair weather would soon end. She spoke without turning around. "Did you find out who Clive Darlington's parole officer is? Maybe he knows where Clive was the night before last."

Nick stopped her. "I was hoping Mark could tell me who he is, but he didn't answer his phone."

"Of course not. He was at the police station this morning. All of Lower Cove's officers were, remember?" She couldn't stop the tiny bit of sarcasm.

Nick frowned at her. She didn't like the shadow of suspicion that drifted across his features. The wind flipped a lock of hair into his hooded eyes. Above the sounds of the busy city she heard him slur out an expletive. "Where was he?"

"After you left me, he walked past the office, heading downstairs."

"Are you sure?"

"Of course I'm sure. I know the man. He was in uniform, too."

Nick pursed his lips, grabbed her elbow and directed her into the garage again.

She pulled back. "Where are taking me?"

"Back to the police station."

"We should walk. It's not far."

"No. It's not safe for you to be out walking the streets."

Nick didn't bother with any more explanations. As soon as they reached the police station, he took her elbow again and practically dragged her down to where he'd left the tape. She saw another officer viewing it on one of those huge monitors that surely was part of a state-of-the-art computer system. He glanced over his shoulder when Nick and Helen entered.

"Hey, I'm not done yet."

"Sorry," Nick answered. "We had to come back here anyway, so I thought I would check on it. Do you know who Clive Darlington's parole officer is?"

Still studying the tape in slow motion, the officer rattled off a name. Nick turned to Helen and indicated that she could sit on one of the vacant chairs. Then he grabbed the police phone book.

Five minutes later, he hung up the phone. "What did he say?" Helen asked, her voice tight.

The other officer, Jones laughed. "Said Nick should stop investigating while he's suspended." He grinned at Nick. "Everyone around here knows what you're doing."

Nick glared at him before turning to her. "He was 'counseling' and I say that lightly, Darlington, at a coffee shop at the time of the hit-and-run. One of the terms of Darlington's probation was to avoid all establishments that serve alcohol. Well, someone called his parole officer from a local bar, saying they saw him in there. The parole officer managed to talk him into going for a coffee, but Darlington figured he was headed for another arrest, so he took off."

Jones twisted around to face Helen. "Are you Helen Eastman?"

She nodded.

"You can pick up your car keys at the front desk. The ones you gave us so the boys could look at your mother's car." He turned back. "Oh yeah, they impounded the vehicle used in the hit-and-run. It's in the compound, waiting for Forensics to go over it."

"Where was it found?"

"Illegally parked downtown."

Nick pulled a face at Helen. "We won't get any fingerprints off it until Forensics is done."

Jones zoomed in on one of the men and began to clean up the image. "But I hear there was an eyewitness. A club owner saw the driver park it around two yesterday morning."

"Let's go," Nick told Helen. "We'll see if the description matches what I saw." He turned to the other man. "Thanks, Jones."

"No problem. Now leave me alone so I can finish this for you. Neither of us needs to be caught doing this before you turn the tape in as evidence."

That was a big, easy hint and Jones was right. Neither of them needed to be caught with any evidence. His suspension would turn permanent pretty quickly, then. He nodded and headed back upstairs.

"Nick?"

He grunted.

"You came back here because I said Mark was here. Why aren't you trying to find him?"

She was too smart. "Never mind. We've got other things to do."

It didn't take Nick long to obtain a description of the driver. It fit the man he'd seen. Tall, heavyset, and unfortunately, built like most of the men on the tape.

Frustration welled in him and he told Helen where she could find her keys. While she was gone, he headed downstairs to Records.

"You're not the first person today who wanted that autopsy report," the file clerk commented. "Don't you guys in Lower Cove have a filing system?"

"Who else was here?" Nick asked, feeling the hairs on his arms prickle as he leaned on the counter and faced the clerk.

"Sandra somebody called from your office. I faxed it to her. Plus Mark..." He peered at his computer screen. "Mark Rowlands. But he hasn't picked it up yet. You guys have to get organized."

"Yeah, we will. Thanks." Nick grabbed the copy of the autopsy report and scanned it, thankful the clerk didn't seem to know about his suspension yet. Jones hadn't opened his mouth to this guy, he figured.

There it was, right below the detailed description of the bullet that had lodged in DiPetri's skull. The cause of death. Gunshot wound to the head. Death was immediate. While the contusions Nick had inflicted were noted, at least they hadn't contributed to the man's death.

Almost hollowly, he handed the report back. Had he hoped his beating of DiPetri had contributed to the man's death, making that horrible revelation become more proof that he wasn't that perfect man Helen was looking for?

Hell, he didn't know.

He vaguely remembered climbing the stairs to meet up with Helen. As his hand found the polished curl of the rail at the landing, he paused. Oh, yeah, he had wanted to be responsible for that death. It would give him a solid, valid reason to stop this relationship with Helen.

Now he had nothing. Blinking, he climbed wearily up the remaining steps. No, he still had the fact he shouldn't be involved with an ex-girlfriend and victim of a local drug lord.

But that reason didn't seem to matter much anymore.

Not now that he knew he'd fallen hard and fast—yeah, really fast—for Helen Eastman. Not even when he realized that he was losing his edge with this investigation. And if a cop loses his edge, he puts himself at risk. Big time.

Opening the door into the bustling front entrance of the police station, he tried to shut out the reasons against falling for Helen. He should just focus on keeping her safe.

"Did you find the autopsy report?"

He spun around in time to see Helen pocket her keys and fold the copy of the receipt she'd signed. "Yeah."

"What did it say? Did you find out what happened to the other copy?"

"No." He shook his head as he led them out the door. The day was graying fast. Rain was due again. "But I know Mark was here looking for it."

"Maybe your clerk had asked him to pick it up."

"No, she'd asked the file clerk to fax her a copy."

"Maybe he noticed it was missing and was doing the station a favor."

"Maybe."

A voice rang out from behind him. "Nick!"

He turned and looked up the wide stone steps to the front door. Jones trotted down to him. "Here," he said. "I was able to clean up most of the people on the video, but not all of them. Some I recognized and I wrote their names on the back." He handed a large brown envelope to him.

Nick took it. "Thanks, man. I appreciate it." He felt the envelope. "Where's the tape?"

Jones looked contrite. "The chief walked in, saw it and...well...you don't need to turn it in as evidence, okay? I was lucky I had already put the prints in that envelope."

"Thanks."

As Jones walked inside, Helen laid her arm on Nick's. "Let's look at them in the truck."

As soon as they both slammed the truck doors, Nick flipped open the file. A few grainy black-and-white stills fluttered onto Helen's lap. She picked them up, studying them one by one, shaking her head. "Jamie, Clive." She paused. "Here's Mr. Parker. Jamie had wanted to schmooze with him. At the time I thought it was so Mr. Parker would lease more of his buildings, but I guess that wasn't the reason." She picked up more stills. "Some I've seen around, but most of these men I don't know. I just know some faces, or what we can see of them."

"Bad angle for the camera. Not many of these faces are useful."

"Well, if you're going to hide a camera, you've got to take what you can get for vantage points." She held up the last picture. It was of her. "I had no idea I was so short. I look like a midget compared to all these men."

Nick took the stills and folded them all up before shoving them into the inside pocket of his lightweight jacket. "You are short," he said. "Was your dad short?"

Helen nodded. "Yes, but he was always a big man to me. Even when he lay in his casket. He looked small, but I can still remember thinking of him as big."

Nick glanced up at her melancholy expression. "Cooms wasn't a big guy, either." Why was he bringing this up? Because he was a foot taller than her?

Her features darkened. "I told you I only dated Jamie because he promised no strings. I wasn't trying to replace my father. No one could do that."

He should tell her to remember that. He should remind her that she wasn't ever going to find anyone good enough.

But the words wouldn't come out.

"So, where to now?" she asked.

He tugged his jacket closed. "I find Mark Rowlands. I want to know why he's so interested in the autopsy report and why he thinks it went missing."

"Do you know where he is?" Helen asked him as he pulled out of the parking space.

"It's nearly noon and he's been up all night. If he's not here anymore, he's got to be on his way home."

"You're going to keep him up?"

"Yep." Mark wouldn't like it, but frankly, too bad. A lot of things were adding up and some of the answers were pointing back at Mark.

Helen clenched her fingers until they were damp and half-numb. She wasn't sure why she was nervous. Perhaps because she knew Mark Rowlands wasn't going to be too happy to be awakened by a suspicious Nick. There seemed to be enough tension between the two of them.

Nick pulled the truck into a small house just west of Lower Cove. They'd driven though a local fast-food drive-through on the way there and eaten on the run. The scent of French fries still filled the cab. Of course it would, half of Helen's were still cooling in the paper bag.

"It is really okay to call on him?" she asked.

"He'll be mad as hell, but there are some things I need to know."

"Wasn't he on the undercover case with you? Why did I see him in uniform this morning?"

Nick shut off the engine. "He was doing the follow-up work. He wasn't actually undercover, but rather my contact man."

"So you would have to trust him to relay information, wouldn't you?"

He shifted in his seat. "Yeah."

"Do you think he knows something he's not telling?

Do you think he's one of the crooked cops Jamie hinted at?''

''Look, I'm not assuming anything. Can I do this my own way?'' He unlocked his seat belt. ''Now stay here. Quietly.''

Helen shut her mouth. He was having second thoughts about bringing her here, but whether they were because Mark posed some level of danger or because she was asking too many difficult questions, she wasn't sure. She leaned toward him, scrutinizing the doubt on his face. ''Be careful.''

He chuckled. ''I'm always careful.''

Helen watched him ring the doorbell, holding her breath. His back to her, he stood tall and strong, all confidence.

That strong sense of desire—as strong as the day she first saw him—still hit her. Last night, she'd tasted the very essence of the attraction and her desire for this man hadn't diminished a single bit.

Abruptly, Mark opened the door. After a short talk, Nick signaled for her to come in.

''I wasn't asleep yet,'' Mark told her as she crossed the threshold. To Helen, he looked tired and drawn. She offered him a cautious smile before glancing furtively at Nick.

''Can we talk to you about DiPetri's autopsy report?'' Nick asked.

Mark rubbed the back of his neck. ''Nick, I can't discuss the case with you.''

''Can you tell me when you noticed it was missing?''

''You like breaking the rules, don't you? Was that why you were in Saint John today seeing Jones?''

''Mark,'' Helen interrupted gently. ''I know you're tired and we won't stay any longer than necessary. But both of you, try to understand each other's position, okay?" Though the sense of rivalry still lingered between the two men, she noticed it didn't feel as strong, especially from Nick. Why, she'd consider later. "We found the missing tape and noticed a short segment of a surveillance tape recorded on it. We took it into the Saint John police. I also got my car keys back. Now, before you say anything, the tape is at the police station. As evidence." She was counting on her instinct that Mark was innocent, but he didn't need to know that they hadn't originally planned to turn it in right away.

Nick cut in. "We know the autopsy report went missing and we know you asked for a copy of it. Why?"

Mark sat down on the couch and folded his arms. He looked like he wasn't planning to say a thing, until he glanced at Helen. "At work last night, I went over the whole investigation again. That's when I noticed the report was gone. I made a mental note to get another copy. When I gave it to Sandra, she told me she'd already had a copy faxed in."

"Do you have any idea where the first copy went?"

Mark said nothing. Helen knew he was holding something back. Had they uncovered something so important that he felt he needed to keep it from Nick and her?

She sat beside him. "Please, Mark. Regardless of your regulations, I can't just sit back and wait for someone to try to kill me. We know Clive Darlington didn't try to run me over. Do you know who did?"

Mark glanced up at Nick's dark, clenched expression before he looked down at her. Helen reached out and squeezed his arm, feeling the tension in him.

"You should let the police do their job, Helen," he said, "and keep Nick from getting in the way." He stood to face Nick. "I don't know why the report went missing.

DiPetri was shot and the autopsy detailed the beating you laid on him, but that was all. It was pretty straightforward, as far as autopsies go.'' He stopped. ''Mind you, I haven't seen the ballistic report, nor have the toxicology tests come back yet. They may tell us more. But if that's so, why steal such a basic report?''

''Who was at the station yesterday?''

Mark shrugged. ''Everyone. We were in and out all day. Even had a couple of officers from Saint John in.''

''Why?'' Nick asked.

Mark yawned. ''Setting up the new computer system. The chief had done some of the work, but didn't have time to finish it.'' He looked at Helen. ''They have all the experts, so they often loan us some computer whiz.''

Helen stood. Nick's frown was starting to deepen and Mark was losing steam fast. They had to leave so he could sleep. ''Thank you for all your help—''

The phone interrupted her. Mark strode over to it. ''Yeah?'' he answered in an exasperated tone.

He listened, rubbing his brow and finally saying, ''Thanks. Tell him I'll be in later to talk to the guy.''

He hung up and turned to Nick. Helen watched and waited.

''That was Sandra,'' Mark told him, suppressing a yawn. ''The hospital called. Ron Mills says he's ready to talk. The chief thought I should know. I'll talk to him tonight and to whoever takes his statement.''

Chapter 13

"What?" Nick took a jerking step toward him. He could hardly believe his ears. Mark was going to sit on this? "You're going to wait?"

Mark stifled a yawn. "Nick, I've been up for twenty hours. I'm in no shape to drive in, let alone question anyone. Besides, he's still in ICU. The guy can't even stand up, let alone walk away. Saint John is sending someone over."

"I'll drive you." Nick strode to the front door. He flung the thing open, hoping it would bang against the front hall closet. Mark had always been so damn by the book and yet it didn't take a psychiatrist to see he was holding back on this. Nick didn't know what he was holding back, but he was sure as hell going to find the guy who wanted Helen dead.

Mark tossed a tired glance at Helen and Nick could see her dark eyes grow wide against the pale skin of her face. She was tired herself. Tired and scared and unable to find safety anywhere, except with him. She was also tired because he'd had her up a few times in the night.

"Come on," he growled at the two of them. "Mark, you can sleep in the truck."

Muttering under his breath, Mark grabbed his briefcase and gestured to Helen to precede them out the door. With her head tilted down, she slipped past Nick. He purposely exhaled to avoid drawing in any more of her gentle scent. Without waiting for Mark, he walked out to the truck.

Mark climbed into the back of the SUV and threw his briefcase to the far end of the bench seat. Helen quickly clipped on her seat belt and sat in the front passenger seat as rigid as a nun.

Nick flipped up the sun visor. It was early afternoon, but the sun was gone. The sky hung down close to them, threatening rain.

Within minutes, they were on the highway, heading west into Saint John. Nick rotated his stiff neck and tried to relax with a short, controlled sigh. It wasn't working. And why should it? He hadn't been able to relax since he carried Helen off the cliff.

A shudder ran through him. It was hard to believe only a few days ago he found her, a tiny bedraggled wisp of a woman who was so desperate, she was ready to fake her own suicide. He didn't want her to go anywhere near that damn cliff again.

Not that she would. Out of the corner of his eye, he noticed she still remained prudently upright, her hands clenching each other in her small lap.

She'd never handle being a cop's wife. She simply wasn't strong enough.

A cop's wife? Nick gripped the steering wheel and swallowed. That was stepping a bit too far into the future. They had to get through this day first. Just because he'd fallen head over heels in love with her, didn't mean she was ready to return that love. Hadn't she already told him she didn't do relationships?

His stomach hurt.

A soft, vibrating noise rumbled from the back seat. Both he and Helen turned around at the same time. Mark was snoring behind them, his mouth open and his head flung back at an awkward angle.

Nick faced the front, ignoring Helen's soft smile.

"What's wrong?" she asked. "He's just asleep."

He kept his attention on the road without saying anything. The very sound of the gentle question sent ripples of unwelcome pleasure through him. He must be getting soft because he didn't need to catch a glimpse of her wearing a quiet smile, the kind of smile that stretched out her lips enough to tease him with erotic images of really making her smile. Or better still, making her too limp with sated exhaustion to smile.

"He's asleep," he muttered.

"You heard him. He'd been awake for twenty hours. I can't blame him for passing out."

Nick refused to answer. Over the drone of the engine, he listened to Mark's snoring. So what if Helen thought he was being unreasonable? Mark should remember that two men had been murdered, one man clung to life in the ICU and someone wanted Helen to join the list of casualties. Permanently.

"You can't be upset he's fallen asleep, surely?"

"I expected more out of him," he snapped. "Personally, I'd like to know he can stay awake if I needed him. It's as bad as freezing up the first time you draw your weapon."

Helen frowned at him. "Did Mark do that to you?"

Nick flexed his fingers. They ached from clenching the

steering wheel. "No. Years ago, I had a partner who was fresh from the academy. He froze up right when I needed him the most."

Helen let out a small gasp. "What happened? Did he get shot?"

He rolled his shoulder, trying to loosen the tight scar. "No, I did. So did the suspect."

"So your partner did end up shooting him."

"I shot him. I wasn't much for negotiating back then."

Helen raised her eyebrows, but thankfully kept to herself the comment he knew hovered on her lips.

"I didn't want to shoot the kid," he went on to explain. "He was still in high school, and my partner was supposed to be covering me. But the kid panicked. We both knew he was going to fire. If the bullet he'd fired had hit me three inches to the right, I would have been killed." He tilted his head to stretch out the tense muscles of his neck.

"What happened to the boy? Did he…"

"No. I had to shoot him. But I couldn't take the kid down. His own mother was standing nearby and she looked directly at me when I'd been shot. I could see her begging me with her eyes."

For a long time, Helen said nothing. Eventually, she asked, "Has Mark ever given you reason to believe he would do the same?"

"Look, Helen, you don't understand." Glancing in the rearview mirror at his snoring ex-partner, Nick continued in a quieter tone. "Mark is by the book, one hundred percent. Only thing is, sometimes the book doesn't help an officer who's out there in the real world. Sometimes we need instinct, speed and guts. We have to be willing to break the law if need be. Mark would rather check with the chief first."

"What would you have wanted to do with that boy?"

He couldn't answer. He'd broken the rules and shot the kid in the leg simply because he was a kid. His chief had been furious, not happy that Nick had risked not only his life, but the lives of the people around him, by allowing the kid to live. A kid who, for a few seconds, was injured and carrying a deadly weapon.

But would Mark have followed the standard operating procedures and killed the boy? Now, reliving it all, he wasn't sure.

A raindrop splattered the windshield, directly in his line of vision. Immediately, it raced up the glass away from his vicious stare.

Helen twisted around to study Mark, whose snoring had increased. "Yes, Mark isn't the same as you. But did you really want your partner to kill a boy when you wouldn't do it yourself? Is that what you wanted your partner to do?"

He didn't know. Anger and bitterness and the urge to work alone had ate at him and fed his desire not to sort out his feelings. "You're making it sound like I wanted someone else to shoulder the blame. Forgive the pun."

"I know you didn't. Maybe it's time to accept that Mark isn't like your first partner. I think you two make a good team. You need the balance."

"I need to find out who has been trying to kill you. And I'm hoping Mills will tell me just that." Glad that he was able to terminate the conversation, he reached for some change they'd need for the toll booth over the Saint John River. He threw in one of his quarters. When the light ahead turned green, and the gate lifted, he gunned the engine.

"If Mills talks, you'll be able to get your job back?" Helen's question was cool.

They needed to talk. He didn't want her to think he'd

been using her only to clear his name, or prove his suspicions that Cooms had more than just an illegal drug trade going on. He had control of some public officials.

But now wasn't the time. They'd reach the hospital in a few minutes. Besides all of that, Nick didn't want to tell Helen how he felt. What if she reminded him that she didn't do relationships? What would be his argument? He was still suspended and it looked more and more like he'd stay that way. A relationship wouldn't be the answer to his problems, then.

They said nothing until they reached the hospital. It was then that Nick turned around and grabbed Mark's knee, shaking him awake. ''We're here.''

At the main desk of the ICU, a nurse told them that Ron Mills had been taken down to the surgery ward. She gave them the number of his room.

It wasn't hard to spot which room, Nick thought, stepping off the elevator. Another officer was guarding the door. Nick headed toward it, but Mark grabbed his arm. ''This is my job, Nick. Now let me do it.''

Helen's gaze ping-ponged back and forth between the two tall men. She waited, holding her breath as she fully expected Nick to have it out with Mark right then and there.

He didn't. He stole a quick glance at her, pursed his lips and nodded. ''We'll be in the TV room if you need us.'' With that, he grabbed Helen's elbow and directed her to a nearby corner room.

There were several people watching TV. They turned when she and Nick entered. One was a patient, the others obviously family members.

She refused the seat Nick offered. How could she sit down and relax while Mark found out, this very minute, perhaps, who wanted her dead? She felt useless, forced into a corner. Like that night she'd tried to fake her own suicide.

Not quite. Somewhere along the way, she'd begun to see herself in a different light, like she'd begun to see Nick differently, too.

She wandered to the tall, tightly shut window. The view was unremarkable. The other side of the hospital. She hadn't wanted to trust Nick but he somehow managed to get under her skin. That clean tang of aftershave that was uniquely him still lingered in her nostrils. The memory of seeing his strong, chiseled muscles that first night still weighed heavily in her mind. Nothing could erase it. Not the busy hum of the ward around them, not the television, not the astringent odor all hospitals had.

She couldn't get him out of her system.

She was a fool. She'd been looking for a white knight, someone to sweep her away and protect her. Nick wasn't that person, and though she knew it was foolish to think she might find such a man someday, she wasn't crazy enough to try to mold Nick into him.

He wasn't into the kind of caring relationship she needed. That much was obvious.

With a hard pivot on the tiled floor, she turned and strode to the open door. Behind her, the strains of a TV sitcom tried to reach her, but she ignored them. "I'm going to the washroom," she muttered without looking at Nick.

To her left, Helen noticed the curtains hanging in the window of Ron Mills's private room were open. Several people were standing by the bed. One was Mark. He glanced at her through the old-styled observation glass.

The door swung open and her boss stepped out of Mills's room. Helen swallowed the urge to cringe. She had been hoping that it would be days before she would have to confront Mr. Parker. By then, hopefully, everything would have been sorted out and she could be exonerated. She had, after all, abused the privilege of knowing the alarm system codes as well as stolen the warehouse keys. Even Mr. Parker didn't have access to them right now. The police had taken them away and sealed the warehouse. Production was probably at a standstill.

Mr. Parker noticed her immediately. He shut the door behind him and strode over to the still and silent Helen, who stood in front of the nurses' station.

"I'm glad I ran into you, Helen."

The tone of his voice chilled her. No, she told herself. What she did was the right thing to do. Hadn't Nick said the same thing? Hadn't he said that sometimes the rules needed to be bent and a person had to go on instinct and guts to do what was right?

She straightened, catching a glimpse of Nick out the corner of her eye. He was standing at the threshold of the TV room, watching her. She turned back to Mr. Parker's cool stare.

"What is it that you'd like to discuss, sir?"

"A few of your indiscretions. I trusted you with the security of my company, Helen. We both know how that turned out, and here isn't the time to discuss that, but I'd like to see you in my office as soon as you feel well enough to return to work."

Helen folded her arms, refusing to be stung by the icy barb. She'd even lied to him about needing a few days off, but she didn't feel guilty about that. "Until I return to work, I think you should also consider that I did what I had to do. You wouldn't have done any different under the same circumstances. I didn't set out to deceive you, Mr. Parker, but I'm sure by now you're aware that someone tried to kill me. And had I not taken the initiative to find out who, Ron Mills wouldn't be alive today.''

Her heart was pounding in her throat. When she'd first secured her job at Globatech, the company was new. Parker was a seasoned executive with international experience. He was also tough. But she wouldn't back down. She wouldn't beg for her job because she'd risked it trying to save her own life and would do it again in a heartbeat if necessary. Despite the wet palms she'd just wiped on her sleeves, her heart pounded and her spirit soared. It felt wonderful.

After watching the elevator doors close in front of a group of people, Parker said, ''Ron Mills is a crook.''

She took a step forward, encouraged by her exhilaration. ''He may be a crook, but he's a live crook. And I heard your welcome-to-the-company speech, Mr. Parker. You put the emphasis on manpower. You said yourself human resources were the most important. That wasn't rhetoric. You meant it.''

Her shoulders ached from holding them back so far. ''I'm sorry if you feel I haven't lived up to your expectations. I've only done what I thought was right.''

Parker said nothing for a moment. Then, slowly, he began to nod. ''Helen, when the police called to tell me what had happened, I was furious. I was ready to fire you right then and there. But I learned a long time ago to temper my initial reactions with time and what I consider good sound judgment. I don't agree that what you did was the most prudent, but I can see where you're coming from. And you're right. People are the most important. I can't say you'll be back with all the privileges you enjoyed before, but I can say, your job will be waiting for you when you do come back.''

Tears stung her eyes, but Helen refused to blink. She

smiled briefly. "Thank you." She couldn't help but glance over at Nick, hoping that her small victory would prove to him that she wasn't looking for a savior. She was strong enough all by herself.

Nick wore a difficult, almost pained expression.

Parker shot his own curious look at Nick as the elevator door open, then he walked onto it, after a big, burly orderly wearing wrinkled scrubs stepped out.

The man had his head down, his hand up scratching his cheek closest to her. Something in the other hand glinted in the stale fluorescent lighting, catching Helen's attention. It looked like a small knife.

The man dropped his hand slightly, exposing enough of his face to—

She gasped.

Clive Darlington! His ugly, distorted features slackened slightly with shock a moment before he swung away from her. His hair was cut short and he'd shaved off the scruff of a beard he always seemed to have, revealing deep acne scars.

She turned to Nick. "That's Clive!"

Immediately, Nick lunged at him.

Just before they connected, Helen caught another glimpse of the knife, pointed directly at Nick.

But her feet fused themselves to the floor.

Chapter 14

No! She couldn't let Nick fight him unarmed. She couldn't let him die!

The two men hit the tiled floor and rolled against the closed elevator door. Helen wrenched her feet free at the same time she screamed out to no one in particular, "That's Clive Darlington!"

The door to Mills's room flew open and out charged Mark. He knocked Helen out of the way and she staggered backward. Nick grunted out something incoherent, like a groan of exasperation.

Or pain?

Clive yanked his hand free. Helen gasped. The knife! Blood smeared the tip of it. She clenched her jaw, refusing to scream as Mark hurled himself on Clive and grabbed his arms. But Nick finished the battle. One clean sweep of his fist connected with Clive's pockmarked cheek. Clive, as big as he was, took the full force of the hit and slumped out of Mark's grasp to the blood-splattered floor.

His knife slipped out and skittered over to where Helen stood.

She stomped on it to stop it. Then dashing over to the men, she cried, "Nick!"

He caught her and pulled apart her hands. When he saw her empty palms, he scanned the floor. "Just making sure you didn't touch the knife."

She gripped him tightly. "I tried to warn you before he stabbed you!"

"He stabbed himself." Nick turned to Clive, who lay on the floor, face-down, his bloodied wrists already locked in handcuffs, thanks to Mark.

"What the hell happened?" Mark pinned down the semiconscious Clive. By now, a crowd had gathered at the foyer. One old man wheeling an IV bag teetered nearby, until two nurses and an orderly began to disperse everyone. Another nurse asked if anyone was hurt.

"Him." Nick flicked his head toward Clive. "We'll take him down to emergency to see how bad he is."

"I'll get him a wheelchair."

Nick hauled up on the handcuffs, forcing Clive to stand. "No. This bastard's walking."

"Where did you find him?" Mark asked.

"He came out of the elevator," Helen said. She steeled herself to stare at Clive. "He had a knife in his hand. I saw him and called out to Nick."

Still gripping the handcuffs, Nick poked the elevator button. Mark retrieved the knife, asking the nurse for a plastic bag.

Helen drew in a deep, shaky breath. "He was here to kill Ron Mills. I don't think he expected to see us."

Nick frowned at her. Had her words surprised him? She knew by the look on his face he was still trying to fit the pieces together. She shivered, the cold sweat of shock finally seeping in.

He yanked on Clive's handcuffs. ''It's over, buddy. No more thirty days in the local jail for you. Where you're going, you won't see the light of day for about twenty-five years.''

''I'll call the station. They can come get him,'' Mark said. ''We're lucky to get that bastard, Nick. Ron Mills has decided he needs a lawyer before he says anything.''

''What?'' Nick shoved Clive against the wall. Only then did Helen see where Clive had accidentally stabbed himself. The top of his pant leg was dark with a small stain of blood. Nick leaned into Clive. ''Who tried to run down Helen?''

''It wasn't me,'' Clive snarled back, his words muffled by the plastered wall and his groggy state.

''We know it wasn't you, jerk,'' Nick snapped. ''You were busy violating your probation at a bar. So who was it?''

''I don't know!''

Nick did something to make Clive yelp, but Helen couldn't see what. She shot a hasty look over to Mark, who turned his back to pick up the nurses' phone, all the while holding the knife in a plastic bag.

''Who's been trying to kill Helen?''

''William Townsend. Ah!'' Nick crushed him farther into the wall. Helen stepped forward, biting her lip, afraid Nick would go too far.

Clive let out another gasp. ''Ron Mills! He was the one driving the car!''

Nick let go of him and Clive slumped down. The elevator door opened and Nick dragged him in. When they turned around, Mark called out, ''The boys are waiting downstairs for him. Wait down there for me. I won't be long."

Helen caught Nick's stare. His eyes burned so dark and hot into her, she could hardly breathe. Her heart hammered in her throat, and only now did she realize she was standing in the middle of the foyer, all alone.

"I'll be right back," he said, quietly, his voice a far cry from the angry tone a minute ago. The elevator door shut on them.

Disoriented, she turned around. The curtains were still open in Mills's room. She could see him lying there, his eyes shut, probably still half-groggy.

The foyer began to spin. The guard who'd been in the room with Mills and Mark caught her as she slumped. "I'm fine," she said. "I'll just sit down for a minute."

The guard nodded and guided her into the now empty TV room.

A few minutes passed alone and quiet for her. "You okay?"

She looked up to find Mark standing in the doorway.

"Where's Nick?"

"Giving his statement downstairs."

Tears sprang in her eyes. "I'm sorry," she whispered, not knowing why she was apologizing.

"Don't be." He sat down beside her. "Everything will be all right."

She lifted her head. "Is Nick okay? Really?"

Mark gave her a confident smile. "He's fine. Nick's tough. But good. Too bad he doesn't like to work with a partner, though."

"Do you know why?" It seemed impossible that Nick wouldn't have said anything to Mark.

Mark nodded. "Yeah, I know."

"He told me on the way in here. It must be hard for you to work together."

"Sometimes. But trust is something you earn. I trust Nick to do what's right. And that in turn will help him trust me." He stood. "I have to get back to Mills. There are a few things I need to read to him."

His rights, she assumed.

"Will you be okay in here?" he asked. "I'll be just across the foyer, if you need me."

Helen nodded and Mark left her alone. For a long time, she sat in the dim room, still not believing it was all over. It had all happened so fast, she had trouble getting it to sink in. Her hands were shaking, her mouth dry, even her heart still thumped furiously, hurting her when she tried to swallow.

Leaning back, she shut her eyes. She wasn't the sort to faint. But then again, all her sheltered life, she'd had nothing like this happen to her before. So maybe she was the kind to collapse, after all.

But Nick was safe, despite the fury of the fight with Clive. That was all that mattered.

He hadn't followed the book. He'd let his anger get a hold of him and had pressured Clive to admit who was behind all of the killings and attacks.

He wasn't a white knight, a perfect cop. Just like he'd said.

A sob bubbled up and choked her. Dear Heaven, was she going to cry? Did that mean she was still looking for that perfect man?

But she wanted to spend her life with Nick, didn't she?

Helen lifted her head and let the tears well up in her eyes. A dark shadow to her left moved within her blurred vision and she snapped her head over.

Nick stood in the doorway. Behind him the ward had

returned to normal, only a few inquisitive visitors peered out of their loved ones' rooms. A short announcement of someone looking for a doctor cut through the murmurings.

"That was quick," she commented, hastily blinking away the tears.

"I still have to give my statement down at the station."

"Where's Clive?"

"He's in custody downstairs. We got lucky again. There was a patrol car just leaving the hospital." He closed the distance between them.

With a nod, she swiped the tears away. "I didn't think I would fall apart like this. I guess it's shock."

"A damsel in distress?"

"That's not funny."

"I didn't really mean it." His words were soft, not mocking, but they may as well have been. She didn't want to be weak. She wanted to be in control of her own life.

Maybe share it with him at the same time.

"It's over, Helen. You can cry if you like."

She stood. "I don't want to." Her voice quivered and she had to rush out the words before it failed her altogether. "And I don't want to be a damsel in distress, either."

Nick's features clouded. He stood, more slowly than she had. His clothes were rumpled and there was a small tear in his shirt at the shoulder. Smeared down his right leg was some of Clive's blood, no doubt from the fight.

She shivered.

Nick pulled the hem of her sweater down and rubbed her arms. "Darlington came here to kill Mills. They must have been battling for control. Full share of the profits ever since Cooms died."

"Do you think Clive killed him?"

"Maybe. Maybe Mills told him to. I'd always figured

Darlington wasn't smart enough to run things, but with the amount of money involved, he might have been thinking he could.''

''I know Ron Mills. I worked with him when they were shorthanded. He has a wife and kids who need braces. They have his small jaw, he said. I can't believe he would stoop to this.'' She hugged herself.

''Like I said, the chance to get some big money can tempt a lot of people. More than you realize.''

''Is Clive talking yet?''

''He hasn't said a word except to say he wants a lawyer. He did say that his confession about Mills wouldn't hold up in court and that he was going to sue me for police brutality.''

''Oh, Nick!''

He drew her into his arms. ''Now, that's a long shot. He's more likely to be declared a violent offender. After all, he was the one with the knife.''

She snuggled deep into the warm folds of his open jacket. Against her cheek, she felt the creased edges of the photos Jones had printed out for them.

Nick smelled wonderful. There was little left of the unique citrusy tang of his aftershave. In its place was a warm, male scent, mingled with musk and heat. She wanted to stay cuddled safely here forever.

Safe.

She straightened. She wasn't safe. Not her heart anyway and that prickly pain couldn't be smoothed over with one simple embrace.

No, she didn't feel safe.

Nick stepped back himself, clearing his throat. ''Look, I want you to go home. To my place.''

She wiped her eyes. ''How? You drove me in.''

"I can call you a cab, if you're not up to driving my truck."

"No," she answered firmly. "I'm fine. I'll take it easy. And when I get there, I'll get my things together. There's no reason to stay with you anymore."

His expression darkened, a frown creasing his angular features. He didn't look like some handsome Latino movie star, anymore. He looked like Nick Thorndike, a world-weary cop.

She stopped her hand before it slipped up and stroked his dark, rough cheek.

"Helen," he said, taking his keys out, "will you do one last thing for me? Stay until I get back? Then we'll talk. I have a lot to say to you."

She wanted to say no. It would be easier for both of them. She didn't do relationships because she'd been looking for that perfect knight. Knowing that now didn't mean she should leap into one with Nick, a far cry from perfect.

Now was the time she proved to herself she could stand and go after life alone.

But something in Nick's tight voice, the way he held himself together, as if he would fly apart if he did so much as exhaled. She hadn't heard his tone before and it made her heart squeeze and her knees liquefy, all at the same time.

"Please, Helen. Stay 'til I get back?"

Her chest felt hot. She gave into the pleasure of touching his warm, rigid frame. He was so solid, so tense compared to her. She ran her fingers up his arm, over his square shoulder, inhaling deeply the whole time to smell again his unique scent. When she reached the area of the scar, she hesitated.

His hand snapped up and caught hers. His other arm whipped out and hauled her in close. "Please say you'll stay. We need to talk, but first I want to help Mark wrap this up. I want to know that when I get back to my home, you'll be waiting for me."

He drew her into his arms, holding her in a squeeze that crushed her breasts against him, and ground her hips into his. "I just want to talk, okay? Will you stay, Helen?"

She wanted more than talk. She wanted to wait in his bed, to have him come and fall into it and cover himself with her and after many languid hours of lovemaking, then they could talk.

She blinked and nodded.

Nick relaxed. Then he tilted his head down and pressed his lips against hers.

His kiss started so gently. Such a tender kiss she'd never even dreamed to be possible, and yet the moment her lips parted to invite his tongue inside, he exploded.

His arms tightened, his tongue plundered her mouth. This was the Nick she'd made love to. The man who, once she'd begged him to release her passion, had taken her, heart and soul.

In the few seconds their kiss lasted, she relived their lovemaking, blocking out the sounds of the hospital around them. She felt loose and pliant beside his lean, hard frame.

Then he lifted his head. "I have to see Mark."

The keys were still pressed in her palm. He covered her clenched fingers with his own and squeezed them. "Drive carefully, okay? I'll call you."

She nodded vacantly. "How will you and Mark get home?"

"We'll get someone from the station here to drive us. Don't worry about that, okay?"

Again, she nodded. He touched her chin with his fingers, his thumb arcing upward to brush her lips. All of his attention was focused on her mouth.

"You have the most incredible lips, did you know that?"

Before she could answer, he turned and left her alone.

On the way home, without thinking, she grabbed one of Nick's quarters for the toll bridge. It seemed so right to be using his truck. Like it was a part of her routine.

She swallowed as she threw the quarter into the basket at the far end of the bridge. It wasn't natural, though. She'd already been through this. She and Nick would never last. He was an undercover cop, a man who didn't—couldn't—do relationships because he didn't trust anyone. His work was the most important thing in his life and he preferred to do that alone.

She'd had a chance to salvage what was left of her heart before she'd lost it totally. But he'd asked her to stay at his place until he returned.

He'd saved her life. Several times. It was the least she could do.

Finally, she pulled into the long, quiet driveway that led to his house. Last time she'd come here by herself, she'd been bent on faking her own suicide.

She shivered and twisted the heat control on the dash. The rain had started just after she left the city. It wasn't a hard rain, but steady. A dull, dreary downpour that seemed to coat the whole world in cold gray.

Nick's house appeared in front of her. Once free of the spindly trees that flanked the driveway, Helen noticed the wind had picked up. A lone gull battled the updrafts above the house.

She quickly parked and dashed for the house. Her head was soaked before she reached the covered porch. After fumbling with the keys, she found the right one and let herself in, careful to lock the door behind her.

The house was cold. Only a few weeks ago, summer had still lingered here along the coast. But not now. Autumn was here, hinting of the icy, damp days of winter ahead.

Helen set her purse and the keys down and kicked off her shoes. She headed straight for the woodstove and quickly made a fire.

What heat Nick's kiss had kindled in her was all but gone. As the papers and sticks caught fire, she sat back on her heels and stuck out her hands.

It was all over. All over. The words echoed and danced in her head. Clive had been caught. Sooner or later, in light of the evidence, he and Mills would confess and the police would close the case.

Those few times she'd seen the big, ugly Darlington ran through her mind. Jamie telling him to do something. Jamie ordering him out when she walked in.

Jamie was dead. It wouldn't take the police long to confirm who killed him. They would have the ballistic report. They could compare the bullet that killed him to the bullet that killed Tony. Providing they hadn't gone missing, as well. The bullets would match, she knew, just as she knew Clive had access to Jamie's handgun.

Helen's ankles ached and she shifted to relieve them. The heat of the stove felt good against her cold face.

And if Mills had been trying to take over the flow of drugs, then he'd have wanted the tape Jamie had made for blackmail purposes. He'd have wanted Helen dead if he thought she knew too much.

Mills. He looked so small, so thin, lying there in that bed. As small and thin as her father had been in his coffin.

Helen tightened her jaw and pursed her lips. No tears.

She'd got over her father's death years ago. And as good as he was, he wasn't her perfect savior.

Mills was so small.

Cold rippled through her, settling in her stomach like a block of ice. Not even the blasting fire in front of her couldn't melt it. She stood, flexing to ease the aches her body had accumulated over the last few days.

Oh, mercy.

Mills was small. And very short. And everyone at that party had towered over her.

The man who'd tried to run her down was big. Nick had seen his silhouette. The eyewitness had concurred. A big, muscular man. As big as Nick or Mark or Clive.

Feeling faint, she dropped to the couch, the truth sinking into her like she sank into the soft cushions.

Mills wasn't the one who tried to run her down. Nor was he going to say anything to the police until he saw his lawyer, which could be as late as tomorrow, or even the next day.

She put an unsteady hand to her mouth, not surprised to find her lips quivering.

A thumping at the front door made her jump. Nick! She had his keys, had kept the lights off on the porch and locked the door behind her.

She hurried to the door, glad she could tell him what she'd realized. He would know what to do. Perhaps even Clive or Mills had finally told the truth.

She found her way through the dimness easily. Quickly, she twisted the deadlock and threw open the door.

It wasn't Nick.

Chapter 15

He couldn't look back at Helen as he left the TV room, so he went straight into Mills's hospital room. Mark turned when he entered. A quick glimpse at Mills told Nick the man had fallen asleep. His eyes were shut, his mouth was slack as he snored lightly, beneath an oxygen mask.

"They just called up for you," Mark said. "They want you down at the station to give your statement."

"I'll leave in a few minutes."

"They want Helen's statement, too. Where is she?"

"I sent her back to my house, in my truck. I'll bring her back in, don't worry."

Mark lifted his eyebrows. "You realize that this means we're stuck here."

Nick nodded, listening to the soft hum of the machines in front of him. One machine seemed to be monitoring Mills's pulse and respirations, while the other looked like it was connected to the IV bag. He wasn't a doctor, but the fact that Mills was out of intensive care and these machines weren't beeping or wailing must mean the guy was going to pull through.

They said nothing for a while and Nick wasn't even sure why he was there.

He sighed, running a hand over his face. "Hey." He cleared his throat. "Thanks for helping out back there. I mean, thanks for pulling me off Darlington."

Mark grinned. "And for looking the other way while you got some 'answers' from him?"

Nick felt the corners of his own mouth quirk up. "Yeah. But I probably would have done a lot worse if you hadn't been there."

"The bastard had a knife, Nick. He would have killed you if you'd done any less."

The moment felt less difficult all of a sudden. Nick walked over to the window and looked down at the parking lot. His truck was gone. If Helen had taken the highway, she'd be home by now.

"Mark," he said, "sorry about trying to get info on Helen's past out of you. She told me everything."

"It's okay. I would have done the same."

He turned and indicated to Mills. "Did he decide to talk yet?"

"Not without a lawyer. He must have overheard Darlington's confession. He won't say a thing. The nurse gave him a sedative."

Nick resisted the nearly overwhelming temptation to shake the man awake. Instead he stared at the monitors, willing them to somehow heal the man.

Globatech?

He peered at the labels on each of the machines. The logo sticker practically glowed at the back of the IV monitor. Globatech had made that piece of equipment.

He'd seen that same sticker on the back of a laptop at the station in Lower Cove.

The chief's laptop.

His gaze flew to Mark's face. "When you were acting chief this spring, did you see any requisitions for laptop computers?"

Mark laughed. "Are you kidding? With Supply and Services now going through the mayor's office? They'd laugh us right out of the town hall." He sobered. "Why? Because the chief had one? Forget it, it's a cheap one. I don't know why he bought it. It's always crashing. He hates it."

Really? Dennis Hunt cursed computers one day and was toting a laptop the next? Then he was back to cursing them?

"But maybe he decided to finally learn something about them, since we were getting a whole new system in the office, anyway," Mark suggested.

"Wait." Nick held up his hand. "Wasn't Jones the one who set up our new computers?"

Mark shrugged. "Sure. We shared the contract for them with Saint John because it was cheaper. Jones set up all the systems. He's a real whiz at them."

"How is he at removing reports?"

"What are you talking about?" Mark then rolled his eyes. "Aw, Nick, the autopsy reports? Your corrupt officials theory?"

"Yeah."

Mark shot him a disbelieving look. "Nick, why would he steal the autopsy report? There were other copies available. He could have taken Saint John's copy, if he wanted one so badly."

That was true. Grimacing, Nick rubbed his face. It didn't make any sense, but he decided to run with the idea anyway. "Listen. What if he only wanted to read it and since it didn't tell him anything of interest, do you think he would check out the ballistic report instead?''

Mark swore as he yanked out his cell phone. He punched out a few numbers, all the while glaring with skepticism at Nick. Then he spoke sharply. A minute later, he hung up, even more grim than before. ''I called Sandra. She says the ballistic reports have now disappeared. She found that out when she tried to file her new copy of the autopsy.''

''Reports?''

''For both DiPetri and Cooms. The chief asked for a copy of Cooms's because I was still part of the op. And that's not all. Sandra says she called Saint John and they noticed that the bullets have walked out of the evidence room, as well.''

Nick swore. The slugs the coroner had dug out of Cooms and DiPetri had been sent for testing. It was standard procedure and everyone expected the findings to tell them that they'd been fired from the same weapon. Only the lab could tell them if they matched, but he wagered even the lab's copies would be missing as well. And with no evidence or reports…

Someone had a lesser chance of being prosecuted.

Mark broke into his thoughts. ''Do you think Jones took them?''

''No. I was just running with the idea.'' He shot his ex-partner a short smile. ''I should have been using logic instead of my instinct.'' He dug through his jacket and pulled out a wad of folded printouts. ''Here are the printouts Jones made for me from the video clip we found on Helen's tape. At least we still have them.'' He spread them out at the foot of the bed, ignoring the unconscious Mills. ''Mind you, Jones printed out a picture of everyone who was at the party that night. He also admitted he had to clean up some of the stills so we could see them clearly. Helen said that Cooms had hinted to her that there was more than one crooked cop involved. If Jones had seen his own face on the video, wouldn't he have 'cleaned' it up so much, we wouldn't recognize it? Or eliminated it entirely?''

Mark shoved the bed table out of the way and peered at the printouts. ''But how will we be able to tell? Assuming he had the time to do it.''

''We have a printout of the party as a whole. Let's start comparing pictures to see if we have everyone.'' Nick pulled out a pen and began to mark off the obvious ones. Helen, Cooms, Darlington—

His hand froze over the next one he picked up. A trail of icy cold whipped up his arms as the short hairs stood on end. It seemed as if his breath was suck from his lungs just as every hair on his body stood at rigid attention.

The blowup was grainy at best and didn't show more than a quarter of the man's heavy features. But the shape of the head, the ruddy complexion, the heavy jowls prevalent in middle-aged men who were big-boned and heavyset. How had he missed him before in his truck?

Nick glanced up at Mills, who was still oblivious to the world. Mills was thin and small-boned. He looked gaunt and drawn in the bed, his thin, sloping shoulders not at all like the ones of the man whose silhouette he'd seen against the streetlights the night Helen was nearly hit.

He swore. His hand shook as he handed the paper to Mark. ''Recognize him?''

Mark's curse was fouler.

The chief.

Nick grabbed the cell phone from where Mark had laid it and punched out his home number.

One ring. Two rings. Three rings. She should have been there by now. Where could she be? Where did she go?

"Who are you calling?"

"Helen. She isn't there." He disconnected and dialed the Lower Cove Police Department. Sandra answered.

Nick was going to ask her to send a patrol car to his house, but he caught the order before it reached his lips. "Sandra? Where's the chief?"

She sighed. "He said he wasn't feeling well right after Mark called. Since it was quiet here, he decided to go home to lie down. I had to call in the auxiliary officers. Good thing, they're all out at the tavern answering a noise complaint."

Nick's stomach lurched. No! No! Pivoting sharply, he raced to the door and flung it open, only to skid to a stop. Damn! He didn't have his truck!

The guard outside the room looked at him questioningly. Nick shoved the cell phone into his pocket and grabbed the man's shoulder. "Do you have a car here?"

"Sure. One of the new ones from the compound."

"Quick! Give me the keys!"

The guard glanced over Nick's shoulder to Mark, who nodded. Nick grabbed the keys as soon as they were produced and bolted toward the stairs.

The chief! Nick's mind raced as he reached for the handrail in the stairwell. It seemed impossible and yet...

Yet it all made sense.

On the ground floor, Nick roared for the front doors. Outside, ignoring the steady rain that had begun to fall, he snapped his head from one side to another to orient himself.

There! He spotted the cruiser and leapt out in front of a parked ambulance to race to it.

Keep her safe, he prayed, slamming into the hood of

the cruiser in his haste to whip around to the driver's door. Keep her safe! Please!

He roared out of the parking lot, cutting off two small cars and getting sharp, angry honks for his effort.

Once out on the highway, he pulled out Mark's cell phone. He had one more suspicion to confirm. He punched out the city's jail number.

The corrections officer told him Darlington had two visitors, apart from his lawyer and parole officer. His mother and Dennis Hunt.

Someone had told Darlington to kill Helen, and Nick was guessing it wasn't the guy's mother.

The windshield wipers beat a rhythmic slapping against the window, swishing away the downpour. Nick gripped the steering wheel to stare past them. Dennis Hunt had suggested that they start the undercover investigation at the local seasonal fishing industry. It was an obvious point to start, so no one, even Nick who'd had his doubts, had said any different. But it had also been designed to thwart the investigation from the start. Then Nick had suggested to move the investigation closer to Cooms, Hunt must have become nervous. When DiPetri was murdered, he used that excuse to suspend Nick, afraid he was getting closer to the truth.

Helen had said, quite absently, that she thought the reason was picky, but she had suggested he was merely protecting Nick's butt.

In a way, Helen had been right. Only the chief had been protecting his own butt.

Nick fished out a coin from his jacket for the bridge toll, cursing the fact he was wasting precious seconds. Once past that and cruising westward, with lights flashing, Nick grabbed the cell phone again and dialed his home number.

Still no one answered.

* * *

Helen gaped at Dennis Hunt. Why was he here? The man stepped over the threshold and turned to close the door. The sounds of the steady rain died into the soft click of the door being locked.

"What's wrong?" she croaked out. Please let it not be Nick.

The chief walked into the living room, not bothering to remove his wet shoes. Helen glared down at the shiny footprints he was leaving on Nick's clean, wood floor.

"Nick called me to ask if I would come by. He said he needed someone to keep an eye on you."

"But Clive has been caught and..." She trailed off, wondering if it was a good idea to mention that even though Clive had ratted out Mills, she didn't believe him. "And Nick sent me back here."

"Caught?" Chief Hunt turned to face her, his expression clouded with confusion.

"Yes, he tried to sneak in and stab Mills."

Hunt glanced around the semilit room. Helen could smell the dampness of his uniform over the comforting smells of Nick's house. Outside, the sky seemed grayer and darker than a midwinter's twilight. A gust from the bay slashed a sheet of heavy rain against the window beyond the wood stove and Helen half expected to hear a peal of thunder in the distance.

She rubbed her arms. "Well, thanks for checking up on me, but I'm fine."

"I don't think so. You opened the door without checking who it was."

Helen studied his frown. "I thought you were Nick. You're right, though. I'll be more careful." She made a movement toward the door.

"You should be. Not even a cop's home is necessarily safe. You're lucky Nick asked me to stop by."

Something wasn't right. Helen reached the door and stood staring out the door's window at the rain-drenched driveway. Nick trusted the chief? She doubted that. He didn't even trust his own feelings, his own heart. She shifted her gaze from the middle distance beyond the door glass and focused on the faint, blurry reflection of the chief behind her.

She squinted. His face. She'd seen his face before.

Then it came to her.

At the party Jamie had found so necessary to tape.

She whirled around. "You're him! You're the crooked cop that Jamie had hinted about. You were at the party that night. The one Jamie videotaped."

"Clever girl. Keep up the good work. And thank you for telling me exactly what evidence Cooms had on me." He whipped out a gun and pointed it at her. "And since Darlington is in custody, I think it's time I finished the job." He shook his head. "If you want something done right..."

Helen felt her breath coming out in short, dry gasps. She couldn't take her eyes off the gun. Never in her life had she even seen one this close, let alone pointed at her.

"Oh, I knew you would recognize me sooner or later," Hunt said, matter-of-factly continuing the conversation. "You really should have disappeared. I would have found what Jamie Cooms had on me and destroyed it. And you'd have been too scared to show your face in this province again. Not that you would have, after faking your own suicide. That's a criminal offense here."

She gaped at him. Then slowly, like the way daylight was seeping from the landscape, she truly, truly understood. She tried to swallow, but her throat hurt. She had to somehow slow down her thoughts, get control, and find a way to stop this crazy nightmare.

She backed up toward the door. "Jamie was blackmailing you, wasn't he? But why would he blackmail you when you could turn him in? Unless you were selling drugs? Or were you taking protection money from him?"

Her words sounded garbled to her ears. She wasn't even sure she was making sense.

"I'm six months away from retirement and Cooms was a greedy bastard. He paid me to keep him safe and then found a way to get the money back."

It was all sinking in too fast to make any sense. "You didn't know about the videotape he'd taken from my apartment?"

"Keep talking. It'll save me having to bring Mark in for a full report. Damn shame I have to rely on a civilian for information."

Helen's hand reached back to touch the doorknob. It was cold, even in her already cold hand. She'd seen the chief shut it and lock it. She'd never get it open before he could leap on her. And he stood between her and the rest of the house, filling the far end of the entranceway with his heavyset frame.

She didn't want to keep talking, to let slip to this horrible man something that could jeopardize Nick's life, but if she lapsed into silence, what would he do? Finish off what he came here to do?

"You tried to run me down."

"No, William Townsend did." He chuckled.

Anger leapt inside of her. "William Townsend doesn't exist. And Nick knows that, too."

Hunt nodded. "He's always been a good cop. He likes to have his own way, but he's smart."

"Why do all of this, anyway? You said you were near retirement. It seems like an awful risk to take."

"I have six months left as a police officer. And I'm to retire to what? A small pension in a small town out in the middle of nowhere? Not even able to afford to go south for the winter while people like Cooms are just drowning in money?"

"He got rich on the backs of poor addicts. Hardly something to be envied." Even the thought of it all sickened her.

"Ah, yes, I remember when I had those ideals. But you can't stop crime. It'll always be here, and people like Cooms will always win. My whole career would have been for nothing and I'd retire with a pittance."

But he had gone south. Nick had told her he'd taken his wife on a second honeymoon. "Is that why you went to the Caribbean? To set up a bank account to launder your money?"

He laughed. "You've been watching too much TV. Banks don't launder money, per se. Besides, I prefer to call it putting a little away for a rainy day. Like this one."

The phone began to ring. Both of them jumped slightly.

"Ignore it," Hunt growled.

"We both know that's Nick. He's expecting me to answer it. He's given me enough time to get home."

"Too bad."

Helen swallowed to relieve her dry throat. That had to be Nick, which would mean he must still be at the hospital. At least twenty minutes away. She glanced at Hunt, past the gun pointed at her, all the way up to his face. "What are you going to do?"

His ruddy features cracked into a cold smile. "I'm going to make your suicide real."

Chapter 16

The car slid on the wet pavement as Nick yanked the steering wheel to the left. Immediately, the tires bit into the packed dirt and peppered gravel into the wheel wells before lurching forward.

He slammed the gas pedal to the floor, cursing his long driveway. He took the last curve on two wheels.

Ahead was the house, his truck. And one of Lower Cove's police cruisers.

The one that didn't have a light bar. The one Hunt preferred.

He slammed on the brakes and skidded to a stop behind the cruiser. Ahead of him, the house looked dark and cold. And empty.

He leapt out, ignoring the pelting rain as he took the porch steps two at a time

''Helen!'' he called as he threw open the front door. ''Get down!''

Only the silence answered him, mocking him for pretending to have a weapon.

Where was she? He raced from room to room, galloping up the stairs to check his bedroom.

Empty. He tore back down the stairs, leaping over the last few before sprinting out the door. What had the chief done with her?

His gaze fell to the ground. Rainwater had already begun to fill two sets footprints.

One a big set, the other, much smaller. The smaller prints were smudged and twisted, like the owner had been dancing around the bigger person.

Not dancing. Fighting.

Nick looked up. The rim of his cove rose in steep, pale gray rocks. Wind and rain lashed at the spruce, contorting the short branches. He squinted, focusing on the very outer rim of the cliff, the edge where he'd seen Helen standing.

Nothing.

Looking back down at the footprints, he followed them with his eyes, all the way to the path that led to the cliff.

Beside him was the police cruiser and he automatically reached out to touch the wet hood.

It was warm. The chief had just gotten here.

Nick bolted up the trail. Wet, prickly branches slapped at him, taunting him to run faster, to catch Hunt. He stumbled over a slick root, as if the damn thing had sprung up just to trip him.

The trail seemed twice as long as it ever had been before. He tried to call out to Helen, to tell her to keep fighting, but nothing but a gasp spewed from his mouth.

Damn it, reach the end! Panic welled up in him, urging him to stretch out a little more, to drive himself into the thick forest.

One long, nasty branch scraped across his face, leaving a burning line that even the cold rain couldn't relieve.

There, ahead! He blinked, flicking back his wet hair as he focused on the snatches of Helen's bright jacket he could see through the trees. Again, he stumbled.

"Helen!" He leapt up again and roared through the few remaining trees, to the cliff's edge.

"Stop!"

Nick skidded when he heard Hunt's angry command. The chief waved a handgun to catch his attention.

"Another step and she dies, Thorndike."

But Nick was no longer thinking. "No!" he thundered. He flew forward while the gun was still high above Helen's head.

She ducked. Nick's arm clipped her hair as he aimed for his chief's throat. He caught it in his right hand, his left forearm ramming the gun up and out of the way.

Somewhere behind him, Helen fell free.

His momentum drove both men to the ground, inches from the jagged ledge. The thin layer of sand and sediment scraped under the chief's body.

Nick shoved his right knee up to Hunt's left arm, pinning the elbow under him. He then let go of his neck and with both hands, grabbed the hand holding the gun.

The gun fired. Immediately, dirt and rock chips hit the side of Nick's head. The weapon's report echoed across the wet cliff until it was absorbed into the lament of the wind and rain. Nick wanted to turn around, to make sure that the bullet hadn't ricocheted and hit Helen.

Instead he slammed Hunt's hand into the rocks. The gun fell away and tumbled over the cliff.

Nick loosened his grip, easing off the man's elbow at the same time.

The chief's big fist connected with Nick's jaw.

Nick felt his head snap over to his right and his teeth grind sickeningly against each other. He tumbled away, barely noting that the chief had leapt to his feet.

"Nick!" Helen screamed. It was too late. Hunt brought his knee straight up under Nick's chin, the tip of his boot driving itself deep into Nick's solar plexus.

Breath swooshed out of him the same time pain shot through his jaw.

"No!" Something scraped past his head. Helen had swung a large tree limb above him and into the chief's face.

The man swore violently, before throwing away the half-shattered branch. Nick shook off the swimming confusion and pain. Helen was okay, still alive, fighting back. He staggered to his feet and plowed into Hunt with an agonizing yell.

And the cliff edge disappeared behind them.

Helen tried to shout, but her vocal chords froze. Before her knees could collapse, she lurched to the edge of the cliff. Her heart pounded, pumping fear through to the very pores of her rain-soaked skin.

She threw back her long bangs and peered over the rocks. Lord, keep Nick safe, she prayed. Keep him—

The ledge below was empty. She gasped, her whole body vibrating as she collapsed to the jagged rocks and lowered herself down.

A gust of bay wind buffeted her, slamming her into the cliff face as she struggled to set down on the soft sand of the narrow ledge. There were scuff marks all around, leading to the edge that honestly, truly fell straight down to the raging surf.

Over the wind that roared in her ears, she heard something. A moan, a throaty gasp, she wasn't sure what it was, but it propelled her to the edge.

She wiped her drenched face and saw it. A hand. A big, meaty hand that tempted her to charge over and step on it and kick it away in anger.

Another hand. The coat was dark, lightweight.

Nick! It was Nick's hand!

She dropped to her knees, ignoring the battering they were getting on the hard, jagged stones.

"Nick!" She bent down and grasped on wrist. "Hang on!"

His other hand gave way and slipped down. "Helen..." He sounded so weak, her name garbled and pained.

No! She dug her fingers into his skin. "Grab my wrist."

He looked up at her. His jaw was swollen and misshapen. An angry slash, black with chips of dirt and wood, cut a line across his face. His lower lip was bleeding, dripping down his wet chin.

"Grab my wrist!" she repeated.

"You...not strong enough..." He looked up at her then, his eyes blurred with pain. He blinked, his lip quivered and he wore an expression of such terrible uncertainty, she wished she could halt time and reach out to stroke the doubt away.

She flattened herself down on the rocks and sand and reached over to grab his right elbow. "The hell I'm not strong enough!" Wind flicked his jacket up, entangling it with her cold, wet hands. She threw it off. "Trust me, Nick. I'm plenty strong enough."

He shut his eyes. His legs flailed uselessly around. For a panicked moment, she thought he was going to give up, let go and disappear down to the killer surf below.

She tightened her grip. "Use your other hand, Nick. And your feet. Don't let them dangle. Find a foothold."

He tried. Yes! His left arm reached up as she pulled on his elbow. He found a foothold and together they got his shoulders up above the ledge. She leaned forward to grab his belt, anything to help him.

She saw the chief.

Daylight seemed to be draining from the sky quickly, but she could still make out his blank features before another powerful wave swamped over him, battering his lifeless body against the rocks.

She blinked away the rain and focused on Nick's drenched back. Finding his belt, she let out a loud grunt and leaned backward.

Nick heaved himself up and together they crawled away from the edge. When she banged her head against the rock, she turned. Nick was close at her heels and she pulled him into her arms before rocking back.

He fell on her, burying his face into the soft, wet crook of her neck. She could feel the heat of his bleeding lip pressed to her skin. She tightened her own grip on him until he flinched.

"I'm sorry," she said, pushing away and peering into his face. His jaw looked sickeningly deformed and her heart squeezed at the sight.

She looked down his frame. Pulling him over the cliff had caused the rocks to scrape him from his chin to his waist. His shirt was open, torn in one spot and the skin on his chest was abraded and bleeding.

"Oh, Nick, for a while there, I didn't think you would ever come. You were so far away and the phone kept ringing and I knew it was you—"

He dragged her back into an embrace. Helen immediately shut her mouth, blocking the futile words of remorse. They held each other tightly, rocking with the wind, ignoring the steady downpour, the cold, the fear.

She opened her eyes, finding her gaze directed toward Nick's house. Another police car plowed up the driveway and several men threw open the doors. She lifted her hand to wave, but the men were already charging into the house. Forget it. They'll find them soon enough.

Nick released her. He looked horrified, his expression a mix of disbelief and wonder. "Helen, I—"

He swallowed and touched his lip. Then his hand gingerly probed the outline of his jaw. "I think my jaw's broke," he mumbled. "But hell, before they wire it shut, I want to say something to you."

"Don't." She covered his uplifted hand with her own and moved it to his side. "It can wait." She didn't know what he felt he must say, and she didn't want to know. He was safe. His career would resume and his life would go on. That was all she dared to hope for.

"No." He grabbed both her hands. He could barely move his mouth and his breath sounded labored. "No, Helen. Let me say this. It has to be said, not written down or kept inside of me until I heal." He stared directly into her eyes. "Until five minutes ago, I didn't know if I could trust you, or anyone for that matter. I didn't think you could pull me off the cliff, either. You always wanted a—"

She touched his lips, gently enough to avoid hurting him. "A white knight? Oh, Nick, you were right. I've always wanted a man who could protect me. And yet, at the same time, I was too scared to look for one. My father had always been there for me. But I got mixed up with Scott Jackson and Jamie. I was afraid to trust my own judgment."

Nick flinched with pain as he tried to smile. "You don't need a white knight."

"But I need you. You, Nick! When you went over the

cliff, I thought I'd lost you forever. I love you, Nick. I love you so much it hurts me inside to think of it. I know you're not a white knight.'' She let out a breathy laugh. ''You know what? I felt like a superhero fighting with you. And these past few days have shown me I can survive without a protector. But I can't survive without you.''

He looked pained, blinking away the rain as it streamed down his now puffed-up cheeks.

Suddenly, a loud crashing and shouting started above them. Helen looked up, spying Mark and another officer shining a flashlight down on them.

Mark took one look at Nick and turned to the other man. ''Call an ambulance.''

Helen cringed over the hospital bed. ''He looks so different in the daylight. Are you sure he'll be allowed to leave tomorrow?''

Mark nodded when she turned to him for an answer. ''His doctor only wants to keep him here one more night for observations.''

''But he took a wicked tumble and two of his ribs are cracked. His jaw is broken in two places, don't forget.''

''He'll be fine at home.''

Pulling a face, she turned back to Nick just as his eyes fluttered open. ''Hi,'' she said softly to him.

Unable to speak, he grunted something.

She smiled. ''Now I have permission to tell you to shut up. The surgeon's wired your jaw shut, sewn up your lip and reset your ribs. Amazingly, he thinks you can go home tomorrow as long as you have someone to take care of you.'' She let her smile widen. ''I volunteered.''

Nick's gaze wandered to Mark. He frowned slightly, flicking his head and communicating something with his eyes.

''He's dead. They pulled him off the rocks last night.''

Helen stared at Mark. ''Who? The chief? How did you know what he was asking?''

Mark shrugged. ''He's my partner. We know what each other is thinking. It comes in handy when you can't communicate verbally.''

Nick shook his head, wincing all the while. He pulled his lips to say something. Helen reached out her hand.

''Ellis?'' Mark interpreted.

''Chester?'' she asked. ''What does he have to do with this?''

''Ellis's actions were suspicious at best. Sneaking into your apartment. Selling real estate to Cooms. But we've pretty much got it figured out.''

Helen felt Nick's grip on her fingers tighten.

Mark nodded. ''Seems you were right, Nick. He was—is—in love with Helen. But rather than sending her roses, he decided to win her heart proving that Jamie Cooms was no good for her.''

Helen shook her head. ''What? How?''

Mark looked at her. ''Remember, he was once a Customs Officer. He knew who to suspect, who to watch. He'd sold Cooms that land in hopes he'd get in tight with Cooms and do his own undercover investigation.'' He chuckled. ''A bit of an amateur, and Cooms knew it, too, I bet. That's why he removed the tape from your apartment and hid it at your mother's. Ellis has been advised about leaving the investigative work to us.''

Helen stole a glance at Nick. He shrugged. She refused to allow this conversation to continue. ''I don't think now's the time to get a rundown of all that's happened. You're loaded up with morphine. And decongestants so you don't sneeze and blow your brains out your nose.'' A nervous giggle slipped out as she set down his hand.

''There'll be plenty of time to talk tomorrow when you're feeling better.''

Nick stared at her, his eyes soft and pleading, his swollen, stitched lip moving down slightly. He reached out his hand, awkwardly, with the back of it covered with tape where the IV still remained lodged in his vein. His eyes were limpid, glistening with urgent emotion, but his grip was surprisingly strong. She stroked a section of his dark hair away from his forehead. ''Now that I understand. I love you, too. And we'll talk about it later. I promise. Get some sleep.''

He nodded and shut his eyes.

By the next morning, Helen decided she was used to the change in Nick's face. Still swollen, but not as much, his face looked heavy and strong. While it changed his whole appearance, his eyes remained the same dark, deep pools.

With a straw, he sucked up the last of the meal replacement she'd found in the ward kitchen. ''All right,'' she said, taking the glass. ''That's the last of the chocolate, but there's one more vanilla and two strawberry packets.''

''Hate fanilla.''

She smiled. ''I'll go to the store later and buy some chocolate. I'd never have pegged you a chocoholic.''

''Imma cop. We eat choc-lut.''

''The dietitian you met this morning would have a fit if she heard you weren't planning to stick to the diet she gave you.''

Nick pulled a face as he tried to get more comfortable. Quickly, she helped him get resettled. The IV had come out earlier and they were just waiting on the doctor to release him.

''Fanks,'' he mumbled.

When she sat down next to him, he took her hand. "We need ta' talk."

She nodded. He needed to find out every last detail. And she needed to tell him how she felt, what she'd realized the day before yesterday.

"Yes, but I'll talk, you listen." She took a deep breath, steeling herself against the grisly details she'd learned from Mark yesterday. "They scooped Dennis Hunt's body out of the water after the ambulance left. He'd broken his neck in the fall. Yesterday, they found his gun lodged between two rocks about halfway down. Oh, yes, he had the two missing bullets in his pocket. He must have been planning to get rid of them after he was through with me."

Nick swallowed. With a frown, he muttered, "G'on."

"Well," she said, settling down on the bed closer to him, half-hoping that touching him would help her cope with all the facts. "After you went into surgery, they interrogated Clive and Mills again. Mills still isn't talking, but Clive is hoping to plea bargain, Mark said. He's been in enough trouble and knows if he doesn't plea bargain, he's looking at life behind bars. He said your chief had visited him in jail and offered him more money than he earned with Jamie, if he did a few jobs when he got out. Shortly after he was released, Jamie was murdered.

"They also found the missing ballistic reports in Hunt's briefcase. The same gun killed both Jamie and Tony. It looks like it's the one your chief had."

Nick shook his head in confusion.

"The handgun was registered in Hunt's name. Mark said Hunt had it for target practice only. Clive admitted that Jamie told him to steal it from the chief's house. Jamie then killed Tony with it, to keep Hunt involved."

"Like he did with me. It doesn't surprise me. Why was the chief involved in all of this?"

"For the money. To pad his retirement fund. But I think the whole business got out of hand, too much for even the chief."

She shuddered at the thought. "He'd known about Jamie's entire illegal empire for ages and for a price, he was willing to thwart the undercover investigation. When he found me at your house, he admitted he knew Jamie had something on him, but didn't know what." She paused. "I accidentally let it slip about the tape."

"G'on."

"Well, thanks to you remembering that Globatech had made the laptop, Mark was able to piece together most of what happened. Clive filled in the rest. The laptop was like my VCR. It had been imported through Globatech, filled with cocaine. Jamie, in one of his generous moods, I suppose, gave the laptop to your chief, who made a mistake when he asked Jones to look at it. It had kept crashing and Jones was computer savvy enough to spot a knockoff. He reported it after you were suspended."

"Told ya doze cheap models are no good."

"It seems some components inside were missing, too. Mark said they found traces of cocaine in it. A bag must have broken."

"But why did he kill Cooms?" His speech remained slow and stilted.

"Hunt told me Jamie had become greedy and wanted his protection money back. That must have been after Jamie had videotaped the party. Invite Hunt to the party, tape him schmoozing with Jamie's clientele. Maybe even get Hunt involved in a few small sales, or have him promise a bit of protection to some big-name clients. Then blackmail him. But Hunt shot him instead."

"It's hard to believe he was that foolish."

"Money seduces, they say."

Nick wet his dry lips. "But he didn't know 'bout the videotape."

"That's true, he didn't. But Jamie would need proof Hunt was involved and the chief knew that. He also knew that Jamie would have hidden the proof and since I was the latest girlfriend, he figured I'd probably know something."

She looked at her tightly clenched fists. "I did, but I hadn't realize it until I saw his reflection in your front door. While Clive was still in jail, Hunt asked him to kill me. When Clive failed, Hunt tried to run me down using Jamie's car." She shivered.

Nick leaned forward and with a painful gasp, pulled her up closer to him. "Mills?" he whispered after a lovely embrace.

"He's still in here, down the corridor, in fact, under guard. He's not talking, but Clive said that Jamie approached him ages ago with an offer of money to look the other way when certain shipments arrived. I know Ron's finances. He's always broke. He needed cash badly."

She settled into Nick's arms, glad for the comfort he offered. "Jamie's plans go back several years, before he even bought the warehouse and rented it to Globatech. He knew he could always buy the right people and knew who they were. Mark said I was probably part of his plan, too. Or some other female Globatech employee was, rather. Dating me gave him another way to gain access to the warehouse in case Ron Mills failed. Ron knew about the cocaine, but never expected Hunt to order Clive to retrieve it and then kill him. Ron should plead guilty. It's his first offense." She looked up from the embrace. Mark had filled her in with most of the details of how Nick figured out who the real killer was. She knew Hunt realized Nick was getting close to discovering the truth. Because he didn't trust Jamie one bit, Hunt had murdered him and suspended Nick, almost stopping the investigation dead in its tracks.

But he hadn't counted on Nick's persistence. In a few weeks, he would return to his job. Maybe even return to undercover work. Either way, there was no room in his life for a woman, especially the ex-girlfriend of a drug lord, despite his admission that he loved her.

But she'd promised she would nurse him back to health, and she would. A short time with him was better than nothing.

She inhaled the clean smell of the hospital gown Nick wore. Gone was his trademark scent of citrus and musk. At least until she got him home. The cotton beneath her cheek had warmed up nicely, transferring the heat from Nick's broad chest through to her. Somewhere outside the hospital room, someone dropped a metal tray and behind the clatter, the P.A. paged some doctor.

But she tuned out all the sensations except Nick. She wouldn't have long with him. Enough to take care of him at home and then he would probably ask her to leave, accepting the logical decision that they were worlds apart.

As if sensing her despair, Nick pushed her back and peered at her. "You were pretty scrappy out there on the cliff, Helen. You scared the hell out of me."

"I was pretty scared myself, but I realized something. I don't need someone to protect me. I can do it myself." She smiled, knowing it was sad.

She'd told him that much out on the cliff. She had to say it again, so he wouldn't need to feel obligated to keep her around after he healed.

Nick nodded. "I know. But are you willing to let me do some of it, sometime? I'd like a crack at that superhero stuff once in a while." His words were slow and deliberate, as he struggled to pronounce each syllable. He tried to smile, too, but the swollen, sutured lip must have restricted his mouth's movement and made his "v's" and "w's" sound a bit odd.

His eyes, so urgent and pleading, conveyed without another word an emotion she wasn't sure she was reading correctly. Her heart gave a little leap, forgetting that her mind had already prepared it for a future breaking.

"What are you saying, Nick?"

He stroked her hair. "I love you. I wish I could explain so much more, but I can barely put a sentence together. Don't leave me. Ever."

"What about your career? My reputation can't be good for that."

"I want you. I'm a cop, Helen. And I want to be a cop, but I want you more."

"And your undercover work?"

"Cops get married, too. And some of them do undercover work. I don't have to do it. I can be in uniform for the rest of my career, if I want."

"But you didn't want a relationship."

"Not at first I didn't. I was always too wrapped up in my work. Then I'd told myself I couldn't trust anyone enough. When I met you, I wondered if it would be better to be responsible for DiPetri's death. It gave me an excuse not to get involved with you. But it was all a matter of trust."

"Like you didn't trust Mark?"

"I was unfair to him. I thought I could do it all myself. I thought I didn't need you because I figured I couldn't trust anyone..." He swallowed. "...with my heart."

"But you've realized that you can trust Mark with your life like you trust me with your heart?" Mercy, how could she sound so calm? Inside, her whole being shook and tears threatened.

He nodded, swallowing and waiting with caution in his eyes.

She bit her lip, blinking to clear her vision. "You can trust me, Nick. I won't ever break your heart. I promise."

"But you don't need me."

"Oh, yes, I do. To love me and share my life with me and hey, maybe to fight crime with me."

He tightened his grip on her. "Whoa, girl! That's my job."

She laughed, the bubbly silly giggle full of relief. "I'm only teasing. I promise to leave the policing to you. I don't need someone to baby me, but I do need you to love me, like I love you."

"That'll be the easiest thing in the world for me." He pulled her back against his chest.

"Mind you, with Hunt gone, who will be chief?"

"Mark, probably."

"So, you'll be short one officer."

"We've got auxiliary officers, so you can forget the idea of enlisting. Besides, you have a career at Globatech."

"And it would be nice to earn Mr. Parker's trust again." She smiled, her cheek touching his chest. For a while, it looked to her like Mr. Parker had known about Jamie's illegal activities, but he'd been completely unaware of what was happening in his warehouse.

Her gaze wandered to the window. The last few days of rain and drizzle had moistened the early fall, and now with the sunshine beating down through the window, the day looked fresh and crisp.

The first day of the rest of her life, made stronger with Nick's love.

* * * * *

MIRA®

Your opinion is important to us! Please take a few moments to share your thoughts with us about your experiences with Harlequin and Silhouette books. Your comments will be very useful in ensuring that we deliver books you love to read.
Please take a few minutes to complete the questionnaire, then send it to us at the address below.

Send your completed questionnaires to:
Harlequin/Silhouette Reader Survey, P.O. Box 9046, Buffalo, NY 14269-9046

1. As you may know, there are many different lines under the Harlequin and Silhouette brands. Each of the lines is listed below. Please check the box that most represents your reading habit for each line.

Line	Currently read this line	Do not read this line	Not sure if I read this line
Harlequin American Romance	❑	❑	❑
Harlequin Duets	❑	❑	❑
Harlequin Romance	❑	❑	❑
Harlequin Historicals	❑	❑	❑
Harlequin Superromance	❑	❑	❑
Harlequin Intrigue	❑	❑	❑
Harlequin Presents	❑	❑	❑
Harlequin Temptation	❑	❑	❑
Harlequin Blaze	❑	❑	❑
Silhouette Special Edition	❑	❑	❑
Silhouette Romance	❑	❑	❑
Silhouette Intimate Moments	❑	❑	❑
Silhouette Desire	❑	❑	❑

2. Which of the following best describes why you bought *this book?* One answer only, please.

the picture on the cover	❑	the title	❑
the author	❑	the line is one I read often	❑
part of a miniseries	❑	saw an ad in another book	❑
saw an ad in a magazine/newsletter	❑	a friend told me about it	❑
I borrowed/was given this book	❑	other: ______________	❑

3. Where did you buy *this book?* One answer only, please.

at Barnes & Noble	❑	at a grocery store	❑
at Waldenbooks	❑	at a drugstore	❑
at Borders	❑	on eHarlequin.com Web site	❑
at another bookstore	❑	from another Web site	❑
at Wal-Mart	❑	Harlequin/Silhouette Reader Service/through the mail	❑
at Target	❑	used books from anywhere	❑
at Kmart	❑	I borrowed/was given this book	❑
at another department store or mass merchandiser	❑		

4. On average, how many Harlequin and Silhouette books do you buy at one time?

I buy ______ books at one time ❑
I rarely buy a book ❑

MRQ403SIM-1A

5. How many times per month do you shop for any *Harlequin and/or Silhouette* books? One answer only, please.

1 or more times a week	❑	a few times per year	❑
1 to 3 times per month	❑	less often than once a year	❑
1 to 2 times every 3 months	❑	never	❑

6. When you think of your ideal heroine, which *one* statement describes her the best? One answer only, please.

She's a woman who is strong-willed	❑	She's a desirable woman	❑
She's a woman who is needed by others	❑	She's a powerful woman	❑
She's a woman who is taken care of	❑	She's a passionate woman	❑
She's an adventurous woman	❑	She's a sensitive woman	❑

7. The following statements describe types or genres of books that you may be interested in reading. Pick *up to 2 types* of books that you are most interested in.

I like to read about truly romantic relationships	❑
I like to read stories that are sexy romances	❑
I like to read romantic comedies	❑
I like to read a romantic mystery/suspense	❑
I like to read about romantic adventures	❑
I like to read romance stories that involve family	❑
I like to read about a romance in times or places that I have never seen	❑
Other: ______________________________	❑

The following questions help us to group your answers with those readers who are similar to you. Your answers will remain confidential.

8. Please record your year of birth below.

19 ____

9. What is your marital status?

single ❑ married ❑ common-law ❑ widowed ❑
divorced/separated ❑

10. Do you have children 18 years of age or younger currently living at home?

yes ❑ no ❑

11. Which of the following best describes your employment status?

employed full-time or part-time ❑ homemaker ❑ student ❑
retired ❑ unemployed ❑

12. Do you have access to the Internet from either home or work?

yes ❑ no ❑

13. Have you ever visited eHarlequin.com?

yes ❑ no ❑

14. What state do you live in?

____

15. Are you a member of Harlequin/Silhouette Reader Service?

yes ❑ Account # ____________ no ❑

MRQ403SIM-1B

MIRA®

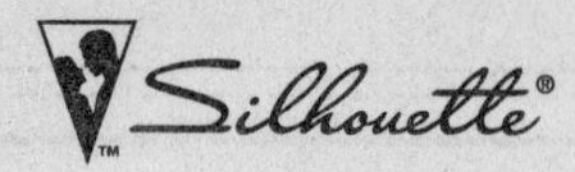

INTIMATE MOMENTS®

COMING NEXT MONTH

#1249 RACING AGAINST TIME—Marie Ferrarella
Cavanaugh Justice
Judge Brenton Montgomery was devastated when his daughter was kidnapped. Detective Callie Cavanaugh made it her mission to find the little girl, and he was grateful for her help despite the unsettling and long-burning attraction the two had shared for years. Would this crisis finally bring them together?

#1250 DEAD CERTAIN—Carla Cassidy
Cherokee Corners
Homicide cop Savannah Tallfeather was on a desperate mission to uncover the truth behind her father's injuries and her mother's disappearance. When she met Riley Frazier and discovered his parents had met eerily similar fates, the two teamed up to find the truth—and discovered an undeniable attraction!

#1251 A WARRIOR'S VOW—Marilyn Tracy
City slicker Leeza Nelson had taken over her friend's orphanage ranch, so when ten-year-old Enrique ran away, it was up to her to find him. Little did she know that brooding Apache tracker James Daggart planned to help her. But would their journey into the wilderness lead them to the lost child and salvation in each other's arms?

#1252 A DANGEROUS ENGAGEMENT—Candace Irvin
When U.S. Navy Lieutenant Anna Shale agreed to turn her back on her family and go undercover to infiltrate their crime organization, she met Tom Wild, who seemed bent on seducing her! What she didn't realize was that he had his own secret agenda, which might not align with hers....

#1253 LINE OF FIRE—Cindy Dees
When political activist Kimberly Stanton and Special Forces soldier Tex Monroe were kidnapped, she found herself fighting her attraction to the sexy soldier. As a military brat, Kimberly knew falling for an enlisted man was trouble. But when the two escaped and were forced to hide out together, would she fall prey to the passion that stalked them both?

#1254 MELTING THE ICE—Loreth Anne White
When journalist Hannah McGuire's best friend turned up dead, she set out to investigate the murder. Then she ran into her ex-lover Rex Logan, and was shocked to find that he was investigating the same case. Now they would have to put aside their differences if they wanted to solve the mystery—and fight their growing passion!

SIMCNM0903